SUMMER IN THE ORCHARD

Fay Keenan

First published in the United Kingdom in 2018 by Aria,
an imprint of Head of Zeus Ltd

Copyright © Fay Keenan, 2018

The moral right of Fay Keenan to be identified as the author of
this work has been asserted in accordance with the Copyright, Designs
and Patents Act of 1988.

9 7 5 3 1 2 4 6 8

A CIP catalogue record for this book is available from the British Library.

ISBN 9781786694904

Aria
an imprint of Head of Zeus
First Floor East
5–8 Hardwick Street
London EC1R 4RG

SUMMER IN THE ORCHARD

FAY KEENAN was born in Surrey and raised in Hampshire, before finally settling back in the West Country. When Fay is not chasing her children around or writing, she teaches English at a local secondary school. She lives with her husband of fourteen years, two daughters, a cat, two chickens and a Weimaraner called Bertie in a village in Somerset, which may or may not have provided the inspiration for Little Somerby.

To Mum and Dad... for everything.

I

Sophie Henderson looked out at the sea of impassive faces and swallowed. No matter how often she'd told herself that it would be fine, that coming back to her old school to talk about her job would be a breeze, it really, really wasn't. *There's a reason I never wanted to go into teaching,* she thought as Mr Jones, the Head of Year Twelve, droned on with his introduction.

Churchwell School's main hall had changed little in the ten or so years since she'd left, and Sophie was uncomfortably aware of feeling simultaneously like a student again, but also realising how much time had passed since she'd been the one sitting down there, and Matthew Carter, Managing Director of Carter's Cider, had come in to give this same talk. Seeing those distinctly bored looking, but admirably fresh faced students sitting on the plastic chairs, staring back at her, did little to banish her nerves. Had she looked the same, when Matthew had come in on Careers Day? She hoped not.

'And so, I'm sure that Sophie will be more than able to not just dispel the myths about her job as a cider maker, but also explain the very good reasons why a job at

Carter's Cider might just be for you.' As Mr Jones finished his introduction he glanced over at Sophie, who stood up a little too hurriedly from her chair, causing it to totter precariously on its back two legs before it righted itself with a thud on the wooden boards of the stage. Trying to ignore the trembling in her knees, she looked out at her captive audience, a fixed grin on her face.

'Good morning, everyone,' she said, her voice echoing slightly back at her from the walls of the main hall. 'It's great to be here.'

As she drew breath she was sure she didn't imagine the whispered, 'Yeah, right,' from somewhere in the front row.

'I hope I can answer your questions today about what it's like to work for Carter's Cider, and that some of you might consider applying for the apprenticeships, which, for you, will begin after your exams finish next summer.'

'Only if we get to drink the cider!' A voice came from the audience, and was greeted with raucous laughter.

Sophie's grin got a little more fixed. 'Well, it's funny you should say that,' she said quickly, 'as part of my job actually involves cider tasting. So, who knows, perhaps you might get to do that, too? If you're old enough to drink alcohol, of course!'

Recognising that the heckler had been, as they would put it themselves, 'burned', or at least mildly singed, by Sophie's instant response, the audience laughed a little more enthusiastically, and, encouraged, Sophie started to relax. She'd only agreed to speak at the careers day because David Armitage, Chief Cider Maker, had double booked himself and was, by his own admission 'a little too long in the tooth to be down with the kids anyway, these days.' At twenty-nine years old, Sophie felt the age gap keenly as she continued to speak, but, she figured, a lot had happened to her in the years since she'd left school. After ten years in the cider business, now having risen through the ranks to be Deputy Cider Maker, she was an enthusiastic and eloquent speaker, and found that the words came easily.

As her speech drew to a close, and she paused for any questions, Sophie felt a flutter of nerves again. What if none of the students had any questions? Should she just continue to stand there, or should she sit down again? Mr Jones had been a little hazy on what happened after she finished talking. Thankfully, a hand shot up a few rows back from the front. Sophie breathed a sigh of relief.

'So, like, you try all the cider before it leaves the factory, right?'

'That's right,' Sophie replied.

'So, what happens if you're not happy with it? Does it just get, like, chucked down the drain?'

Sophie smiled. 'Well, thankfully that doesn't happen very often, as we're pretty good at making cider both we and the customers will be happy with. Although...' she paused tantalisingly, keeping her audience hanging for a moment '... there was an incident just over a year ago that meant we did have to get rid of about seventy thousand pints from one of the oak vats in the barn.'

'Seventy thousand!' Mr Jones echoed. 'That seems like a criminal waste. I'm sure someone could have found a use for it!' He pointed to himself and grinned. His audience laughed at the attempt at a dad joke.

'I don't think you'd have wanted to drink it.' Sophie shook her head good naturedly. 'After all, if you throw someone in a cider vat, it tends to contaminate the product a bit!'

Suddenly the sixth form audience looked a whole lot more interested. 'Does that happen often?' Mr Jones asked.

'No, thank goodness,' Sophie said. 'And I think you can only get away with doing it if you happen to own the business.' She was referring, of course, to the night Jonathan Carter, co-owner of Carter's Cider, and erstwhile Lord of Misrule, had thrown a man into the top of one of the Vintage oak vats after he'd been threatening the love of his life. Jonathan had released the man into the waiting hands of the local police, and, while the details of the case had never been made public, the episode had gone down in local folklore as the most dramatic thing to be added to cider since his late father, Jack Carter, had changed his grandfather's recipes back in the early eighties and several local farmers had staged a go slow tractor protest outside the front gates of the cider farm.

'It took four days to empty and clean the vat, and refill it with more of the Vintage blend, and it did slow us down for a little while, but thankfully the guy didn't do too much damage.'

'Wouldn't he have drowned?' a voice called out from the floor.

'There's a stainless steel ladder inside each of the vats so that the coopers can get in and repair them,' Sophie replied. 'I think he'd have been pretty cold, but he would have been able to tread water – or cider – until he was released.'

'Wouldn't be a bad way to go, anyway,' Mr Jones replied, grinning. The audience dutifully laughed again. 'Thank you, Sophie, for giving us such an enlightening talk about your job and the business you work for. And if anyone's interested in applying for an apprenticeship for after your exams next year, we have the paperwork at the back of the room, which needs to be completed by November this year, so do please pick it up on the way out.' Shaking Sophie's hand, and uttering a low, 'Well done,' he released her from the stage.

As she walked back behind the curtain and tried to make her way down the steps and out into the auditorium towards the exit, she was brought up short by the scent of a familiar, and distinctly unwelcome aftershave. Pausing in the gloom, cursing the fact that her knees had started to shake, she waited at the top of the steps.

'After you, Soph,' a voice whispered in the darkness. 'Good speech, by the way.'

'What are you doing here?' Sophie muttered, trying to hide her discomfort with defensiveness.

'Same as you, I expect.' The figure drew closer as Sophie gingerly trod the rickety wooden steps away from the stage and into the corridor. 'Lecturing this lot about having to work for a living.'

'I doubt you'd know much about that.' Sophie tried to push past him, but he reached out a hand to stop her. Looking up from her feet, she met the cocky gaze of her ex-boyfriend, Mark Simpson, who was the manager of a

5

dairy farm a few miles from the school. Her heart thumped painfully as she remembered the last time she'd seen him, and she hoped that he wasn't going to try to remind her of that now, in earshot of all the sixth formers.

'Don't be like that,' Mark replied, his hand still resting on her elbow. 'Why don't we go for a drink tonight? Talk things through.'

'I've got nothing to say to you,' Sophie said, pulling away from his touch. 'And since the last time you wanted to talk was because I caught you shagging your admin assistant in that excuse of an office of yours, I doubt you've got much to say to me either.' Resisting the urge to look back, Sophie raised her head and walked straight down the corridor and out of the entrance to the school, pausing only to sign herself out of the visitors' book. By the time she'd got to her car, her hands had almost stopped shaking.

Before she started the ignition, she pulled her phone out and checked her emails. At the top of her inbox was yet another email from a rival cider firm, Martingtons, based in Herefordshire. A long standing contact there had been trying to poach her from Carter's for years, and every time Alannah emailed her the job offer got more lucrative. Sophie was still dithering about what to do: should she hand in her notice and start a new phase in her career, get away from what was safe and familiar and step out of her comfort zone, or should she hang on in there at Carter's and hope that some time soon David, much as she liked him, would hand his tasting jug over to her?

Resolving to look at the offer in more depth when she'd finished work that day, Sophie checked her other messages, which included an image heavy email from her grandmother, Lily. A romantic novelist by trade, Lily had recently discovered Pinterest, and was busily compiling virtual boards of pictures of 'swoonworthy romantic heroes' to aid her with her current novel. Lily's current 'hero' of choice was Keanu Reeves, and Sophie had spent a fair few evenings over the past few months snuggled up on Lily's sofa as they worked their way through his extensive back catalogue. Lily, predictably for a romantic novelist, was most keen on *The Lake House* and *Sweet November*, whereas Sophie was rather fond of the *John Wick* films. Grinning as she scrolled down the email, which contained at least ten different pictures of Keanu, Sophie resolved to look in on her grandmother after she'd finished work. At least, she thought as she pulled out of the school car park and headed back to Carter's Cider, her grandmother's email had lightened her mood after the encounter with Mark. He was someone she certainly didn't want to think about any more than was strictly necessary.

2

'Bloody hell… look at who's just walked in with the boss.'

Sophie's head snapped up at the exclamation from her colleague, Laura. She'd been busy on the filtration floor all morning since she'd returned from Churchwell School, and was, momentarily, lost in the world of tannins, timings and taste. 'What? Who is it?' She checked the pressures on the batch of cider she was currently testing and then turned to where Laura was none too subtly indicating with a thumb on her hip. Striding across the filtration floor was Matthew Carter, and alongside him was a tall, dark and extremely handsome stranger. Dressed in mid-washed blue jeans, a white T-shirt and an unbuttoned checked shirt over the top, he was the same height as Matthew, and just as broad. Sophie tried not to notice the slightly bowed knees on endless legs, muscular arms and lean torso, and the friendly smile that seemed to rest on all who crossed his path. *Bloody hell indeed*, she thought as the two men drew closer.

David, her boss, crossed the floor from the other direction as the two men approached. Shaking hands with the new arrival, he motioned to Sophie to join them. Ignoring Laura's jealous look, she did so.

'Sophie, I'd like you to meet Alex Fraser,' Matthew said as she approached. 'David's suggested that you mentor him during his summer internship, since he'd like to learn about the various Somerset bred apples we press here.'

Alex held out his hand, and Sophie took it. His grip was warm and firm, and she liked the way he looked her straight in the eye. 'It's nice to meet you, Sophie.'

'You too.' Ah, yes, of course, now Sophie remembered the conversation about taking on an intern. She'd been so preoccupied with giving the talk to the sixth form about apprenticeships that she'd forgotten that she and David would be taking on an intern for the summer. The internship had been advertised separately from the more highly paid apprenticeships, and was from late June until the end of September. Sophie had been expecting some spotty schoolkid, who, doubtless, would spend more time looking at his or her phone than actually learning the ropes. She certainly hadn't been expecting this handsome stranger, who, from the sound of that accent, had come from a little further afield than the local secondary school.

'Alex has come over from Vancouver to see how our native Somerset apples could be mixed with Canadian varieties,' Matthew continued. 'I think it would be good for him to learn about our business from the ground up, so he'll be working with various people during his time with us, but mainly with you and David, to really get a feel for how to blend and taste. I'm hoping, in the long term, that we might learn from each other.' He turned from Sophie and David back to Alex. 'I'll leave you in Sophie and David's capable hands for now, Alex. I hope you'll have a really productive and enjoyable time here. Don't be afraid to seek me or my brother Jonathan, out if you have any questions.'

'Thank you,' Alex said, smiling at Matthew. They shook hands and Matthew departed, leaving Alex, Sophie and David on the floor.

'So, what brings you to Carter's Cider?' Sophie asked as the three of them walked back to where she had been mixing. 'It's a long way to come for a minimum wage internship!'

Alex smiled. 'I've just bought a cider business in a town outside Vancouver, and before I can really get going, I wanted to learn how best to get it on its feet. Carter's came up as the place to learn about English apples, since they're the best in the world for cider. I've learnt a lot about the native Canadian varieties, but I want to produce an original Anglo-Canadian blend that would be a real selling point back home.'

Sophie smiled. 'What about French varieties? We've got one or two from across the Channel that we incorporate into our blends, and surely there must be plenty that came over to Canada with the French settlers?'

'Oh, of course,' Alex said hurriedly. 'But they're mostly used in Quebec, where conditions are a little different. I'm really looking for something English that I can use that's robust enough to withstand a Vancouver winter.'

'Well, you've come to the right place,' Sophie said. She could already hear the enthusiasm in Alex's voice for his project. She knew that artisan cideries were springing up all over the place, so she wasn't surprised that Carter's

Cider was getting international interest; they were one of the biggest brands in the UK, after all. 'If you're going to learn about English apples, this is definitely the place to be. It's just a shame Jack Carter's no longer with us – Matthew and Jonathan Carter's dad. He knew absolutely everything there was to know about growing apples.'

'So I've heard,' Alex said. His tone was light, but Sophie noticed he bit his lip as he replied; he must be pretty nervous about being here and want to make a good impression.

'There'll be a lot to take in,' she continued, 'so don't be surprised if your head is spinning by the end of the day!'

The two began to walk over to the exit of the filtration floor, towards the main yard where the apple baths were housed. 'Have you always been into cider?' Sophie asked as they walked, before bursting out laughing. 'I'm sorry, that was a stupid way to put it. I mean, what makes you want to run a cidery?'

'I wanted a change of direction,' Alex said as they emerged blinking into the strong early summer sunlight. 'I am… I mean, I was, a lawyer before making this change, but I've always wanted to do something more creative. When the orchard came up for sale near to where my parents lived, I thought it was a great chance to change direction.'

'And what do they think about it? Your parents?' Sophie asked.

Alex paused for a split second before replying. 'My mom died at the end of last year, but I think she'd have really liked the idea. My stepdad's been really supportive but he's not in great health himself.'

Sophie's heart lurched. 'I'm sorry to hear that,' she said.

'Thanks.' Alex shook his head and then smiled slightly. 'Mom was really fond of the area where she lived, so I think she'd like it that I'm making a go of something new there. But if I am going to make it work, I need a crash course in cider blending! There's quite a difference between producing a few bottles at home and scaling that up, or so I'm led to believe, so I'm looking forward to learning a lot from Carter's – and you.'

'We can guarantee you that here.' Sophie replied, relieved that the conversation was moving on. 'You'll have plenty of ideas to take back with you.' She glanced at her schedule for the day on her iPad. At this time of year, when the cider business was gearing up for the first pressings at the end of the summer, it was all about planning ahead. 'Shall we get started?'

'Sure,' Alex replied. He seemed to hold her gaze a little too long, and Sophie felt her cheeks growing warm. She made it a rule never to fancy anyone at work, and for ten years she had stuck to it; workplace romances were just too awkward, in her opinion. She'd seen Laura's devastation when she'd split up with her last boyfriend, who still worked in the cannery, and she didn't want to get involved with someone she'd be forced to see every day if things went wrong. After her heartache over Mark, too, she was on her guard even more. There was no doubting that Alex was attractive, though.

Banishing the thought from her mind, Sophie started by showing Alex the cider vat floor, where the forty-eight enormous steel vats stood, ready to be filled with the apple mixture that turned, like magic, into the bestselling varieties of Carter's cider through its own process of natural fermentation. This truly was the industrial arm of the business, and as Sophie explained about the thousands of litres of cider that were produced here every day she saw Alex shaking his head in mild disbelief.

'These steel vats are from Germany,' she said as they looked twenty-five feet upwards at the solid, shining, implacable units that lined the fermenting room. 'Every time one needs replacing, it's brought in on the back of a flatbed truck with a crane, and then winched through the roof into place. The roof slides back, and we need to make sure that it's a dry day when we do it or it gets very messy in here.'

Moving on, Sophie showed Alex her favourite part of the farm, where the oak vats were kept. Pushing open the door to the barn, she paused, inhaling the scent of oak and age. The vats exuded a sense of timelessness, dark and mysterious in their presence. They were the jewel in the crown of the business. 'These go back to the very start of things,' she said, as she pushed open the door further to admit Alex. 'They're what most people think of when they think of cider, although they tend to only hold the speciality varieties these days – Eloise, of course, and the Vintage years, as well as the seriously strong Somerset Sprite.' Walking through to where the first vat stood, she rested a hand briefly on the side of it. Thirty-four feet high, and fifteen feet in diameter, made of oak that once housed the finest Scotch whisky, their slats were roughened and darkened by decades of use. It was as if they were still living, still breathing, still watching.

Alex circled the vat, craning his neck upwards to take in the sheer height of them. 'They're beautiful,' he murmured. 'Breathtaking.' Following Sophie's lead, he placed a hand on the side of the nearest vat, feeling its rough texture under his palm.

'They're stunning, aren't they?' Sophie agreed. She couldn't help herself; her eyes drifted from Alex's face to where his hand, fingers splayed on the side of the barrel, rested, back to his lips and then down his body. He seemed completely lost in the moment, and she felt a jolt of something that felt very definitely like attraction. His eyes were wide, lips slightly parted; he was clearly entranced by the sight, sound, scent and touch of the ancient wooden structures that gave the barn its name. *Get a grip*, she thought. *No relationships at work, remember?*

Coming back to the moment, Alex dropped his hand. 'I wish I could afford something like this for Adelaide's,' he said, 'but I'm not sure I could house something on this scale.'

'There are a couple of smaller ones in the shop.' Sophie smiled. 'I'm sure you'll have plenty of chance to see them and taste it all over the next few weeks, too. Although I'd bear in mind that some of our varieties can give you quite a sore head if you have too much of a good thing!' Sophie remembered quite a few of her own nights lost to Somerset Sprite, back when she was a teenager.

'I hope so.' Alex's gaze returned to Sophie's and she was taken aback by the intensity in his eyes. The oak vats affected nearly everyone the first time they saw them, and Sophie had witnessed their thrall on countless occasions. Their very presence was enough to render even the most eloquent people speechless; and that was before they'd had a taste of what was in them.

'It's so good to be here, to learn how the professionals do it.' Alex continued, seemingly collecting his thoughts. 'Hard cider's not yet such a big deal at home.'

'Hard cider?'

'The stuff with the alcohol in,' Alex explained. 'If you ask for cider in Canada, you're likely just to get apple juice. Although the ice cider's fermented, of course.'

'Ice cider?' Sophie asked, baffled. She knew a lot about cider, but she hadn't heard of that.

Alex smiled, seemingly pleased to be able to impart some knowledge to the cider expert. 'It's made mostly in Quebec from frozen apples and can be really strong.'

'It sounds like you could teach me a thing or two!' Sophie laughed, then blushed. 'Perhaps we should organise an exchange trip.'

Alex laughed too. 'Let me get Adelaide's up and running first, and then you're welcome to visit any time you want.' His eyes were still locked on hers, and Sophie felt herself growing even warmer under his gaze.

To break the tension, she suggested they head back to the office. Alongside all the practical things to take in, an internship at Carter's involved quite a lot of reading and learning about the company, which Sophie wanted to start as soon as she could. After all, there was a lot for Alex to learn, and only a few months to do it in. As they left the barn, Sophie noticed for the first time that Alex's slightly bow legged walk seemed to be more pronounced. She wondered what might have caused it. An ex-professional rugby player she'd once gone out with had a similar gait; perhaps it was a sporting injury? Tearing her gaze away from Alex's back view again, mindful that she didn't want to be caught ogling the intern, she closed the door to the barn and headed back to the office she shared with David, which would also be Alex's base for the duration of his internship.

The rest of the day passed swiftly, and Sophie was relieved. It wasn't that she minded tutoring him, but having someone shadowing her was going to take a bit of getting used to. Just as she was leaving, wondering whether or not to stop in on her grandmother on the way home, she saw Alex and Matthew walking across the courtyard. He'd been summoned back to Matthew's office at the end of the day for a first day feedback session, and Sophie was surprised to see the two of them still deep in conversation. Sophie was once again able to appreciate how in step they were for two such tall men. She decided she'd give visiting Lily a miss tonight; she didn't want Lily quizzing her about the new intern. She was sure that Lily would have found out through the grapevine that the person Sophie was tutoring wasn't some graduate from the local secondary school, and she knew that Lily's mind would only go in one direction. Heaven forbid, Sophie thought, if Lily actually met him. Shaking her head, she began the walk home.

3

'All right, love?' Brenda, the formidable landlady of the Rose Cottage Bed and Breakfast, called as Alex turned his key and pushed the heavy wooden front door open. 'Have you had a good day?'

'Yes, thank you, ma'am,' Alex replied as he hurried through the cool hallway of the cottage, his boots tapping against the tiles of the floor as he approached the stairs. Catching sight of Brenda buzzing around her living room, straightening magazines on the immaculately polished coffee table and whipping out a duster for the ornaments on the mantelpiece, while her husband Roy slumped in his armchair watching the early evening news, Alex quickened his pace. He liked the centrality of the B & B, but Brenda was a talker, and after a long first day at Carter's he wanted to be alone to gather his thoughts.

Taking the stairs two at a time, he headed across the landing and into his room. The bed had been neatly made, once again; almost *too* neatly for his liking, and there was an almost overpowering scent emanating from a jar of sweet peas that Brenda had placed on the small desk in the corner of the room. Under his bed was his wheeled suitcase, and his clothes were hung neatly in the small pine wardrobe on the other side of the room. Reaching under the bed, he retrieved the suitcase, which he'd padlocked again before putting it out of sight.

Glancing around to ensure that the bedroom door was shut, he opened the lock and unzipped the compartment on the inside of the lid. He pulled out the sheaf of papers hidden inside and sat down on the edge of the bed. Untying the red ribbon that kept them all together, his hands trembled as he separated out around half a dozen letters; letters so passionate that when he'd first read them, he'd struggled to acknowledge that they were intended for their original recipient. At the bottom of the pile of documents was a dog-eared photograph, yellowed with time and slightly creased across the middle. The photograph said more than the letters ever could, and for a while Alex just looked at it, trying to connect. He'd looked at it a thousand times since his mother had passed everything on, but it still brought him no closer to the truth.

'Will you be wanting dinner, my lovely?' Brenda's voice called from the bottom of the stairs, so strident that it could penetrate closed doors.

Alex jumped as if he'd been caught in some misdemeanour. 'No, thank you, ma'am,' he replied. 'I'm going to go for a run and I'll get something later.' He couldn't get used to the English bed and breakfast culture, where there seemed to be an obligation to make oneself accountable to your landlady at all times. When he'd watched *Fawlty Towers* with his mother as a kid, he'd thought it was all too absurd to be true, but elements of the beloved British sitcom did seem to exist in the hospitality industry, at least here in Little Somerby. Brenda certainly had a touch of Sybil Fawlty about her. He carefully retied the ribbon and put the papers back into the suitcase, being sure to secure the padlock before stashing it under the bed again. It wouldn't do to leave them lying about.

Changing swiftly into his running gear, he headed back out onto the landing. A run would clear his head, he thought. There was so much to take in, and not just the information overload that Sophie Henderson had joked about when he'd first met her this morning. Crossing continents for the summer, for a job that barely paid enough to cover his weekly rent at the B & B, immersing himself into a whole new career, meeting new people... he felt overwhelmed by it all. Not to mention the more personal reasons for his visit to England.

Alex began to jog, trying to find his own pace on the narrow pavements of Little Somerby until he could reach the Strawberry Line, which ran parallel to the village centre. A former railway branch line that had been closed during the 1960s, it was now a foot and cycle path that ran from the World Heritage site of Cheddar through to the railway town of Yatton, with plans, eventually, to extend from the coast at the picturesque seaside town of Clevedon down to Yeovil. Popular with locals and tourists alike, it was a great introduction to the Somerset landscape – at least that was what the leaflet in the B & B had said. Although Alex didn't fancy doing the whole of the run from Little Somerby to Cheddar, which was an eight mile round trip, he did want to see the disused railway tunnel that was about halfway down the Little Somerby stretch of the line.

Finding his pace, his feet got into a rhythm. The Strawberry Line was bordered each side by elder and oak trees, the elders in full flower, their gentle scent wafting into the early evening air. As Alex passed the local football club, he smiled to see a group of primary school children kicking a ball around. The season was over for now, but clearly the passion still remained. Jogging further, he passed fields of ewes calling throatily to their lambs, and the lambs bleating in sleepy response as the day began to cool. The honeysuckle in the hedgerows waved gently in the breeze, giving off its own sweet aroma, and gradually allowing him to shrug off the pressures of the day.

As he approached the railway tunnel, the air around him changed, becoming cooler and damper. Huge banks of rock reared up on either side of the tunnel's approach, covered in vivid green ferns and moss. Feeling a flutter of apprehension, Alex picked up his pace a little as the yawning mouth of the tunnel approached. In the light from the other side he could see a cyclist approaching, so he kept to the left hand side, assuming that the road rules would be the same here as on the street. Entering the tunnel, he realised too late that the solar lights weren't working, so in the centre of the tunnel he'd be running blind. He hoped the path was even; he didn't fancy a trip to the local hospital if he could help it.

Slowing his pace to adjust to the darkness and the rough path underfoot, Alex could hear his own regular breathing echoing off the walls of the tunnel, which dripped with condensation, splashing into pools in the recesses of the walls. The crags and bumps of the uneven, rock hewn sides of the tunnel reared into view in the almost darkness, like the ghosts of long ago trains. Alex felt his spine tingling in response, and unconsciously upped his pace towards the light. In the distance, he could see the cyclist growing nearer, but the illusion of the tunnel made it seem endless. Breathing more heavily, he pushed on, waiting for the moment when the light would penetrate the all encompassing darkness.

What was he *really* in Little Somerby for? he mused as he pounded on. What was he hoping to find? Was it truly about starting afresh, or was he trying to cling onto the past, to the shreds of memories that weren't even his? Was this decision to run a cidery merely an early onset mid-life crisis, or could he really see himself making a success of it? So many questions were spinning in his head, after only a day at Carter's, that he wondered how he was going to feel when he was weeks into the internship.

As he reached the end of the tunnel, when the light began to infiltrate the darkness, his thoughts turned again to Sophie, whose welcoming smile and bright blue eyes had immediately put him at ease. She'd been completely professional, and was clearly very knowledgeable, and spending the day with her had been as much of a pleasure as a learning process. Emerging fully into the light, he couldn't suppress the thought that Sophie would make a good friend; perhaps, even something more. But there was no point in thinking that way; he was only in England until the end of September, and after that he'd have his hands full with running Adelaide's full time. Not to mention that his recent track record with women wasn't exactly worth shouting about. Messy didn't even begin to cover it. It was probably just as well he'd decided to steer clear of dating in the aftermath of his mother's death; he had enough to work through, without throwing falling in love into the equation. Alex picked up his pace once more, heading out onto the main road and back towards the heart of the village, which, he thought, was the only heart he should be thinking about right now. Pushing all further thoughts out of his mind, he concentrated on throwing off his jet lag, and headed back to the B & B.

4

The first week of Alex's internship passed surprisingly swiftly, and Sophie was starting to get used to having him around as a colleague. He was keen to learn, asked sensible questions and seemed to really listen to the answers she gave. She was actually rather enjoying teaching him. However, they'd not discussed much about their own lives, Alex seeming to prefer to deflect attention from himself to the processes of learning a new trade, and Sophie because she was, by nature, quite a private person; more so since she'd split from Mark, who'd thankfully not contacted her since their impromptu meeting backstage at the careers day. She was curious about one thing, though: how Alex was finding the Rose Cottage B & B. Brenda's reputation preceded her.

'It's fine.' Alex laughed. 'At least as far as living locally is concerned. It made sense to live in the village for the duration of my internship, rather than have the expense of hiring a car and living outside somewhere.' Alex turned back to Sophie, who was waiting by the office door with her iPad in her hand, preparing to check 'the stats on the vats' as she called them: overnight figures such as temperature, acidity and tannin levels, fermentation rates and suchlike. The technology was so advanced that each of the forty-eight tanks on the main fermentation floor could be checked remotely at any given time. The up to date figures were accessible online 24/7. David, who suffered from recurring bouts of insomnia, had been known to log in at three in the morning to check the levels as a way of sending himself back to sleep.

'Means you're a bit landlocked, though,' Sophie said. 'Aren't you afraid you'll get sick of the sight of Little Somerby?'

Alex laughed. 'I grew up in a small country village, so I was used to walking miles to get anywhere,' he said. 'It doesn't really worry me.'

'You'd better download the app for the local bus company, then, if you want to go anywhere bigger than Little Somerby!' Sophie smiled back. 'Or I can always give you a lift if you get stuck.'

'Thanks.' Alex looked surprised by her offer. 'I might take you up on that.'

Sophie blushed. Despite being initially unsettled by the intensity of Alex's gaze when she first met him, she was getting used to his quirks and ways, and just how far to joke with him. If she'd suggested that to one or two of her other male colleagues, they might have construed it as a come-on. Alex just seemed to take it at face value.

'So, what's the schedule for today?' Alex asked as Sophie consulted her iPad.

'The usual checks, first of all,' Sophie replied. 'And then I thought I'd give you a little treat.' She grinned. 'And see how much you've taken in about what you've been learning so far!'

'I'll be sure to try to impress you.' Alex smiled and looked intrigued. 'So long as you're not going to make me eat a whole Dabinett – one mouthful was enough on my first afternoon!'

Sophie laughed. Dabinetts were excellent apples for adding acidity to cider, since they were full of tannin, but they were horrible to eat, tasting dry and bitter, despite their luscious red appearance. Although this year's crop wasn't ready, there were still a few of last year's kicking around in cold storage, and she'd used one to demonstrate a point to Alex yesterday, a kind of variation on a joke that had been pulled on her by David during the early days of her own apprenticeship years ago. She'd not realised he was winding her up until she'd gamely tried to eat the whole apple, such was David's deadpan expression. These days, having worked with him for so long, she knew how to read him better.

As good as her word, after an intentionally unadventurous lunch at the staff canteen, so as not to ruin her taste buds, Sophie took Alex along to the vat barn to take part in the weekly tasting of the Vintage blends. A tradition since the business had begun, the blenders would take their glass jugs and sample the cider from each of the vats to see how the bespoke varieties were doing. Sophie had been assisting David with this task ever since her apprenticeship days, and it was still a highlight of her working week.

This particular afternoon, David was in a meeting, so she and Alex were heading into the barn by themselves.

Usually, one of the Carter brothers would attend the tasting, although for a couple of weeks running now neither of them had. It was a busy time of year, and Sophie had got the testing and tasting down to a fine art.

'Watch your step as you go up to the gantry,' she warned Alex as they walked between the barrels to the foot of the steel staircase. 'It can catch you out if you're not careful and you might come a cropper.'

'Come a cropper?' Alex looked quizzical.

Sophie grinned. 'Fall on your backside.'

Alex laughed. 'Thanks for the warning.'

'David was off work for three weeks when he missed his footing and bruised his coccyx – although he wouldn't stop emailing me, day in, day out, making sure I was doing everything to his specifications.'

'Sounds like he's a bit of a workaholic,' Alex observed wryly. He'd had a bit of contact with David over the week he'd been at Carter's, although David had mostly left his internship to Sophie's tutelage, and he had no doubt that the man took his responsibilities very seriously, from the way he hardly ever cracked a smile. Sophie had warned Alex that David was notoriously straight faced, but it still took a little bit of getting used to.

Heeding Sophie's advice, Alex held onto the gantry rail as he climbed the steps, his boots clanging on the steel as he rose. From the top of the platform, he could appreciate for the first time the scale of the vats in the barn. Standing solid and impassive, they filled the space, the silence in the air at the top of the barn unnerving in its absoluteness. This was a different perspective from his first time in the vat barn; seeing all seventeen vats at once, from the top of the building, was a little overwhelming. He drew in a deep breath as he looked out over the barrels; he could almost smell the history in the atmosphere. Bracing himself against the sudden onslaught of thoughts unbidden, emotions unchecked, he closed his eyes briefly.

'Are you all right?' Sophie asked as she climbed the steps to join him.

Alex's eyes snapped open as he tried to regain his equilibrium. 'Sure.' He laughed nervously. 'Just got a little dizzy.'

'Afraid of heights?' Sophie teased. 'Don't ever try climbing Jacob's Ladder at Cheddar Gorge!' Despite the levity, her eyes were kind. 'Shall we?' She walked across the gantry to the top of the first of the oak vats they needed to check. 'It's OK,' she said. 'You can walk on the tops of them. It's the only way to get to them all!'

Alex smiled as he watched Sophie lean over to unlock the hatch that was set into the top of the nearest oak vat. He had to stop himself staring as her grey T-shirt rode up, revealing a tantalising sliver of pale skin between it and her long, denim clad legs. *Don't go there,* he thought.

'Ready?' she asked, turning briefly back to Alex. 'Let's see how much you've taken on board about what I've been telling you about flavour this week.'

'My first test?' Alex asked lightly, relieved to have something to take his mind off the maelstrom of emotions evoked by being in this place, charged as it was with history and heritage. Not to mention the glimpse of Sophie's bare skin; he was only human, after all, he conceded.

Sophie grinned. 'Don't worry too much about the specifics. Just tell me what you think.' She dipped the jug into the vat, almost up to her elbow to get past the surface oxidisation, and then poured the contents into two tumblers. Deliberately not taking a sip first, she handed one to Alex and then waited for him to taste.

Alex paused, and then raised the glass to look at the colour. It was a deep, luscious gold, and the fermentation had left lazy bubbles rising to the surface in his glass. As he brought it closer to his mouth he first drew a deep breath to catch the scent. It had a deep, oak soaked aroma, which had been given to it from the barrels themselves, and just the finest whiff of cognac from the wood of the vat. It smelt of warm days, orchards and the county of Somerset. Inhaling again, he put the glass to his lips and allowed the liquid to fizz over his tongue, keeping his mouth slightly open to allow the cider to breathe.

'Wow,' he said. 'That's seriously good.'

Sophie looked at him shrewdly. 'And what else?'

Alex felt his stomach clench as her clear blue gaze held his intently. 'It's broad,' he said. 'And feels like it's getting there.' He took another sip. 'Perhaps a bit longer? A bit more sweetness? Seems slightly acidic?'

Sophie nodded coolly. 'Not bad,' she said. She took a sip from her own glass, swirled it around in her mouth and then swallowed. 'So how long would you say it needs?'

'Week or so?'

'Possibly.' Sophie put her glass down and smiled. 'I'd say the acidity is actually about right for the UK market – Brits tend to like their Vintage ciders with a little more bite, but it would be easy to adjust the sweetness for your home market if you felt a sweeter blend was needed. The Eloise variety would be a good bet for that – just tweak the blend to suit your customer.'

'Noted,' Alex said. He took another sip from the glass he was holding.

'Steady on!' Sophie laughed. 'We've got another five vats to sample this afternoon, and if you drink the whole glass each time, you really will go arse over tit on the way back down.'

Alex didn't need her to explain that particular turn of phrase – especially after an illicit mouthful of the Vintage – it seemed fairly self explanatory, and he didn't want to go the same way as David on those steps if he could help it.

On her way home that evening, Sophie was mulling over the schedule for the next few weeks, which crops were due to harvest soon, and the kinds of blends she'd need to put into action, when she saw Alex crossing the road by the Co-op. Before she realised what she was doing, she'd raised a hand and waved at him, and then felt her face turning red at the gaucheness of that gesture. What an idiot, to be waving with quite such enthusiasm!

However, Alex, much to her relief, waved back, and then increased his pace a little to get to where she was.

'Hi,' he said as he approached. 'It's a nice evening for a walk.'

'It is,' Sophie said. 'Although I'm not going far. I said I'd pop in on my grandmother tonight.'

Alex fell into step beside Sophie as she walked in the direction of Lily Henderson's house. 'It's neat that you live so close to her. Must make things easier,' he observed. 'My mom's parents lived about twenty miles away from us, so we saw them quite a lot, but my stepdad's mom and dad were a way upstate, so we only really saw them in the vacation.' Then he stopped, a look of rather attractive uncertainty crossing his features. 'I'm sorry,' he said. 'I've just presumed to join you, without even asking if that's OK.' He shook his head. 'Where are my manners?'

'It's a free country, and an open road,' Sophie replied, smiling. 'Where are you off to, anyway?'

Alex looked sheepish. 'I kind of have to get away from Brenda in the evenings. She and her husband like to sit in their garden, which is fine, but she can talk like no one I've ever met, so I've been getting out of there just for the peace and quiet. It's amazing how far you can go on an English summer evening.'

Sophie snorted with laughter, wondering if Alex was aware of his rather sweet double entendre. 'I did wonder how long you were going to stick it at the B & B when you told me you were staying there. Brenda's pretty well known around these parts for only stopping talking when she's asleep, and sometimes not even then, apparently!' She furrowed her brow. 'But then, you haven't met my gran yet, have you? She's another one who can talk for England!'

'No, I don't think so,' Alex replied. 'Although I did see a lady walking a Weimaraner a couple of nights ago – might that have been her? Wasn't that the kind of dog you told me she had?'

'Yes, that's right,' Sophie said. 'Barney's pretty distinctive, and the only Weimaraner in the village, as far as I know!' She paused, then before she could think better of it, a wicked grin lit up her features. 'Look, if you want to come and say hello, and hide from for Brenda a bit longer, I'm sure Gran wouldn't mind you joining us.' She omitted to say that Lily would probably find out more about Alex in five minutes than Brenda had in a week; Lily had a way of getting information out of people.

'If you're sure I won't be intruding?' Alex replied. 'I don't want to impose on you, or her.'

'Oh, Gran's used to having guests,' Sophie said. 'She's always liked meeting new people.' *And she'll love the look of you,* she added silently, knowing that her grandmother still had an eye for a good looking man.

'Well, if you're sure,' Alex said. 'It would be nice to hide out somewhere until Brenda talks herself to sleep!'

'I could hardly leave you wandering the streets of Little Somerby, could I?' She gestured. 'Besides, Gran's house is only here, and she's got a very big garden to hide in!'

With that, Sophie snapped open the garden gate that topped the paved path to Lily Henderson's front door.

5

Lily's front door was on the latch, in expectation of her granddaughter's visit, and as Sophie pushed open the door she and Alex were met by a frenzy of alternate squeaks and barks as Barney the Weimaraner skittered excitedly between the two of them. Huge, grey and with the energy of a sugar infused toddler, he was ecstatic to see Sophie, and intrigued by her companion.

'Oh, calm down, you big softy!' Sophie smiled, looking semi-apologetically towards Alex as Barney thrust a wet nose into the palm of his hand. 'I'm sorry – he's like this with visitors.'

'It's fine,' Alex said, leaning down to scratch behind Barney's ears. 'He's beautiful.'

'He loves people who love him,' Sophie observed as Barney immediately started to calm down under Alex's touch.

'I miss having a dog.' Alex glanced back up at Sophie and smiled. 'I had a Doberman as a kid, but I haven't had a dog since I've been living in the city. Perhaps now I'm moving back out to the country, I'll be able to have another one.'

Barney, like a big, furry, friendly host, led Alex and Sophie through the hallway and kitchen and out into the long, beautifully kept garden at the back of the house.

As she led Alex through the walled garden, Sophie spotted her grandmother. Lily was standing by one of the extensively populated English rose beds, secateurs in hand, snipping a few blooms for the cut crystal vase that always adorned her dining room table. Wearing a large floppy straw hat to protect her silvery white hair against the still strong summer sunshine and a long linen shirt with matching cream trousers, she looked the picture of elegance as she put the roses down on her garden table and extended a pale hand tipped with discreetly painted pink fingernails, to the man who stood beside her granddaughter.

'Gran, this is Alex,' Sophie said as she, Alex and Barney approached.

'Nice to meet you, Alex,' Lily said, regarding him contemplatively. 'Sophie's told me a lot about you. Are you an Alex, or an Alexander?'

Alex smiled. 'Technically, I'm Alexander, but mostly only when I'm in trouble. It's nice to meet you too, ma'am,' Alex replied, shaking Lily's hand. 'And she hasn't told you too much, I hope!'

'Enough to make me curious to meet you,' Lily said, returning his smile broadly. 'And much as I appreciate your wonderful and traditional mode of address, please feel free to call me Lily.'

'Can I get you a drink, Alex?' Sophie asked hurriedly. Her grandmother was an incorrigible flirt, even now. 'And would you like one, Gran?'

'I'll sort out something cold and wet,' Lily said, picking up her roses again. 'I need to get these into some water. Make yourselves comfortable.' She pointed to the swing seat at the far end of the garden, which had another wooden chair and a small table in front of it. 'We'll have a drink down there, shall we?'

Sophie only just restrained herself from rolling her eyes as Lily gave her a knowing glance. Her grandmother had been trying to set her up with anything male and remotely eligible since she'd broken up with Mark, but Alex, while definitely male and certainly eligible, needed to remain strictly in the business not pleasure category.

'Shall we?' Alex broke into her thoughts.

He smiled down at her, and Sophie's stomach fluttered a little. *You really shouldn't smile like that,* she thought unguardedly.

'I can see that your grandmother isn't a woman to be argued with.'

'You don't know the half of it,' Sophie said, smiling back at Alex. 'The rows she used to have with Jack Carter when he was alive about the wasps from his orchard flying over the fence and going for her roses in the summer… and she was friends with him!'

'Really?' Alex said. 'They knew each other a long time, then?'

'Ever since they were kids.'

'What was he like when he was younger?' Alex asked as they walked towards the bottom of the garden.

'Oh, a bit wild, apparently,' Sophie said. 'He'd dallied with virtually every girl in the village by the time he was twenty-one, then he met Cecily and married her almost overnight. Gran, who will only admit to having kissed him once, was one of the few women who didn't have her heart broken by Jack, or so she claims. But village gossip tends to blow things out of proportion. Especially back in those days when there were fewer distractions.'

Alex looked thoughtful. 'He sounds like an... interesting character.'

'Oh, you know what it's like in villages – everyone knows what everyone else is doing, all the time. That's why so many people get the hell out while they can! Jack and Gran belonged to a generation who stayed put, and as a result she knows most of what there is to know about everyone round here.'

'I'll keep that in mind!' Alex regarded Sophie thoughtfully. 'You didn't leave, though.' They reached the swing seat. Alex had to bend a long way down to sit in it, and it creaked as it took his weight. Sophie couldn't help noticing the length of his legs as he tucked them under the shallow seat of the swing, and the faint stitch line of a scar across his left knee as his shorts rode up slightly. She tore her gaze away hurriedly.

'No, I didn't,' she conceded, sitting down beside him. Lily would want the sturdier comfort of the garden chair, she knew, despite the fact that the swing seat was barely big enough for two adults, especially two as tall as her and Alex. She felt her knee brush Alex's as she shifted in the seat, and pulled it away hurriedly. They'd talked a lot over the past few days, but were still acquaintances really, and personal space still felt at a premium, for her at least. Perhaps it was to do with the slightly odd formality of Alex's manners; she still couldn't quite get used to his sense of reserve; the way he gave her space, held doors open for her and didn't try to wind her up at every available opportunity the way her male colleagues always tended to do. The lack of banter was refreshing, but a little alien to her.

'Why not?' Alex asked, seemingly oblivious to Sophie's hurried break of contact. 'What made you stay here?'

'Matthew Carter offered me a job after my A Levels,' Sophie said. 'And the apprenticeship was great. I never wanted to go to university like my friends, and it meant I could start earning money straight away, which definitely helped out my mum. She and I shared a place until a couple of years ago when she met her partner, Steve, and they decided to move to the South of France.'

'Do you see her often?' Alex asked.

'I pop over from time to time for a holiday, but I like to be around to keep an eye on Gran,' Sophie replied. Her mother had only agreed to move to France on the condition that Sophie would stay in the house in the meantime to make sure Lily, her former mother-in-law, was all right. Of course, now that the Martingtons job had come up, it was another complication that Sophie would need to consider, but that was for another day.

'Gran's had some health problems over the years and she needs keeping an eye on,' Sophie continued. 'When I started training to be a cider maker, it all seemed to fall into place, meaning that Mum could finally do what she wanted to do, without worrying about Gran or me. They were always close, even after Dad died.'

'I'm sorry about your dad,' Alex said, his brown eyes full of sincerity. 'It's hard to lose a parent.'

'Thanks,' Sophie replied. 'I was young when he died, which sort of makes it easier. I guess that's why I wanted to stay close to Gran when I started work; to make sure she stays around as long as possible.'

'I get that.' Alex smiled. 'But haven't you ever wanted to travel, though? Isn't that the dream of all island dwellers: to get off the island?'

Sophie laughed. 'I have actually left the island, as you call it, from time to time,' she said. 'But going straight into a job from school made me grow up pretty fast. A lot of my mates went for the gap year option, and then on to university, and now they're still paying off mountains of debt. I wanted to earn enough to support myself if I decided to travel. And as it turned out, I've been able to visit some amazing places through this job anyway. I've been to orchards in Australia, the United States, Holland... and all paid for by Carter's.' Not to mention the odd deeply unsuitable girls' holiday, paid for by her own wages, she thought, deciding not to share the experiences of her Ibiza and Kefalonia days. Alex definitely didn't need to know about those.

'Carter's invested in you and your training, then?' Alex said. Sophie noticed the peculiarly intense look on his face.

'Yes,' Sophie replied. 'Matthew, well, the whole family really, are keen to develop and then hang onto their people if they can. It's always been a family concern; it's just that the family tends to include a lot of the employees as well these days. Especially those like me who've been working here since school.' Privately, Sophie wondered what would happen when the current generation, Matthew and Jonathan Carter, handed over the reins to the next one. She didn't know Matthew's daughter, Meredith, all that well, and she still wasn't sure if Meredith was, indeed, going to be taking over the business when she was old enough.

Meredith Carter was in her first year of a History degree at York University, her father's alma mater, and as yet showed very little sign of wanting to come in and learn about cider making. It was sometimes difficult for Sophie to remain objective about Meredith; she herself had spent ten years working for a firm she was passionate about, whereas Meredith had been born into the family and would, in all likelihood, just take over the reins when it was time. Part of Sophie resented her for that. She had nothing against her personally, but it didn't sit entirely well with her that someone should just be handed the keys to a very successful business by virtue of birth.

'It's nice to know they treat their family so well,' Alex said quietly. She was just about to reply when she saw that Lily was on her way back from the kitchen with a tray containing a jug of home made lemonade and three glasses, and a plate of scones. 'Here, let me take that, ma'am' Alex said, springing from the swing seat as she approached.

'Thank you, my lovely,' Lily replied, raising an eyebrow at Sophie as Alex turned back to the table and set the tray down. 'Gentleman,' she mouthed behind his back. Sophie ignored her as best she could.

'So, Alex, is this your first visit to the UK?' Lily poured three tumblers of lemonade, passed one each to Sophie and Alex and then settled back into her chair with a creak.

Alex took a sip of his drink, and Sophie was tickled to observe that he was doing his best not to wince at its sharpness. Her grandmother's lemonade was an acquired taste. 'No, although I was quite young when I visited before. Mom was quite the Anglophile, and she brought me to London when I was ten to see the sights. I suppose we just did what most tourists do, although we did head off into the New Forest for a couple of days after seeing the usual places. I fell in love with London, and I wanted to come back some time, but then life and work took over.'

'What was your favourite place to visit?' Lily asked.

'Hampton Court Palace,' Alex said. 'I've always loved history, and it was like walking through a time warp, seeing it all unfolding in front of me.'

'So, now you're back in the country, are you planning to visit again?'

'I hope so,' Alex replied. 'That's why it's so nice to be working with Carter's for the summer. There's certainly enough history and heritage in the business to fascinate anyone. I want to learn as much as I can while I'm here.'

'I'm sure you do,' Lily said wryly. Sophie noticed the odd look on her grandmother's face as she said it. 'And you've got the perfect person beside you to fill you in on the local history. Sophie knows all there is to know about Carter's Cider – she even did a talk to the sixth formers at the local secondary school recently.'

'Only because Matthew Carter asked me to,' Sophie said. 'And the students weren't exactly what you might call receptive.' Although, Sophie thought, the story about Jonathan chucking someone in the vats went down well.

'More interested in drinking it than learning about it?' Alex said lightly.

'Something like that.' Sophie smiled. 'But who knows? Perhaps there will be a new crop of apprentices in a year or so.'

'I hope so,' Alex said. 'It seems like a good family business to be part of.'

'I can't complain,' Sophie said, sipping her drink.

As a companionable silence fell over them, Alex took a last sip of his lemonade and then glanced at his watch. 'I'd better get going,' he said. He put his glass back down on the table and then stood up. For a moment he towered over Sophie where she still sat. She noticed, again, with a jolt, that scar on his slightly bowed knees. She blushed as she realised that she was, yet again, staring at his legs. She really must get hold of herself.

'Thank you so much for the drink, Lily,' Alex was saying as Sophie zoned back into the conversation.

'It's my pleasure, Alex. Please do be sure to pop in again soon. You can go out of the back gate if you'd like.' She pointed across the garden to where there was a wooden gate in the wall. 'It's a bit of a shortcut back to High Street, and since you're staying at Rose Cottage B & B it'll save you a couple of minutes.'

'Thank you.' Alex smiled at Lily and then turned briefly back to Sophie. 'I'll see you at work on Monday.'

'Yes, nine a.m. sharp,' Sophie said. 'See you then.'

Alex gave her a brief smile and then walked across Lily's garden to the gate. With a click, he'd vanished through it.

'You want to watch that one,' Lily observed as she put her glass down on the garden table.

'What do you mean, Gran?' Sophie refilled both of their glasses with the last of the lemonade.

'He's not all he seems.' Lily took her glass in still steady hands and before she raised it to her lips she looked her beloved granddaughter straight in the eye. 'Don't get me wrong, he's perfectly charming, and seems very nice, but he's got more up his sleeve than a magician at a children's party.'

'Oh, Gran!' Sophie laughed. 'You think everyone's up to something. What could Alex possibly have to hide?'

'He's not just here to learn about cider, you mark my words. He could have done that in Canada.' Lily regarded her granddaughter levelly. 'He's here for something else.'

'You spend too much time listening to *The Archers*.' Lily had often tried to get Sophie to listen to the BBC's radio soap opera, but Sophie had made a vow to herself to wait until she was at least thirty before she gave it a try. Sophie offered the plate of scones to her grandmother, but Lily waved her hand away impatiently. Shrugging, Sophie took one instead. Alex hadn't taken one, she noticed. Perhaps he was still acclimatising to West Country stodge.

'You need feeding up,' Lily said, nodding in approval. 'You've been looking a bit thin lately.'

'As if,' Sophie muttered, taking a bite of her scone.

'I mean it,' Lily replied. 'Those Carter boys work you too hard. And as for that chief cider maker of yours...'

'David's all right,' Sophie said, putting the scone back on the plate.

'Mark my words, my girl. If Jack Carter was still alive, things would be very different.'

'Oh, Gran.' Sophie smiled. She knew her grandmother had always had a soft spot for the late chairman of Carter's Cider, and the two had had many a lively chat over the years; they'd even made up the odd bridge foursome when Jack's wife Cecily and Lily's husband Seth had been alive. 'Things change. They have to. We've got to move with the times.'

'But enough about that. Back to that young man of yours.' Lily's eyes twinkled.

'He's not mine,' Sophie said hurriedly. 'I'm just meant to be teaching him the tricks of the trade. David would have been a better fit, but Matthew wanted me to do it.'

'You sell yourself short,' Lily said. 'You've been working there for over ten years now. I'd say that means you know a thing or two about blending and tasting, don't you? If that's what young Alex is really here for.'

'What do you mean?'

'You mark my words.' Lily raised a finger to emphasise the point. 'That boy wants more than just a crash course in which apples go best with what. You only have to look him in the eye to know that.'

Sophie shook her head in exasperation. Her grandmother could sniff out the drama in any situation, whether there was any there or not. Her theory, that all life was a narrative, had both fascinated and amused Sophie since she was knee high to a grasshopper. 'I think you're reading too much into things. As usual.'

'You'll see,' Lily said mysteriously. Her eyes assumed a faraway expression for a moment. 'Time will tell with that one.'

'You've been reading your own novels again, Gran,' Sophie teased. 'Life's not a sweeping love story, you know. Not everyone has an ulterior motive, and not everyone needs a Prince Charming.'

'So, you admit you think he's charming, then?'

'Gran! I've got to work with him. I can't go thinking like that.'

Lily refrained from comment while she had another sip of her lemonade. 'Nothing wrong with thinking,' she said eventually. 'After all, as you say, you will be working with him for the next month or two. And he is a rather good looking chap. Better than the last one you went out with, anyway. And such nice manners.'

'No. Comment,' Sophie said. 'Now, is there anything you want me to do for you before I go home?'

'I'm perfectly capable of doing anything that needs doing,' Lily said shortly. 'You worry too much.'

'I know you are,' Sophie said patiently. 'But since I'm here, it's only reasonable to ask.'

'You get off home and get your beauty sleep, my girl,' Lily said. 'You'd better look your best for Mr Canadian Dreamboat when you see him at work on Monday.'

Sophie stood up and leaned forward, kissing her grandmother goodbye. Lily really was incorrigible.

6

Alex found that the days were slipping past with alarming speed. He'd learned so much already, but he couldn't help thinking that in a few months' time he'd be back home again, and he still hadn't worked out exactly how he was going to come clean about the other, more personal reason he was here in Little Somerby. The more time he spent working with the Carters and their employees, especially Sophie, the more he liked what he saw, and the harder it was getting to envisage a situation where he could tell them the truth.

And, there were other things to consider. He found himself more and more drawn to Sophie. Her passion, her enthusiasm for her craft, her desire to develop new blends and push boundaries in cider making; it was as if she embodied the spirit of the business he was trying to emulate. If only he could bottle some of her ideas and take them back home with him. It wasn't just her passion for cider that he liked, either. She was kind, warm, thoughtful and decidedly attractive. Despite his initial vow to stay away from romantic relationships, in his more confident moments he'd considered asking her out, but what would happen if she said no? That could get really awkward, considering she was overseeing his internship. And, more frighteningly, what if she said yes? Could he handle a new relationship, especially one that would be long distance? Did he trust himself to? Sophie was too honourable to play around with.

He would soon be working his way around the different parts of the business, though; Matthew had arranged for him to do a few days in the different departments, including shadowing him for a day or two, so perhaps he should risk it. But to what end? He'd be leaving at the end of September, and she was definitely a fixture here. What would be the point? He wasn't really one for holiday flings, and he didn't want to start something with Sophie that he couldn't finish.

'Homesick?' Sophie asked as she slipped back into the office to find him staring into space.

Alex shook himself back to the present. 'Sorry. Just trying to get my head around everything you've given me to read. I'm going to be working in the cannery and the tech specs for the equipment are blowing my mind.'

'As will the noise, unless you get fitted with some ear defenders!' Sophie smiled. 'It makes my ears ring every time I have to go in there.'

'I'll bear that in mind,' Alex replied. He glanced back at the paperwork. 'I don't know how much more of this is going to go into my head before I have to see it in action.'

'I wouldn't worry,' Sophie said. 'I might be testing your cider knowledge, but the boys on the canning floor aren't likely to want you to do anything more than observe. And possibly unjam the machines where necessary.'

'That's a relief.'

'Look, since you're not really concentrating on all those facts and figures, why don't you stretch your legs and take an early lunch? I've got some paperwork to finish off, and I'm sure you could do with the fresh air.' Sophie smiled. 'Maybe come back to it later?' She glanced at her watch. 'It's nearly lunchtime anyway.'

'OK, sure,' Alex said. He wasn't making much headway anyway, and fancied some fresh air before he was called to the rather more industrial floor of the cannery. 'I'll see you later?'

'I'll be here,' Sophie replied.

Exiting the small office, Alex wandered out across the courtyard. As he did so, he noticed that the lights were on over in the site's newest building, the museum and archive. Not yet open to the public, it was a repository for all of the papers and photographs that Matthew's wife, Anna, had dug out of the tea chests in the attic at the family home, Cowslip Barn, shortly after she'd married Matthew. Overwhelmed with a sudden craving for information, Alex decided to take a look. Officially, it wasn't open, but he figured, as an employee, he could try his luck. Striding over to the timber and glass building, he slipped in through the door.

Alex couldn't help but take a sharp breath as he looked around him. The custom built museum was a stone's throw from the cider shop on site, its oak beams and glass elegant and reverential. Inside the building was the complete history of the Carter family, from Samuel Carter's early days in the shed with a wooden cider press to the state of the art enterprise that Jonathan and Matthew now presided over. Everywhere were photos and artefacts that showed the long, shared heritage of the Carter family. It was impressive, emotional and very, very tribal.

Alex's eyes were drawn to the photo gallery of the most recent generations of the Carter family. There, on the walls, were Jonathan and Matthew, going back in time to when they were younger men, then teenagers, then schoolboys. In some photos they were posing with the orchards in the background, in others they had pints of cider in their hands. And there, next to his sons in some of them, and then alone as the photos grew more tinted with age, was Jack Carter, their father.

The picture that caught Alex's eye instantly was one that was taken in the early 1980s Jack was standing in what was a much smaller shop, a glass of cider in his hand, caught in the moment chatting to one of the Somerset farmers who used to frequent the farm on their tractors. He was smiling, carefree, totally at home in his environment. Alex searched the expression of the man in the photo. It was a carefully curated image, a crafted moment put on display for public appreciation and consumption. A photograph intended to promote a certain impression of a man who went so much deeper than a snapshot in time.

'Hello! Can I help you?'

A voice broke into his thoughts and he struggled to return to the present, as a tall, willowy, dark haired young woman sidled into the museum.

'Hi,' Alex replied. He realised from the girl's height and colouring that she could only be Matthew's daughter,

Meredith. 'Sorry to intrude – I was just curious to see how the museum was going.'

The young woman extended a hand for Alex to shake. 'Meredith Carter – Merry, to most people. I'm just popping in to add a few more pieces to the archive before I start my shift at The Cider Kitchen.' Meredith was working at the flagship restaurant on the Carter's Cider site during her university holiday, as she had done when she was still at school. Run by her uncle, Jonathan, and her aunt, Caroline, it was going from strength to strength and drew customers from far and wide to sample the very best of Somerset's opulent produce, as well as Carter's own cider. 'You're Alex, right?' she continued. 'You've come over from Canada? Dad was telling me you've got a cider farm in Vancouver.'

Alex smiled. Sophie had warned him that before long everyone would know who he was and why he was here; it was the very nature of the Little Somerby grapevine.

'That's right. It's nice to meet you, Merry.'

'You too.' Meredith threw him an inquisitive glance. 'Are you swotting up in case Sophie and David set you a test?'

'Something like that,' Alex replied. Meredith was so like her father Matthew in looks and mannerisms, it was slightly unsettling. He looked at the paper folder Meredith was clutching. 'Are those a few more pieces for the exhibition?'

Meredith grinned. 'Well, I've got to mount these this afternoon and add them to the collection – do you want a sneaky peek before they go on display?'

'Sure,' Alex replied. He had some time before he was due at the cannery, and he was intrigued as to what else Meredith had to add to the museum. He wandered over to where she was spreading out the documents and photographs on the large wooden table at the side of the room.

'My wicked stepmother Anna's still going through a lot of the documents and photos, and she's a bit of a perfectionist, but she's sorted out a lot of the stuff from the early eighties this summer. She's obsessed with finding out what Dad was like when he was growing up, as they lived so close to each other, but never really met until recently. Come and have a look.' At a glance, the folder seemed to contain mostly more photographs, but also the odd letter, too. Alex scanned the images, picking up one or two, before finding his eyes inexplicably drawn to a particular photo.

'That's your grandma and grandpa?' Alex asked softly.

Meredith nodded briefly before starting to cut out sticky pads to mount the pictures. 'Granny died when I was small; I don't really remember her. She and Granddad were married for forty years before she died. That photo was taken the day they were married.' She went back to sorting out the other pieces.

Alex looked at the photo. In it were Jack and Cecily Carter in the orchard. Jack was in a smart suit, and Cecily had flowers in her hair. They looked intensely glamorous and lit up with happiness. 'They got married in the orchard?' he said, mostly to himself.

'What? Oh, no – they had their wedding party in the orchard. They were pretty broke at the time, apparently, but the party was talked about for years afterwards. Dad and Anna actually got married in the same spot a couple of years back. Granddad really was a party animal, pretty much right up until he died.' Meredith looked thoughtful. 'I still miss him.'

'I'm sure,' Alex said.

'Sorry?' Meredith said, only half listening as she read through one of the letters she had to find a home for in the museum. She looked up again and smiled. 'I hope you're enjoying being here,' she said. 'You seem to have settled in really quickly. I heard Sophie saying how impressed she was with your palate.'

'Thanks,' Alex replied. 'I've got a lot to learn, but Sophie's a great teacher.'

Meredith looked at him speculatively. 'You two seem to have clicked. I guess that helps.'

Alex grinned. 'She's very patient with me. I must be asking an awful lot of rookie questions.'

'I don't think she minds too much,' Meredith replied. 'She's really knowledgeable. I'd say she knows more than Dad or Uncle Jonathan about how to blend a decent cider. I know that Granddad really enjoyed working with her over the years. He used to call her his protégé, which got on David's nerves a bit. But Granddad seemed to get away with stuff like that; stuff no one else could. I guess he was just like that.'

'Well, she's certainly been really helpful to me,' Alex replied, mindful that the conversation was turning back to Jack. 'Your grandfather really knew his apples, didn't he?'

'Yup,' Meredith replied. 'If it was up to Dad, he'd have cut the varieties of cider we produce by half, but Granddad always wanted to innovate, to find new things to do with the orchards. Even when he retired he would still take part in the tastings, still hang out with the blenders. He was a bit obsessed.'

'It was in his blood,' Alex said thoughtfully. 'It must have been difficult to ignore.'

'Dad always knew he'd be a part of this business,' Meredith said. 'He tried to get out, at least for a while, but in the end he came back to it.' She sighed. 'I suppose that's what'll happen with me, eventually. I can go and study what I like, but the business will be waiting for me.'

'Is that what you want?'

Meredith looked up, clear blue eyes serious. 'I don't know,' she replied. 'It's exciting, but it's also really scary. What if I'm the one that the business fails with? What if my heart isn't really in it? What if I just can't do it?' Embarrassed at making such a public admission, and to a stranger, Meredith looked back down at the documents on the table.

'Follow your heart,' Alex said gently. 'If being in this business is what you truly want, then you should go for it. If it isn't, then the family will understand. It sounds like your dad had to make a tough choice at an early age, and that he'll get it if you decide to follow a different path.'

'Are you following the path that you want, now, with this choice to go into the cider business?' Meredith asked. Alex sensed that she was keen to move the focus from her own doubts and fears.

Alex nodded. 'Law was always my first love, and I followed it into some interesting places. But doing this… going into a new place, a new venture, it feels like I've come home. And learning how to make cider… knowing that I'll be able to use that knowledge to create something exciting when I go home… that feels right, somehow. Like I'm finally doing what I'm supposed to.'

'You sound just like Dad!' Meredith laughed. 'He's got a law degree, too, you know, but he came back home to run this place when Granddad had his heart attack.' She looked thoughtful. 'With your passion for ciders, you and Granddad would probably have got on like a house on fire.' She passed him another one of the photos that she'd soft mounted. 'This was him at about your age.'

Alex's heart jumped. Jack looked totally at home in his orchards. The master of his domain, he was as much a part of the landscape as the apples hanging on the trees. Clearing his throat, he handed it back to Meredith. 'Good looking guy,' he quipped.

Meredith laughed. 'And he knew it. He was the most incorrigible flirt, even when he got old. Apparently, he had quite a reputation round here when he was young. But Grandma wouldn't have any of it when she met him. Granddad had to work really hard to win Grandma over, but it must have worked – they were married for forty years.' Meredith smiled sadly.

'They were happy, then?'

'Well, Dad once hinted that Granddad might not have been quite the husband everyone thought he was —but the rumour mill around here always goes into overdrive.

I like to think he still liked to flirt, but perhaps that's all it was.'

Alex said nothing. Meredith was a friendly girl who clearly thought the world of her grandfather, and was obviously having some struggles of her own about finding her place in her own heritage. That was a conversation she wasn't prepared to have just yet with her own family, and her conflict resonated within him, reminding him of his own. The truth was never easy to face, he thought. He hoped that when the time came to face his, he would be up to the task.

7

Still feeling muddled, Alex finished work that day and headed back to the Rose Cottage B & B. While he was happy with the accommodation, he was starting to feel a little claustrophobic living with the ever inquisitive Brenda and her husband Roy. Since he'd met Sophie on her way home, the night she'd introduced him to Lily, he'd taken to mooching down to the local pub, The Stationmaster, for a quiet drink, in the hope of seeing Sophie socially again. It didn't feel right to ask her out on a date during working hours, but he did feel as though he wanted to see more of her. His conversation with Meredith had given him a lot to think about, too. Being conflicted about your direction in life was obviously something that you could feel at any age.

Deep in his thoughts, he hadn't realised that his wanderings had taken him to the back gate of Lily Henderson's cottage once again. When he heard a whirr that sounded suspiciously like the pull cord of a petrol mower, and then Lily's exasperated voice muttering a curse under her breath, Alex's curiosity was piqued. Hesitating for a moment, he was tall enough to peer over the top of the stone wall and when he did, he saw Lily bent over a huge lawnmower, which was obviously not doing what it was supposed to. Without giving himself time to wonder if Lily would appreciate his intrusion, he pushed open the garden gate.

'Can I help you, Mrs Henderson?' he asked as he drew closer.

'Oh, Alex, how nice to see you.' Lily straightened up from where she'd been inspecting the mower with some effort. 'What can I do for you?'

'I think it's rather more what I can do for you,' Alex replied gently, handing Lily her walking stick, which she'd propped by the garden wall. 'Would you like me to take a look at that?' He gestured to the mower.

'Oh, I'll be fine,' Lily said airily, but her eyes told a different story. Alex raised an eyebrow. 'Well, all right. The blasted thing's not usually my responsibility, but my dear gardener's put his back out and hasn't been able to come and cut the grass for a fortnight.' She sighed. 'I got fed up of looking at it, so I thought I might as well have a go.'

'Well, why don't I take a look at it?' Alex said, kneeling down to check over the motor. 'If I can get it going, would you like me to mow the lawn for you?'

Lily smiled. 'That would be very kind. That's if you've nowhere else to be on a fine evening like this?'

Alex shook his head. 'I was going to have a beer at the bar, sorry, the pub, but that can wait.'

'In that case, let me get you something to drink for after you've finished,' Lily said. 'I'm sure I've got a bottle of white wine in the fridge.'

'That sounds lovely,' Alex replied. Getting up, he took hold of the pull cord and, after a couple of false starts, the mower started. Lily, in her haste to cut the grass, had forgotten to prime the engine. In no time he was cutting neat stripes into her lawn, finding the action strangely therapeutic.

'Thank you for taking care of the lawns, Alexander,' Lily said as he powered the lawn mower down. She'd brought a jug of iced water and a bottle of white wine to the table on the small patio outside her back door. 'I can rest a little easier tonight. Much as I appreciate Sophie's offer to wield that mechanical monstrosity, I think some things are better left in the hands of a man.'

'I wouldn't let Sophie hear you say that!' Alex grinned. 'From what I've learned of her so far, she's more than capable of holding her own.'

'Oh, I know,' Lily sighed. 'She's done well in such a male dominated business, but I still don't like the idea of her mowing the lawn. I only tried to do it because I couldn't stand it any longer!' She laughed. 'It's like hoovering the carpet; the more you put it off, the more you think about it. Of course...' she paused mischievously '... the lawn mower is a convenient excuse not to work on my current manuscript, which is due in August.'

Alex smiled. 'I know all about procrastination! The nights I spent putting off writing up case notes when I was practising law were crazy. Is there anything else I can do for you while I'm here?'

'Not at the moment, but thank you,' Lily replied. 'So, do you have anything else planned over the next few days?

I know from experience that Little Somerby can get a bit claustrophobic if you can't get out of it occasionally!'

Alex took a sip of his wine. 'Nothing definite yet,' he said. 'Except that Matthew Carter's invited me to dinner at his place tomorrow night, and I was planning on going into Bristol some time this weekend or next – Sophie tells me the Bristol Museum is well worth a look, and somewhere called The Red Lodge is a bit of a hidden gem.'

'Oh, you'll enjoy dinner with Matthew and his family, they're all such lovely people,' Lily replied. She looked speculatively at Alex, and Alex felt himself shifting uncomfortably under her scrutiny. He was glad when she spoke again. 'And as far as Sophie's concerned, she'd make an excellent Bristol tour guide. Why don't you give her a ring and see if she fancies going with you?'

'Oh, I'm sure she's got better things to do,' Alex replied. 'And she's probably sick of the sight of me.'

'Nonsense!' Lily snorted. 'She loves that end of Bristol, and she doesn't get out nearly enough. Although you mustn't tell her I said that. She's been smarting a bit since she and that Mark Simpson went their separate ways. I'm sure spending a sunny afternoon in town would be just what the doctor ordered.'

Alex definitely got the feeling he was being led. 'Are you trying to matchmake me with your granddaughter, Mrs Henderson? Because I don't think she approves of office romances.'

'Oh, I wouldn't let that put you off!' Lily said. 'She's not got out much at all since Mark. Frankly, my love, if I was fifty years younger, I'd be trying to make a date with you myself!' She paused as Alex burst out laughing. 'Sophie needs some fun, and you should go and see some of the sights while you're this side of the Atlantic. Time marches on so quickly, and before you know it, you'll be back on the plane to Canada.'

'Very true.' Alex topped up both of their glasses with the chilled white wine. 'But perhaps it's a little short notice to ask Sophie to come with me. She's bound to have other plans.'

'No harm in asking,' Lily said. 'Speaking of which, I've had an idea.'

'Oh, yes?'

'How long are you booked into Rose Cottage?'

'Until tomorrow night. Brenda likes to keep things fairly informal and suggested a weekly booking.'

'Well, you can't stay there forever,' Lily said. 'After all, nice as it is, it's not cheap, even if it is tax deductible, and from the look of you you've not exactly been availing yourself too often of Brenda's famous breakfast option. If you had, you'd be twice the size you are by now.'

Alex laughed. He liked Lily's directness; she reminded him of his own grandmother. 'Perhaps you're right. But do you know of anyone who might take a temporary lodger for the summer?'

'Well, I've got a decent sized spare room with its own bathroom, which, while not exactly en-suite, is just down the landing. If you can bear the thought of sharing a breakfast table with me in the morning, you're more than welcome to take it.' Lily's eyes twinkled. 'And since I usually let it out to students from Langford Veterinary College just down the road, the rate is a lot more reasonable than Brenda's at the B & B.'

'That's a very kind offer, Mrs Henderson,' Alex said. 'But are you sure you want another stranger in your house over the summer? After all, I'm going to be working some pretty long hours, and I'm also up quite early to run. I wouldn't want to disturb you.'

'Oh, don't you worry about that.' Lily brushed away his concerns with a brisk hand. 'I'd appreciate the company, and, truth be told, I've missed having someone in the house since the last student from the vets' school moved out a few weeks ago. You'd fill the gap nicely between the end of term and the next academic year, if you can cope with a flowery duvet and a few copies of my own novels on the shelves.'

'Well, then, thank you,' Alex said. 'I'd like that. And it sounds like I'll have plenty to read, too!'

Lily smiled. 'I'm not sure you're quite my target market, writing romantic fiction as I do, but you're very welcome to read a few if you'd like.' She sighed. 'After thirty-one novels, you'd think I'd be finding the process easier, but sadly it seems to get harder every year.'

'I'm sure you'll get there,' Alex replied, impressed by Lily's output as a novelist. 'It must be a passion for you.'

'Well, I had to do something to take myself away from things when my son died.' Lily smiled, but it was a smile that thinly masked the pain. 'Writing novels allowed me to escape the ordinary, and it turned out that I was rather good at it.' She paused, as if to collect herself. 'Of course, I've been waiting for that lucrative screen deal, but in the meantime the words, and my readers, will do.' Shaking her head slightly, as if shrugging off the painful memories, she topped up their glasses. 'So, when would you like to move in?'

'As soon as you're ready for me,' Alex replied, realising too late to diplomatically comment on the fact that Lily's son must have been Sophie's father. It seemed they were all plagued by losses.

Lily stood up from the table and reached for her carved walking stick. 'I'll show you the way to the room so you can have a look, just to be sure.'

'There's no need, Mrs Henderson,' Alex replied, standing as soon as she had. 'I'm sure it'll be lovely, and, nice as it's been staying at Rose Cottage, it will be equally lovely to make my own bed again without coming back to find someone's made a better job of it!'

'Ah, yes, Brenda and her famous hospital corners!' Lily laughed. 'She used to be a psychiatric nurse, you know, and the training never really leaves you. She's often joked it comes in handy when dealing with her more, er, eccentric guests. Present company excluded, I'm sure.'

Alex smiled back, feeling relieved to be offered an escape from Brenda and her endless small talk. Living with Lily, he thought, would be far more fun and hopefully give him more of an opportunity to spend time with Sophie. Much as he still had his reservations about starting a long distance relationship, he couldn't help feeling more and more drawn to her.

8

After a lazy Saturday morning catching up on some sleep, and a lunchtime spent doing a little housework and having a Skype call with her mother, who was keen for her to take some time off soon and visit her in the South of France, Sophie decided to wander down to the village to get some supplies in for a quiet evening at home. She'd earmarked a series on Netflix that she fancied binge watching that weekend, and needed wine, pizza and ice cream to accompany it. Having skipped both breakfast and lunch, she was feeling hungry. She'd popped in on Lily after heading down to the shops and was now on her way back from giving Barney, her grandmother's Weimaraner, his afternoon walk when she saw a familiar figure coming down High Street towards her. Surmising from the shorts and T-shirt that he must be on his way back from a run, Sophie wondered whether she should cross the road so that she didn't disrupt his momentum, but, as she drew closer to him, he caught sight of her and smiled, taking out his earphones.

'Hi,' Alex said as they reached each other. 'Nice afternoon.'

'It is,' Sophie replied, gesturing towards Barney. 'It was too hot to walk him earlier, so when I popped in on Gran

I offered to take him out now it's cooled down a bit.'
Barney panted by her side, exhausted from the dash down
the Strawberry Line, but as Alex extended a hand he lifted
his big wet nose and nuzzled it into Alex's palm.

'Oh, Barney!' Sophie shook her head. 'You don't have
to show everyone quite so much love when you see them.'

Alex laughed and ruffled behind the Weimaraner's
ears. Barney rested his huge head against Alex's thigh.
'Good boy. Barney's pretty much the size that Prince, the
Doberman I had as a kid, used to be.'

'Don't be fooled.' Sophie snorted. 'He's as lazy as he is
huge. Which is just as well, since Gran's struggling to do
the walks she used to. I take him out when I can, but he
could really do with a bit more exercise, just so he doesn't
get any fatter.'

'How much exercise does he need?'

'Oh, only about half an hour a day,' Sophie said. 'But
he'll do more if he's pushed.'

Alex was still stroking Barney's big, lugubrious face,
and the dog reacted ecstatically to his touch, belying his
sombre appearance. Sophie found herself feeling strangely
jealous. Alex did have such wonderful hands, after all.
Tearing her gaze away from them, she tried to focus on his
face again, but that combination of hair, eyes and glorious
bone structure was equally distracting. Clearly it had been
too long since she'd been on a date; she needed to get a
grip.

'I don't mind taking him out,' Alex said. 'I run most
days, and it would be a good way to get to know the
countryside round here.'

'I'm sure Gran would appreciate the help,' Sophie said. 'Although bear in mind that Weimaraners can be quite particular about whom they'll listen to. Barney can have selective hearing sometimes!'

'I'll bear that in mind,' Alex said. 'Anyway, since I'll be sharing his living space from tomorrow, it's the least I can do.'

'You decided to take Gran up on her offer, then?' Secretly, Sophie wasn't surprised; Lily could be very persuasive once she'd set her mind to something, and she'd obviously taken a bit of a shine to Alex. Lily had told Sophie she'd be having a house guest for the rest of Alex's internship when Sophie had popped in to get Barney. Sophie had felt a genuine flutter in her stomach when Lily had broken the news to her; the knowledge that her path would cross with Alex's in her downtime as well as at work made her uncertain how to feel. Would it be crossing professional lines a little too far to be socialising with him as well as working with him?

'Your grandmother has a knack of talking people into things, I'm guessing.' Alex smiled, then glanced at his watch. 'I ought to get going, anyway, or I'm going to be late for dinner.'

'Where are you off to?' Sophie asked, and then cursed herself for sounding so curious. It really was none of her business.

'Matthew's invited me to dinner at his place. I guess I'd better be on my best behaviour, as an intern.'

Sophie grinned back. 'I wouldn't worry. He's got three children and a dog, and from what I can gather things are pretty informal.'

'I've got to get to the wine shop and grab a bottle anyway,' Alex said. 'I wonder if they already know what his favourite wine is.'

Sophie laughed. 'He and Kelli are pretty good friends, so I'm guessing they will.'

'Uh, speaking of going out...' Alex said, suddenly looking hesitant.

'Yes?' Sophie's stomach fluttered a little more at the sudden change in direction of the conversation.

'Would you like to, er, go out for a drink with me some time?'

Sophie's stomach suddenly started turning somersaults. For a second she paused.

'Not to worry if not,' Alex said hurriedly. 'It was just a thought. But I didn't want to make things awkward between us. We've got to work together, after all.'

Sophie's head was screaming at her to politely turn Alex down; that it couldn't go anywhere, even if they did go on a date or two, and that mixing work and play was definitely a bad idea. But her heart was fluttering in her chest, and she was flattered to be asked. The way her body had been responding to Alex was sending her a very definite signal that she was attracted to him. And anyway, turning him down would make things awkward between them, at least for a little while. Perhaps it was better to say yes, and if things didn't work out after one drink, they could agree just to be colleagues for the duration.

Taking a deep breath, and before her head could win, Sophie took the plunge. 'I'm a bit wary of going out with people I work with.' Seeing Alex's face drop slightly, she continued hurriedly. 'But I think I'd like to go for a drink with you. Let's sort something out next week and see how it goes, shall we? Since you've got to rush off now.' *So much for not crossing professional lines*, she thought. One offer of a date and she'd caved right in quicker than a landslide on Cheddar Gorge.

'Sure.' Alex replied. 'I'll look forward to that.' He gave her a final smile, and then set off at a jog, leaving Sophie alone with Barney tugging on the lead beside her. Realising her heart was still racing, she breathed out, wondering exactly how to play things over the next few days. Working with Alex was one thing, but seeing him socially added a whole new dimension. She hoped it wasn't going to be an awkward one, especially since he was moving in with her grandmother, too. What if Alex broke her already fragile heart? After Mark, she wasn't sure she could cope with another trauma.

9

Alex wandered up the driveway to Cowslip Barn, Matthew Carter's white farmhouse, three quarters of an hour later, having showered, changed and remembered to bring the bottle of red wine with him. Kelli, Little Somerby's top sommelier and owner of the village wine shop, had proved useful when quizzed about what the Carters' CEO's favourite tipple was, and Alex had been relieved to discover that they shared similar taste. A bottle of full bodied Tinamou Cabernet Sauvignon was in his hand, ready to have with dinner. He hoped it was compatible with whatever Matthew or his wife was cooking.

As he neared the house, along with the unmistakeable aroma of a barbecue, he could hear voices emanating from the back garden: the sound of a young child burbling happily, a slightly older one chatting away, presumably to Matthew, whose low, earthy rumble he could hear in response, although he couldn't quite make out the words, and then a sudden laugh, which threw Alex off guard for a moment. This was a happy family, he thought; a stable family. How he missed that, in the wake of his mother's death and his stepfather's illness.

Steeling himself, he headed towards the back garden. The tall, wooden side gate was on the latch, and he clicked it open and walked through, hoping they wouldn't mind his presumption, but he doubted they'd hear the doorbell from the back. As he entered the back garden, the sense of completeness, of unity, that the Carter family immediately presented, almost knocked him sideways.

Over by an ancient oak tree in the back of the garden was Matthew's stepdaughter, Ellie, being pushed by her mother, Anna, on the swing that was attached to one of the heavy boughs. Matthew himself was tending to the gas barbecue and taking a sip from a bottle of lager while he turned the cooking meat. Their youngest child, little Jack, named after his paternal grandfather, sandy haired and brown eyed, eighteen months old and into everything, was toddling around on the grass, a little away from the barbecue, pulling a green wooden dinosaur on a red string behind him as he made his way over to Anna and Ellie. The only absentee was Meredith.

'Alex, hi,' Matthew said, putting his beer down on the picnic table and loping over to greet his guest.

'I hope you don't mind me just coming round, but I didn't think you'd hear me if I rang the bell.' Alex's palms were immediately, cursedly, sweaty, and before shaking Matthew's outstretched palm he wiped his own on his jeans.

'Not at all,' Matthew replied. 'Actually, the bell hasn't worked for years. We kind of like it that way – keeps the cold callers at bay!'

Alex laughed a little too loudly, and felt relieved when Matthew called to Anna, who wandered over to the patio, taking little Jack's hand on the way.

'This is my better half, Anna,' Matthew said, smiling down at his wife and picking up little Jack to get a better look at their guest. 'And this is the most recent addition to the family, Jack.'

'Named after your father,' Alex said without thinking.

'That's right.' Matthew smiled. 'Sadly he died before they could meet, but this little one seems to be the spitting image of his grandfather in looks and temperament.'

Anna laughed. 'Yup, he's inherited your father's ability to charm, and no mistake!' She brushed a lock of hair out of the child's eyes. 'And over there on the swing is his big sister, Ellie.' She smiled fondly at the six year old, who was swinging higher and higher, shrieking every time she flew up into the air. 'And I hear you've already met Merry?'

Alex nodded. 'We got chatting when she was adding some things to the museum. Will she be joining us tonight?'

Mathew shook his head. 'She's got, er, other plans,' he said. 'She was a bit cagey about where, and with whom, but, as my wife keeps reminding me, she's nineteen now, so she should be able to be trusted away from the house.'

Alex grinned. 'Not easy as a father, though.'

'You could say that.' Matthew gestured to the bottles of beer that were in a bucket of ice on the patio. 'Help yourself to a drink. Dinner'll be ready in about ten minutes.'

'Thanks,' Alex replied, leaning down to grab a bottle, and handing Matthew the bottle of red wine. He must try not to drink too much, for fear of saying something he shouldn't.

Matthew nodded in approval when he saw the label on the bottle. 'Have you been talking to Kelli?'

'She pointed me in the right direction.' Alex grinned.

'Makes me think I'm spending a little too much time there.' Matthew smiled back. 'But it's useful having a shop in the village that really knows your tastes.' He put it down on the table. 'I'll open it to breathe, and we'll have a glass after these, shall we?' He gestured to the table. 'Take a seat if you like.'

'Thanks,' Alex replied. Relieved for a moment that the pressure was off, he watched as Ellie came skipping across the garden, obviously tired of the swing, and plonked herself down on the opposite seat to him.

'Hello,' he said.

Suddenly shy, the little girl smiled, but said nothing. She helped herself to a slice of the thickly buttered white loaf that sat on the table and nibbled at it, watching Alex speculatively. Alex tried again. 'Have you had a good week at school?'

Ellie swallowed her mouthful and then, deciding Alex was worth talking to, she nodded. 'Yes, thank you. We're doing a project about the Romans.'

'Really?' Alex smiled. 'And what have you learned so far?'

'That they ate with their fingers,' Ellie replied, grabbing another slice of bread.

'Not too much, darling,' Anna chided. 'Or you won't eat your dinner.'

Ellie rolled her eyes in a curiously teenaged gesture before putting the slice of bread onto the plate in front of her. 'OK, Mum.'

Matthew was beginning to load up the serving plates with the cooked meat, and as he walked back to the picnic table Alex sprang up and took the plate from him, setting it down in the middle of the table. 'Here, let me,' he said.

'Wow,' Ellie said as Alex remained standing. 'You're as tall as Daddy Matthew is!'

Alex felt his stomach flip again with nerves. Even the most innocuous comment from a child was enough to make him anxious.

'Ellie's right.' Anna smiled. 'There's not much in it between you two. Although everyone looks tall when you're six years old, I suppose!' She looked as if she was about to comment further, but then seemed to think better of it.

'Help yourself, Alex,' Matthew said as he returned to the table. 'Don't stand on ceremony or it'll all go before you get the chance!'

Alex looked at the laden garden table, covered with bread, salads, freshly cooked food and even a pudding for after, and he smiled. 'It all looks great.'

'Shall I plate some up for Merry for later?' Anna asked.

'Could do,' Matthew said non-committally. 'I'm not sure what time she'll be back, though.'

'She said she was in need of a girls' night out,' Anna said. 'And I know she hasn't seen much of Izzy since she's been back for the summer, so I dare say they'll be catching up for a while tonight.'

'It's great that she still keeps in touch with her school friends, even now she's at university,' Alex said, keen to keep the conversation going. 'She was telling me the other day she's starting to think about what happens when she finishes her degree.'

Matthew gave a short laugh. 'Be sure to let me know if she commits herself to anything,' he said. 'She's been as cagey about that as she has about her social life!'

'Oh, she didn't say anything specific,' Alex said hastily, not wanting to imply that he'd gained any earth shattering confidences from the boss' daughter. 'Just that she was starting to consider her options.'

'Well, she knows we'll support her, whatever she decides,' Matthew said, picking up the wine bottle and filling up three glasses. Passing one to Alex, he smiled. 'So how are you finding things at work?'

Alex took a sip of his wine, which was, as he'd hoped, exactly to his own taste as well, before he answered. 'It's been great so far.' Even if that hadn't been true, he thought, he'd at least have tried to be diplomatic. 'Sophie's been showing me the ropes – she's a great teacher.'

'She's one of the most gifted blenders in the business,' Matthew replied. 'Long may we keep hold of her.'

'There's so much to take in with a business the scale of Carter's,' Alex said between bites of his barbecued chicken legs. 'Four months isn't really enough to get my head around it all.'

'Well, you're welcome to keep in touch after you go back,' Matthew said. 'It would be great to see how you incorporate what you learn here over in BC.' He looked speculatively at Alex as he picked up his wine glass. 'Perhaps I'll take a trip over – see what we can learn from you.'

Alex laughed. 'I don't know what I could teach you about cider making that you and your family doesn't already know!'

'We're always open to new ideas,' Matthew said. 'But enough shop talk. What do you like to do when you're not learning about apples?'

Alex took a moment before he responded. It really didn't sit well with him that he had to be so careful about what he revealed to a man who had welcomed him so easily into his home, but the time needed to be right. 'Well, as you know, I was a corporate lawyer until about six months ago,' he said, hoping it was fairly neutral ground. 'But when Mom got sick, I decided it was time to realise the dream she had about moving out to the countryside and doing something more connected to the land. Land's not something we're short of in BC, and the time seemed right to make a move away from the city.'

'Matthew studied law at university,' Anna said, seizing on the common ground.

'It's a seductive mistress.' Matthew smiled ruefully. 'I nearly got to practise it, too, but it wasn't to be.' Matthew had been forced to give up a prized internship at a large legal firm in the north of England after Jack, his father, had suffered a heart attack and had to hand over the cider business to his elder son before either was truly ready for that to happen. Despite making peace with his choices some years ago, occasionally Matthew still wondered what might have been if he'd had the chance to follow his own path for a few years. That was why he was so keen for Meredith to take her time before she made any long term decisions about her future career. Whether she joined the family firm or not, Matthew wanted her to be absolutely sure that she chose what she wanted.

'It was a great career to have,' Alex replied. 'But in the end, the pull of the countryside got too much. It was time to make a change.'

'Well, you couldn't get more different than renovating an old cider farm!' Anna said. 'It must be taking some work.'

Alex laughed. 'It was a wreck when I first saw it, but it's starting to get there. We hope to be pressing in the late summer next year, if everything goes to plan.'

'And we're back to cider again.' Matthew joined in with the laughter. 'Anyone would think we're obsessed.'

'I'm saying nothing.' Anna raised an eyebrow. Matthew's energy was legendary when it came to the family business. She couldn't help noticing a similar light of enthusiasm in Alex's eyes when he spoke.

Dinner passed swiftly, in a back and forth of amiable conversation, and before long Alex found himself sitting on one of the garden chairs further down the lawn, sipping his second glass of red wine. Anna had excused herself to put Jack and Ellie to bed, and so he sat with Matthew, enjoying the still warm rays of the mid-evening sun, and the man's company.

'This is certainly a beautiful place,' Alex said as he looked around the garden and then glanced back at the large white farmhouse, turned slightly rosy by the rays of the sleepy evening sun.

'Thanks,' Matthew replied. 'It was my great-grandfather's house, originally, and kind of goes with the territory. My first wife didn't like it much, and before I met Anna it had kind of fallen into a state of bloke-ish decay, but she's been putting her own stamp on it since we got married. Meredith's relieved it's not about to fall down around our ears any more!'

'The farmhouse at Adelaide's is in a pretty wild state,' Alex said. 'Which isn't a major problem while the weather's warm, but it's going to need some work before the winter if I'm going to survive the cold. There's a builder in there at the moment, trying to plug some of the bigger gaps and make it a bit more comfortable before the weather turns.'

'Brave of you, leaving him to it while you're over here,' Matthew observed. 'Not sure I'd be able to put that much trust in someone from four thousand odd miles away.'

'He's an old friend.' Alex smiled. 'And I've promised him a few gallons from the first presses as a sweetener if he can get the place sorted out by the autumn.'

'I like your thinking.' Matthew laughed. 'My great-grandfather used to pay his labourers in cider back in the day, too!'

They sat in companionable silence for a while as they waited for Anna to join them. Drifting across from the window of Ellie's bedroom was the sound of Anna reading her daughter a bedtime story, and the little girl protesting that she wasn't remotely tired.

Matthew raised an eyebrow. 'Six going on sixteen at the moment,' he said as Anna's soothing tones gave way to the faintest trace of motherly exasperation. 'Thinks she knows everything.'

'My niece is the same,' Alex said. 'My older sister tells me to take it as a warning for the future!'

'Is that on the cards?' Matthew asked.

Alex laughed. 'Not unless there's something I don't know about!' Then, as he realised what he'd said, his heart thumped painfully. 'I mean, uh, there's no one waiting back home just at the moment.'

Matthew smiled gently. 'Sorry. None of my business.'

'N-no, it's fine,' Alex said, heart still thumping uncomfortably. 'To be honest, I've been so caught up with work up until now that I haven't really given much thought to settling down.' He smiled ruefully down into his half-empty wine glass. 'And with Adelaide's getting started, I'm pretty sure I won't have time for anything else any time soon, either.'

'I wouldn't rule it out,' Matthew said, a soft smile lighting up his features as Anna finally came back to join them. 'These things can happen when you least expect it.'

Alex smiled into his glass. Sophie had told him all about the way the hitherto aloof Managing Director of Carter's Cider had fallen head over heels in love with the custodian of the village tea shop after both had suffered emotional upheavals, and, the way she'd told it, it had been the Somerset love story of the decade. From the way that Anna and Matthew looked at each other, he didn't doubt their deep and abiding love. For the moment, though, he had enough to focus on with Adelaide's. But he had to admit Sophie was intruding on his thoughts a little more than was professional. Especially since she'd tentatively agreed to go out for a drink with him. The Somerset air had a lot to answer for; especially when it was sweet with the scent of cut grass and honeysuckle.

'I guess I should get going,' Alex said, shaking his head as Matthew passed him the wine bottle. 'I'm moving into a new place tomorrow and I need to make sure I've got everything together.' Besides, he thought, he'd had a couple of emotional near misses tonight; it really wouldn't do to have his lips loosened any further by more booze.

Matthew stood to walk him out. 'Thank you for coming over,' he said as they ambled towards the back gate.

'Thanks for a lovely meal,' Alex replied. 'It's not every day you get to have dinner with the boss!'

Matthew laughed. 'As I said, my door is always open.' He thrust forward a hand and shook Alex's, clapping a hand on his shoulder as they parted. 'Anything you need, just give me a shout.'

'I will.' Alex felt the warmth of Matthew's hand and, for an achingly unsure moment, he desperately wanted to level with the man. In Matthew's eyes, he saw friendliness and warmth, and the understanding of just how much hard work was going to be ahead of him to get Adelaide's off the ground. For now, though, he needed to keep his secrets. He left Cowslip Barn that night feeling more conflicted than he had in a long time.

10

The next Monday morning, Anna was preparing little Jack's breakfast and chivvying along Ellie with hers, when Meredith slunk around the kitchen door and quietly started making herself a coffee. With her back to her stepdaughter, Anna continued to try to get some Weetabix into Jack before he was due to go to nursery. Meredith had been a little elusive all weekend, after deciding to spend the night at her friend Izzy's house on Saturday. On Sunday, Anna had been so caught up with baking a few extra summer season supplies for the Little Orchard Tea Shop and keeping the younger children amused that she hadn't kept track of her stepdaughter's movements.

'Were you late last night?' she asked as the whirr and grind of the coffee machine started.

'Not too late,' Meredith replied. 'But I didn't want to disturb you and Dad.'

Something in Meredith's voice didn't sound quite right. For a second, Anna thought about chiding Meredith about drinking too much, but Meredith wasn't much of a drinker, and certainly wasn't prone to binge drinking. Abandoning little Jack's breakfast bowl on the tray of his high chair for a moment, Anna turned around and saw Meredith's red eyes and contrasting pallor.

'What's the matter, sweetheart?' She walked over to where Meredith was still waiting for her coffee, and put an arm around her stepdaughter. 'Did you have a row with Izzy?'

Meredith shook her head. 'No, nothing like that.'

'Come on,' Anna said. 'Come and sit down.'

Meredith allowed Anna to lead her to the kitchen table. As Matthew came into the kitchen, chomping on the last of the toast that he'd made five minutes earlier and taken to his study, Anna shot him a warning look.

'Do you want me to drop Jack and Ellie off?' he said, clocking his daughter's stricken face.

'Thanks, that would be great. Jack just needs his teeth brushing and Ellie's got to find her shoes.'

'Come on, you two,' Matthew said, picking up Jack out of his high chair and ruffling Ellie's hair to get her going. Anna breathed a sigh of gratitude; Matthew was a godsend in the mornings, especially when the unexpected happened, and Meredith clearly needed a bit of gentle handling.

'Tell me what's happened,' Anna said softly, once Matthew had left with the younger children.

'I got a text on Saturday night.' Meredith sniffed, her voice trembling slightly. 'Flynn's broken up with me. He's met someone else.'

Anna's heart dropped through the floor. Flynn O'Connell had been Meredith's boyfriend since they were at school together. Their relationship had endured the distance of both being at university at different ends of the country, as well as a car accident a few years ago that had seen Meredith in hospital with a serious head injury. 'Oh, Merry.' She put her arms around her stepdaughter as the tears, not the first ones since she'd read the text, spilled over.

'I should have seen it coming.' Meredith sniffed again, blowing her nose loudly as with her free hand Anna handed her a tissue from the box on the kitchen table. 'He started getting all weird after I accepted my offer from York, if I'm honest.'

'Oh, sweetheart, you weren't to know,' Anna replied gently. She reached forward and brushed a strand of hair out of Meredith's eyes. 'And it is incredibly difficult to keep a relationship going over such a long distance. You're both having so many amazing experiences.'

'Are you saying it was only a matter of time?'

'Not exactly, but people change. Especially at your age.'

Meredith shook her head. 'It's just really hard because he was my first in so many ways.' She laughed and her cheeks coloured at the memory. 'Although you knew that, of course. I'll never forget *that* conversation.' Meredith reached forward and hugged Anna. 'I'm so glad I ended up having it with you and not Dad – he'd have probably gone round to Flynn's with a shotgun!'

Anna shook her head. 'I think he probably guessed. He just wanted to make sure you were safe.' She didn't add that she'd actually tactfully informed Matthew that Meredith's relationship with Flynn had gone to the next level soon after she'd had the chat with Meredith – and although he'd been concerned, he'd accepted it was the way of things. So long as she was careful, he'd said.

'Guess I won't need to worry about that for a while now, though.' Meredith's voice shook.

'Give yourself time to heal,' Anna said softly. 'It will get better, I promise.'

Meredith smiled shakily. 'I know it's not like... like you went through with Ellie's dad, but it hurts.' The tears started to fall again.

Anna drew Meredith in closer and let her cry. She remembered once saying to Matthew that everything felt so much more intense at Meredith's age. Sadly, that also included the heartbreak. At nineteen, it was an inevitable lesson for Meredith, but no less a hard one. Thankfully, Flynn had pushed off to work in France for his university holiday so there was no chance of Meredith bumping into him in Little Somerby this summer.

Just as she was passing Meredith another tissue, Matthew came back through the door into the kitchen, having strapped the two younger children into the car. Glancing at Meredith, his eyes met Anna's, and as his wife almost imperceptibly shook her head the question died on his lips. Instead, he crossed the kitchen and dropped a brief kiss on the top of his daughter's head before speaking.

'If the office calls, can you tell Jen I'm going out into the Royal Orchard with Joe Flanagan?'

'Will do.' Anna looked quizzical. 'I'd forgotten Joe was starting work this week. God, how time flies.'

Meredith glanced at her father. 'Joe Flanagan? I haven't seen him in ages. What's he doing now?'

Matthew grinned. 'Well, much against his father's wishes, he's working as a tree surgeon. Paddy wanted him to go to university, but Joe was adamant he was going to work with Jim, and now he's been given his first commission here. The orchard maintenance team are going to show him the ropes, and then he's going to prune the Royal Orchard over the next couple of days. Jim's keen for him to get the feel of things as soon as possible.'

Meredith turned back to Anna. 'I'd better get myself sorted out,' she said. 'I've got a shift at The Cider Kitchen at lunchtime.'

'Will you be OK?' Anna asked. 'I can always ring Caroline and tell her you're unwell.'

'I'll be fine,' Meredith replied. 'It'll take my mind off everything.' Caroline had offered Meredith some more hours back at the restaurant during her summer break in addition to the couple of nights a week she'd been doing since she came home. The restaurant was going from strength to strength, and now that they were opening on weekdays for breakfast she needed a few more hands to the pump to cover the increased footfall. Standing, Meredith blew her nose again and then headed out of the kitchen to get ready.

Matthew watched her leave, a look of concern on his face. 'How is she?' he asked Anna.

'Hurt.' Anna sighed. 'She and Flynn have broken up. But she says she saw it coming. I guess it was inevitable with four counties between them.'

'Shall I pick up some Chew Moo's ice cream from the shop on the way home?' Matthew smiled down at his wife. 'I remember what you said to me when she started with Flynn – that ice cream would be useful when the time came.'

'She might like that.' Anna said. 'At the moment, she doesn't seem to be off her food, thankfully.'

'I'll clear out one of the cider vats and fill it with the stuff, if needs be.' Then, more seriously, he said, 'I wish I could protect her from the heartbreak. I know that's daft, but I hate seeing her hurt.'

'She'll handle it in her own way, in time,' Anna replied. 'All we can do is be here for her.'

'You're right, as ever.' Matthew glanced at his watch. 'I'd better get going. I'll drop Jack and Ellie off.' He sighed. 'I've also said I'd talk Alex through the Royal Orchard this morning, and Joe'll need settling in.'

'I thought you were learning to be more hands off,' Anna chided. 'Do you really have to be there, too? Can't someone else handle it?'

Matthew grinned. 'I promised Paddy I'd keep an eye on Joe. But it won't take long. I've not got any meetings until later this morning, and it'll be nice to get out into the open air for a bit. I'll see you later.'

Anna tilted her face up towards Matthew for a kiss. 'See you later.' Vowing to make sure that she gave Meredith as much TLC as she needed, she also hoped there'd be a few slices of cake left over at the Little Orchard Tea Shop to bring home later.

I I

The next week flew by, and before Sophie knew it Saturday
morning came around again. She'd been particularly busy
as the first of the Eloise crops would be off the trees in mid
August, which would mark the beginning of the picking
and pressing season for Carter's. The honey rich scent of
the sweetest apples in the orchard as they were washed
and then gradually pressed would infuse the air, gently
at odds with the alcoholic kick that the finished Eloise
cider would have. Sophie loved seeing them coming in,
beginning their journey from tree to bottle. She'd tried
not to wax too lyrical about it to Alex, for fear that he
might think her some apple obsessed weirdo, but it was
definitely the marker of her favourite time of year. Eloise
was unusual in that it ripened in the late summer rather
than autumn, but this meant that it was out of the way
before the heavier, denser apples came in from September
onwards.

As was her usual routine, but mindful that she might be
invading Alex's space now that he was residing with Lily,
Sophie dropped in on Lily that morning with a couple of
cream cakes from Bird's Bakery. Lily was fond of a strong

morning coffee to counteract the effects of her habitual Benedictine nightcap, and was of the age where 'none of this dieting makes a scrap of difference, anyway, darling,' so cake was always welcome. Lily opened the door with her usual smile, and when she'd finished making the coffee, from a coffee pot she'd had since the 1970s – 'No new fangled machines and pods for me,' – they settled themselves in the front room, sipping the coffee and munching contentedly on the vanilla slices Sophie had chosen this week.

'Best cakes in the county,' Lily said, stabbing the pastry base with her cake fork. As she finished her mouthful, she topped up Sophie's cup with coffee and cream and passed it back to her. 'So, what's new with you then, love?'

'Not a lot,' Sophie said. 'And I'm sure Alex has filled you in on most of the comings and goings at work, and there's really not a great deal else gone on this week.' Alex had checked out of Brenda's B & B and moved into Lily's spare room the previous Sunday evening, where he was proving himself to be the model house guest. Sophie had smiled when her grandmother had texted her on Tuesday morning to extoll the good manners of her new resident, who had insisted on taking Barney for a walk before work, and unloading the dishwasher when he'd come back that evening.

'What about this job offer from Martingtons Cider? Have you made a decision yet?'

'Not yet,' Sophie hedged. 'But I've scheduled a meeting with them for late October, when the picking season's well and truly over.'

'It sounds like a good opportunity,' Lily said. 'I'm beginning to wonder what's keeping you from saying yes here and now.'

'Oh, I don't know, Gran,' Sophie said, rising from the far too comfortable armchair in her grandmother's parlour. 'I honestly don't know which way to jump. Martingtons have made me a brilliant offer, and I might not get another one like it, but I'm just not sure it's what I truly want.' She crossed the parlour to take her grandmother's coffee cup back to the kitchen. 'Shall I put another coffee on?'

'No, thank you, my love, but could you just dash upstairs and get my reading glasses? I left them on my bedside table last night when I was proofreading on the Kindle and forgot to bring them down with me this morning.' Lily was in the late stages of completing her current romance novel and since she'd discovered the Kindle, she'd taken to reading her manuscripts on there, as it made errors easier to spot.

'Sure,' Sophie called over her shoulder. She could hear the water running as she padded up the winding staircase to the landing. Alex must have come back from his run before she'd popped in. He'd told her that he'd taken to jogging around the perimeter of the village before work during the week; he'd obviously taken to doing it at weekends, too. As she got to the top of the stairs and turned right onto the landing she glanced down at her phone, which she'd been checking on the way up. Her grandmother always complained if she checked it too regularly in her presence, so she was just scrolling down her Instagram feed as she passed the door to the guest bathroom. Not looking where she was going, she ran slap into Alex, who was coming out of it, dropping her phone, hands going up to block the collision and landing on some very warm, very wet, bare flesh.

'Whoa!' Alex laughed. 'Too much traffic this morning. Excuse me.'

Dropping her hands immediately, mortified, Sophie found herself nose to chiselled jaw with Alex, who was wearing nothing but one of her grandmother's fluffy white towels slung low on his hips. His body still wet from the shower, hair slicked back from his face, she immediately noticed the toned torso, the towel so low that she could make out the top of a faded appendix scar running over his abdomen towards his hip, the long limbs and the fine dark hair that dusted his chest, thickened and then disappeared tantalisingly below the line of the towel. Immediately, her face felt hot. This was not going to help her caution about socialising with him one little bit. 'Sorry,' she muttered, taking a step back. 'I wasn't looking where I was going. I just came up to get Gran's glasses.'

'No problem.' This time, Alex's laugh was a little nervous. 'Here, let me get that for you.' He knelt down and picked up Sophie's phone from where it had fallen onto the carpet. Sophie immediately found herself willing his towel to slip, and then started thinking even more unsuitable thoughts as his sleek, dark head raised and he looked up at her, all damp tendrils of hair and melting dark brown eyes as he handed her back her phone. As he stood back up, they were still a little too close to each other to be comfortable. Sophie took a step one way, dragging her eyes away from

Alex's near naked body and up to his face, but as she did so, Alex stepped the same way and they ended up close together again. Sophie could feel the heat emanating from Alex and had to fight the urge to reach out a hand and trace a line over that tantalising curved scar on his abdomen.

'Sorry. I'll just, er… I'll see you downstairs, OK?' she said, finally getting a hold of herself. She turned back to the stairs and away from Alex.

'Sophie?' Alex's voice held a trace of amusement.

'Yes?'

'Hadn't you better go and get your grandmother's glasses first?'

'Bugger. Yes, of course.' Face flaming again, Sophie scuttled past Alex, eyes down this time, and into her gran's room. As she turned to close the door behind her, she caught sight of Alex disappearing into his room, and her heart flipped at the sight of his muscular back. She let out a deep breath. She already knew that she fancied Alex; it was hard not to when she spent so much time with him at work, and, after all, he was incredibly good looking. However, coming so close to him had really jolted her. Her heart was hammering so violently in her chest, she was surprised it hadn't echoed off the stone walls of the landing, and she couldn't get the image of Alex, clad only in that towel, out of her mind. Not to mention what was hidden by the towel. To make it worse, her phone had obviously snapped a shot of him as it had fallen, and a rather blurry image of his chest now took its place as the most recent photo. She really should get rid of it, she thought. Then didn't.

'Oh, for fuck's sake!' Too late, she realised she'd said it out loud. She hoped Alex had closed his door behind him; she'd have trouble explaining that it was thoughts of him that caused the outburst, rather than struggling to find her grandmother's glasses, which were, unsurprisingly, exactly where she'd said they would be. Grabbing them off the bedside table, Sophie hurried out of the bedroom door, back across the landing and then down the stairs before she could encounter Alex again. She definitely needed to compose herself before that happened.

'Everything all right?' Lily asked as Sophie came back into the parlour. 'You look a little flushed.'

'Fine,' Sophie replied shortly. The last thing she wanted was to give her grandmother any more ammunition. 'Here are your glasses.'

Lily took them with a smile, and then glanced down at her feet, where Barney the Weimaraner had crashed out. 'He's not used to quite so much exercise as Alex keeps giving him,' she said wryly. 'But I'm sure it's good for him. He's a fine specimen.'

Sophie wondered for a moment whether Lily was talking about Alex or the dog, but was deflected from asking the question by the former's appearance in the parlour. He was more suitably clad in tan cargo shorts and a black T-shirt now, but his hair was still wet from the shower. Sophie felt her face flaming again as she remembered their encounter in the upstairs hallway.

'Did you have a good run, dear?' Lily asked.

'Yeah, thanks.' Alex smiled at the two women.

Please don't smile like that, Sophie found herself thinking. He was heartbreaking when he did.

'Any plans for this afternoon?' Lily stroked Barney's silky grey head, which had snaked its way up to her lap.

'I thought I might head into Bristol and see some sights,' Alex replied. 'There's a bus on the hour from High Street, isn't there?'

'Oh, yes, you mentioned something about that last weekend, if I remember correctly,' Lily replied. She glanced at her granddaughter. 'Do you have any plans for the afternoon, love?'

Sophie bit her lip, vaguely irritated with her grandmother for calling attention to her. 'No, not really,' she conceded. She supposed sitting in the garden and sunbathing didn't really count.

'Why don't you and Alex go into town together, then? I'm sure you'd make a good tour guide. You said the other day you'd been meaning to go in and take a look at the new exhibition in the Bristol Museum.'

'I'm sure Alex has seen quite enough of me at work this week as it is!' Sophie replied, giving a nervous laugh. She glanced at him. Was that merely a polite smile, or was he mortified about being put in this position by Lily? Perhaps, because he hadn't mentioned getting together for a drink again, he'd changed his mind and was embarrassed?

'Not at all,' Alex said, still smiling. 'Although I'll understand if you feel that way. It can't be much fun answering my questions all the time.'

'Well, you do have a lot of them!' Sophie replied. 'But I like teaching you.'

Alex laughed. 'That's a relief! So, do you want to come with me this afternoon?'

Sophie felt herself blushing, both because of the prospect of spending the afternoon with Alex and because she was a bit gutted she didn't have anything else to do, and she felt like quite the saddo for it. Much as she hated to admit it, her social life had taken a dive since she'd split with Mark. Lots of their friends were in couples, and inevitably had not quite known what to say when the relationship ended. 'Yes, thank you,' she said eventually. 'Gran's right, I have been meaning to go to the museum for a while, and it would be nice to get out of the village for a bit.' She glanced at her watch. 'I'll just nip home and get my handbag. Shall I meet you at the bus stop?'

'Yeah, sure,' Alex replied. 'I look forward to it.'

'You kids have fun,' Lily said as Sophie kissed her goodbye. If Alex hadn't been standing there, she'd have chided her gran for the knowing look she gave her, but this time she decided to let it slide. There was nothing wrong with spending an afternoon with a work colleague, after all, was there?

12

Bristol on a warm summer's day was a wonderful sight. Sophie couldn't remember the last time she'd taken the bus into the city, but she didn't want to seem to be pre-empting Alex's plans by offering to drive. Besides, a cool pint in one of the many pubs on the waterfront, or al fresco on Clifton Down, would be a lovely way to spend the afternoon, without having to worry about driving home. As the bus rattled and bumped its way towards the city centre and she caught sight of the Clifton Suspension Bridge cat's-cradling across the Avon Gorge, she thought about the route they should take through the city. There was so much to see, and she found herself wanting to share her favourite places with Alex; to make him see just how much they meant to her.

As if reading her mind, Alex, who'd been looking out of the side window admiring the view of the bridge, turned back to her with a smile. 'Where should we start? I'm in your hands.'

Sophie smothered the thought of just what it would be like to really have Alex in her hands, especially after their encounter in the hallway that morning. 'Well, if we walk up Park Street, we can go to the Red Lodge and the Bristol Museum and then head up onto the downs for a wander, if you like.'

'Sure, sounds good. And hopefully there's somewhere to stop for lunch on the way.'

'Oh, lots of places,' Sophie said. 'There are quite a few pubs or we could try a brasserie – Browns or Pinkmans are worth a go.' She felt her phone buzz in her handbag and, distracted, pulled it out.

'Everything OK?' Alex asked, seeing Sophie's expression darkening momentarily.

Sophie paused a fraction too long before replying. 'Fine,' she said. She was reluctant to switch her phone off altogether, as Lily might need to get in touch with her, but she did switch off the vibrate function. There was no way she was going to answer that text message today. Or ever, for that matter. Why did Mark keep texting her? Hadn't she been clear enough the last time they'd met?

'So…' Sophie dragged her mind back to the present and away from her phone '… we'll jump off the bus outside the aquarium, shall we?'

'Sounds great,' Alex said.

In no time, the bus was nearing their stop. Sophie reached up and rang the bell. Standing as the bus slowed and then juddered to a halt, she found herself careering into Alex's back as they dismounted the steps from the top deck. 'Sorry,' she murmured, taking a step backwards to put some space between them.

'No problem.' Alex smiled back round at her.

Sophie felt her stomach flip. *Get a grip, girl,* she thought.

It was a beautifully sunny day, and as Sophie and Alex headed up Park Street the light caramel stone of the buildings looked warm and inviting. They passed the city library, and headed up towards College Green, where students were lounging on the grass eating lunch al fresco, laughing, and even playing frisbee in the larger spaces. A couple of dogs, panting to be let off their leads, dragged their owners towards the fountain outside the pillars of City Hall, and the enticing scents of coffee and street food blended in the air. Sophie's stomach gave a rumble; those pastries with Lily seemed like an age ago.

'It almost seems too good a day to go inside, but you really ought to see the Red Lodge,' Sophie said. 'It's not only a gorgeous house, but it has the most amazing herb garden.' She gestured to the traffic on Park Street. 'Let's cross here, and start with the lodge, if that's OK with you.'

'Sure,' Alex replied. They headed over the road and then Sophie led Alex down a steep, narrow cobbled street to the garden gate of the Red Lodge. They could smell the garden before they saw it. Enticing scents of thyme, rosemary and honeysuckle drifted through the warm summer air, and as Sophie pushed open the wrought iron gate that marked the entrance to the Red Lodge's walled garden, the riot of colour and scent was a huge contrast to their brick and urban surroundings.

'I thought this might be a nice place to check out how good your nose is getting,' Sophie said playfully as they walked up the cobbled path. 'The garden used to be a lot bigger, but this is all that's left now.'

The garden was arranged in a geometrical formation with small pathways of hedge separating the aromatics and flowers that clustered in colourful and fragrant beds. Sophie reached out and rubbed her thumb and forefinger against the leaves of a light silvery green, roughly textured herb. 'Can you identify this one?' she asked, picking a leaf and then handing it to Alex. Their fingers touched briefly as he gave it a sniff.

'That's easy,' Alex replied. 'Sage.'

'Variety?' Sophie teased.

Alex wrinkled his brow. 'There's more than one?'

Sophie laughed. 'Of course! This one's Berggarten sage. Doesn't flower often, but it's really pretty in a garden like this, as well as smelling great.'

She leaned forward and buried her nose in one of the large, loose petalled Old English roses that rambled along the far wall of the garden. In full bloom, their scent was a marked contrast to the sage, and made her think of long sunny days, and the sweet, fizzy taste of Carter's Eloise cider, which was one of the blends she'd been proudest to help create. It was a cider that, when you drank it, made you yearn to share a warm afternoon with a lover. For that reason, it was best to limit your consumption if you had anything substantial to do after drinking it.

Snapping back to reality, Sophie straightened up, her face colouring as she noticed that Alex was staring intently at her. 'What?' she asked, slightly on the defensive.

Alex smiled and shook his head. 'Nothing. It's just...'

'Just what?'

'You get this look on your face when you're smelling or tasting. I've noticed it at work. It's as if those senses are taking you to a whole different world. You seem to just drift off, as if you really are somewhere else.' He glanced away, embarrassed. 'Sorry. I didn't mean to make you feel uncomfortable.'

Sophie smiled to try to defuse the moment. 'Not at all,' she said. 'I'm flattered that you've been paying so much attention. To the process, I mean.'

Alex smiled back. 'So why don't you show me the rest of this place, and then we can decide where to go next?'

Relieved that the focus was shifting away from her, Sophie nodded. 'It's not huge, so it won't take long, but it's got a very interesting history. And you wait until you see what's in one of the rooms on the ground floor!'

Mounting the steps to the front door, with Alex loping behind her, Sophie had just about regained her sense of equilibrium by the time they crossed the threshold. Trying to be cautious on such a warm day, with such lovely scents in the air, was going to take some willpower, she thought. The atmosphere itself seemed to be singing love songs.

As they entered the cool, marble floored hallway of the Red Lodge, they were immediately assailed by that very English scent of wood polish underpinned with dust. The open hallway led off to a room to the left that had a rather unusual feature, and as Sophie stepped over the threshold she gestured to Alex and pointed.

'I dare you to walk over it,' she teased.

Inset into the floor, around a metre in diameter and nearly twelve and a half metres deep, was a sixteenth century well. It had been uncovered during renovations to the lodge in 2010, having been incorporated into the house at some time in the distant past during an extension, and was now artfully lit, topped by thick glass and a feature of the room. Schoolchildren, students and visitors alike dared each other to step on the glass without feeling dizzy.

'That's pretty cool,' Alex said, leaning over to get a better look down the well. 'I'll walk over it if you will!'

Sophie laughed. 'Such a gentleman, getting the lady to go first!' She stepped into the middle of the glass top and beckoned. 'Come on, scaredy cat!'

Alex glanced down, shook his head and took a step. 'Are you sure it'll take both of us?'

'What are you suggesting?' Sophie took a little step back so that they could both stand over the glass covered gap. She looked down again. 'Although it *is* a long way to fall if the glass cracks.'

A discreet cough behind them signalled that there was someone else in the room. 'I wouldn't worry about that,' the guide said. 'It's built to take a lot more strain than you two could put on it.'

'That sounds like a challenge.' Alex's voice was low with amusement. Stepping forward again, he joined Sophie in the centre of the glass panel. Sophie felt a shiver of anticipation run down her spine at his nearness; it reminded her yet again of their collision in the hallway at Lily's.

'I guess you're right,' Alex said as the guide gave a smile. 'We seem to be holding up OK.'

Speak for yourself, Sophie thought as she once again found herself nose to jawline with Alex. Suddenly feeling awkward, she stepped backwards off the glass panel. 'Come on,' she said. 'There's still loads to see in here, especially if you want to go to the Georgian House, too.'

Alex stepped over the well and grinned. 'Well, you're my tour guide, so I'd better do as you say.' In step as they left the Well Room and headed upstairs to see the rest of the house, Sophie realised just how much she was enjoying spending time socially with Alex; she definitely wanted to make the most of the day.

13

After getting through her shifts at The Cider Kitchen that week on autopilot, Meredith had been consoling herself with the tubs of her favourite Chew Moo's ice cream in the freezer that her father had bought. Knowing that this was his way of expressing concern, she'd given him a hug. Anna had also suggested a film and popcorn night on the sofa on the Thursday evening, which had cheered Meredith immensely. She never stopped being thankful that her father had married Anna, who had glued the fractured Carter family back together with her patience, her kindness and her emotional intelligence. She dreaded to think how her father would have initially reacted to the news of her and Flynn's break-up – with well meaning, but truly terrible advice, she assumed. And a shotgun. She felt pleased that Flynn was in France for the summer, though – it meant she didn't have to worry about bumping into him before she was ready. Getting dumped by text was rough, but at least she hadn't actually had to see him face to face.

She'd been sleeping better than she'd thought she would, too, and she'd woken up on Saturday morning, a week after being dumped, completely ready to face a shift at The

Cider Kitchen. Still unable to face breakfast, though, she left the house, cutting across the cider farm's site towards the restaurant. She was a little early, but Caroline never minded her getting in before her shift started. Meredith was so preoccupied with her own thoughts that she failed to notice the tree surgeons still working on the taller trees of the Royal Orchard. Although they wouldn't normally work on a Saturday, there was a lot to do and they were independent contractors so they were putting in a few extra hours.

Whereas the commercial stock was kept to a standard height and width, and organised in neatly regimented rows on the fifty or so acres of the site, the Royal Orchard was left intentionally a little freer, a little wilder. A standing monument to the Carter's Cider heritage, it contained a couple of dozen ancient varieties of apple trees, some of which were growing increasingly rare as the years passed. Blends from the orchard were occasionally produced on a boutique scale, but for the most part it was a monument to their past. Every few months the tree surgeons would come in and maintain the trees, ensuring that the varieties would live to see another spring.

Meredith, however, failed to notice the bright yellow signs that had been put on the boundaries of the Royal Orchard, and, as it was her usual route, she headed straight through the middle, head down, eyes on her own feet, earphones connected to the phone in her pocket, playlist deliberately loud and distracting. It wasn't until a huge branch crashed to the ground, landing virtually at her feet, that she looked up in alarm. Whipping out her earphones, she took a step back, just in time to hear someone shouting from the boughs directly above her head.

'What the hell are you doing down there? Didn't you see the signs?'

Meredith's head snapped up and, dazzled momentarily by the sun glinting through the branches of the ancient tree, she couldn't quite make out the tree surgeon's features. What she could see was a long pair of jeaned and booted legs leading to a harness around a rather muscular bottom, and, unnervingly, hands holding a huge, still running chainsaw.

'Sorry,' she muttered. 'But you could have checked below you before you chopped that branch off and nearly decapitated me.'

'I shouted the moment I saw you.' The tree surgeon's voice was still raised. 'You must have had your music up so loud you didn't hear. Perhaps you should think about turning it down in future.'

Meredith felt a prickle of irritation at his condescending manner, and then surprise as he switched off the chainsaw and attached it to a hook on his belt and then abseiled down a little. It was only when he was directly above her head, and out of the dazzle of the sun, that she thought he looked familiar.

'You don't remember me, do you?' Mocking blue eyes, as clear as her own, stared down at her from the vantage point above her head. Still harnessed to the thick upper limbs of the oldest tree in the orchard, he grinned.

Meredith was irritated by his insouciant manner, and even more irritated with herself that she'd noticed his pert backside in those tight blue jeans; although, to be fair, his arse was pretty much in her eyeline now he'd abseiled down that bloody tree.

'You'll have to remind me,' she said more coolly than she felt.

'My dad and yours are still good mates,' he said as he adjusted the harness and slid back down to ground level. Extending a hand sardonically, he grinned. 'Although since you've been away for a while, I'm not surprised you don't recognise me. I'm Joe Flanagan.'

Meredith's mouth dropped open in amazement. The last time she'd seen Joe Flanagan he'd been sixteen years old, gangly and spotty and had a shock of red hair so colourful it clashed with his face every time he blushed, which she remembered him doing a lot. Now, four years later, he was taller, broader, the spots had gone and in their place was an air of self-assurance that was far more attractive. And his hair might have still been red, but it was cut in a far more flattering style.

'Crikey,' she said unguardedly, 'you've, er, changed.' She cursed herself for being so gauche, and felt a blush creeping up her cheeks.

'Whereas you seem exactly the same,' Joe replied. 'I recognised you immediately. The boss' daughter, come home to take her place in the empire. Right down to the total disregard for your own safety, and that of others.'

'You're the one who nearly took my head off with that flaming branch!' Meredith bit back, not in the mood to be told off by some apprentice tree surgeon.

'Oh, and I suppose you're going to run straight to Daddy and tell him all about it, are you?' Joe sneered.

Meredith's temper flared. 'That's a bit patronising. What makes you think I'd do that?'

Joe laughed. 'Daddy's set you up since the day you were born to take over this place. I suppose that starts now, does it?'

'Why should you care?' Meredith retorted. 'You don't know me.'

Joe's grin got a little harder. 'I know your type well enough.'

'What's that supposed to mean?'

'Why don't you ask your boyfriend? I'm sure he'll tell you everything.' And with that he strolled off out of the orchard, leaving Meredith lost for words and feeling distinctly uncomfortable. Hurrying on towards The Cider Kitchen, she found herself wondering just what she'd done to make Joe Flanagan so offhand with her. Perhaps the tree branch was intended as a warning, she thought darkly. The question was, of what?

After a short walk, Meredith arrived at The Cider Kitchen to the sound of raised voices, one male, and one unmistakeably female. Hesitating outside the front door of the restaurant, which had been converted from a historic barn on the Carter's Cider site a couple of years back and had become the destination venue in the village, Meredith sighed. *Not again,* she thought. Aunt Caroline and Uncle Jonathan had been arguing a lot lately, and not just in the usual snippy way that characterised their relationship. Whatever was going on between them felt deeper, more hurtful somehow. She hoped they weren't going to call time on their marriage after just over a year.

'No, *you* don't understand, Jonathan,' Caroline was saying as Meredith pushed open the door. 'It's like talking to a fucking brick wall, sometimes.'

'I don't know how you can say that when you've spent the past forty-eight hours barely talking to me at all,' Jonathan, from his position by the bar where he was sorting out the cutlery for the lunchtime service, retorted. 'I'm not a frigging psychic, Caroline.'

'No one's asking you to be,' Caroline said. 'I just need a bit of space, that's all. But that's clearly too much to fucking ask.' She headed up the stairs, oblivious to Meredith's entry into the restaurant, and the door to the mezzanine level above the serving floor of the restaurant slammed.

'Hi, Uncle Jonno,' Meredith said brightly, instinctively wanting to relieve the obvious tension.

'Merry, darling.' Jonathan put the cutlery back down again on the bar with a clatter. 'How are you doing?'

Meredith noticed the dark shadows under her beloved uncle's eyes, and her heart leapt in concern. She'd waited so long for him to find his own happiness; she couldn't bear it if that happiness was now under threat.

'I'm fine, thanks,' Meredith replied, glad on some level of the distraction from her heartbreak over Flynn. 'And you?' Her eyes flickered up to the mezzanine level of the building, where Caroline had so recently vanished.

'Oh, we're OK,' Jonathan replied, but his smile didn't quite light up his eyes the way it usually did. Meredith wasn't convinced, but, mindful of her own fragile emotional state, she decided not to push her uncle for details just yet. She hoped that whatever was causing the upset between him and Caroline, they'd manage to work it out. After all, they'd overcome some pretty incredible odds in their relationship, including the threat from an insalubrious old acquaintance of Caroline's, who had been determined to ruin her new life in Little Somerby. She was sure, whatever it was, that they'd eventually be fine.

14

A little while later on Saturday afternoon, Sophie and Alex were ambling towards the downs with a brown paper bag of freshly made panini from one of the artisan delis on Park Street, and a couple of bottles of water. Stashed in a carrier bag were also two bottles of cool lager, perfect for a summer's day overlooking the glories of the Clifton Suspension Bridge.

'Bristol's a beautiful city,' Alex said as the ground started to even out after the long steep climb up Park Street and then Whiteladies Road.

'It is,' Sophie agreed. 'Although that beauty came at a price, of course.' The city had long and controversial links with the slave trade, the gains from which had built many of the beautiful buildings that they'd spent the morning exploring. The Georgian House, for example, was built on the proceeds of the owner's profits from the sugar plantations of the West Indies. It was a history that Bristol had long tried to atone for, with Pero's Bridge on the Harbourside being the latest memorial to the losses and tragedies of that time in history.

'Of course,' Alex replied. 'After all, John Cabot discovered a lot of territory in the name of the British

Crown. My middle school history lessons consisted of a lot of British Colonial History.'

They were nearing the flat of the downs, now, at the top of the Avon Gorge. Wandering in step together, they walked along the top of the gorge, staring out across the river to the Clifton Suspension Bridge.

'Shall we stop here and have our lunch?' Sophie asked. She was reasonably fit, but they'd been walking for a while and she felt like a breather.

'Sure.' Alex gestured to one of the park benches that looked out over the expanse of the Avon Gorge. 'Will this do for a view?'

Sophie smiled. This was a romantic place to eat their lunch, and, despite her concerns about mixing business with pleasure, it had been fun exploring the city so far.

As they munched on their panini, Sophie tried to focus on the view, rather than her companion. Despite the breathtaking beauty of the panorama, she found herself glancing sideways a fair bit, taking in Alex's long legs in his cargo shorts, the hint of toned biceps as his T-shirt rose up his arms and his large hands as he reached for the second half of his panini.

'This was such a good idea,' Sophie said between bites of her own sandwich. 'Gran keeps telling me to make the most of my days off, and the fact that we live near such a great city, but I suppose it's like anything; if it's on your doorstep, you just don't visit it.'

'That must be a British thing,' Alex said wryly. 'Back home, the tourist trail is done as often by locals as it is actual tourists. But I guess when you're surrounded by as much history as you are, perhaps you take it for granted.'

'Maybe you're right,' Sophie replied. 'I mean, I live three miles from Cheddar Gorge and I haven't actually been to the caves since I was a teenager.'

Alex cleared his throat. 'Perhaps we could go together before I go home,' he said. 'Although you don't sound like you'd be much of a tour guide!'

Sophie punched his arm playfully. 'I bet I'd still know more about it than you!'

'Really?' Alex raised an eyebrow. 'What do you know about it, then?'

'Um, er, well…' Sophie stalled for time, put on the spot. 'There are a lot of caves. And some of them have been used to store cheese in.'

'Brilliant,' Alex said dryly. 'I feel like I know the place already!'

Sophie laughed. 'Well, how about we go and discover it together next Saturday?'

'I'd like that.' Alex's voice softened, and, in that slightly unnerving way that he had, he looked Sophie deep in the eyes. 'I'm having a really nice time today.'

'Me too,' Sophie said equally softly. 'It's been ages since I've had so much fun.'

There was a pause between them that felt loaded with something akin to longing. Sophie's hand crept closer to Alex's where it rested on the bench between them, and she felt the warmth as Alex shifted ever so slightly closer to her, his head tilting to one side. She could feel his breath crossing the short space between them, and her heartbeat quickened. He was going to kiss her, she knew it. Despite her reservations about what it might do to their working relationship, her lips parted in anticipation. Just as their mouths were about to bridge the gap, the theme tune from *The Muppet Show* cut into the moment like a discord.

Sophie jumped away, cursing inwardly. She had been aching for that kiss. Alex pulled back, too, smiling gently, signalling without words that it was all right, that there would be *time*. Seeing that the call was from Lily, she pressed the green button.

'Hi, Gran. Is everything OK? Did you want me to pick you up anything in town?' At Lily's response, Sophie felt her stomach sink through the park bench, and her heart begin to beat faster. 'Oh, my goodness. How? OK, explain when I get to you. I'll be there straight away. Yes, don't worry, I'll make sure to let Barney out, or Alex can. Is there anything you need from the cottage? OK, I'll be right there.'

With trembling hands, Sophie pressed the red End Call button and stared, speechless at the phone.

'What's wrong? Is Lily all right?' Alex's concerned tone broke into Sophie's thoughts.

'We need to get back to Little Somerby right away,' Sophie said, her voice trembling as much as her hands were. 'Gran's had a bad fall and she's been taken to Weston General Hospital.'

15

In the end, not worrying about the extra expense, Alex and Sophie took a taxi back to the village. As the car ate up the miles between Bristol and Little Somerby, Sophie went through agonies of worry. Lily had been quite vague on the phone, merely saying that she'd had a fall on the street near her cottage and that the hospital suspected a broken hip. She knew that Lily hated talking on the phone, and wasn't surprised at the lack of detail, but she still feared the worst. A badly broken hip could immobilise Lily for quite some time, and Sophie knew how restless her grandmother got when forced to slow down. Being put on bed rest would both irritate and depress her, Sophie was sure of it.

Stopping in at her grandmother's cottage to grab a few necessary items, Sophie had almost forgotten about her near miss of a kiss with Alex on the park bench.

'Will you be OK?' he asked gently, seeing her set jaw and shaking hands.

'I'll be fine,' Sophie said. 'I just hope Gran will.' She blinked furiously. 'I'd better shoot straight to the hospital. Can you stay with Barney and walk him later?'

'Sure,' Alex said. They'd let Barney out into the back garden of the cottage when they arrived, and the Weimaraner was now stretched out on the warm paving stones, enjoying the sunshine and oblivious to the drama around him. 'But call me when you know how Lily is, and let me know if there's anything else I can do.'

'I will.' Sophie went to turn away, but Alex caught her arm.

'Will you be OK to drive?'

'Honestly, I'll be all right,' Sophie said. 'And I'm glad you're here to keep an eye on Barney. I just need to find out exactly what happened. It's so unlike Gran to lose her footing like that. She prides herself on her sense of balance for someone her age.' A shard of worry prickled in Sophie's heart. What if Lily was finally starting to deteriorate? She'd been so strong for all of Sophie's life; what if her grandmother was becoming too frail? Trying not to panic, she hurried to her car, grateful at least that she didn't have to dash away later to get back to Barney. Alex lodging at Lily's was certainly a godsend. It was only as she pulled away from Lily's cottage and glanced back to see Alex in her rear view mirror that her heart lurched with longing again; she felt as though they'd been on the cusp of something.

'Honestly, it's all a fuss about nothing. I'm all right.' Lily's expression was verging on put out as she struggled to sit up in the hospital bed. 'I can't think why they want to keep me in. I'm more worried about Barney.'

'Barney's fine,' Sophie said, passing Lily the glass of water she'd requested. 'And he'll continue to be fine. Alex is going to walk him in the morning and evening, and I'm going to pop in on my lunch break and let him out for a pee until you're home. And probably for a while after that, too.'

'Don't be daft,' Lily said, taking a large sip of her water. 'It's just a bit of bruising; I'll be back on my feet in no time.'

'We need to wait and see what the result of the X-rays is,' Sophie replied. 'Hopefully the doctor will be here soon.' She glanced at her watch.

'Somewhere to be?' Lily asked.

'No, of course not,' Sophie replied. 'But I promised Mum I'd give her a call when we know what the prognosis is, and I want to be able to put her mind at rest.'

'I'd just ring her anyway,' Lily said. 'They'll probably let me out of here tonight.' She sank back against the starched white hospital pillows. 'I hope so, anyway. I loathe sleeping anywhere but my own bed.'

At that moment, the door to Lily's private room opened and a stern looking doctor in his mid fifties entered the room. 'Mrs Henderson? Good to see you've been made comfortable.'

'As comfortable as can be expected,' muttered Lily. 'But not overly so. I'm hoping I won't need to be *too* comfortable, since I'll be going home tonight.'

The doctor glanced down at his notes. 'I'm afraid not,' he said crisply. 'The X-ray shows a hairline fracture on your right hip where you hit the ground, so you'll be staying with us on bed rest for a few days at least.'

'Ridiculous!' Lily snapped. 'I'm as fit as a fiddle. There must be some mistake.' She struggled to sit up, but couldn't disguise a wince as she tried to swing her legs across the bed.

'Just you stay put,' the doctor said. 'Or you'll end up doing more damage.' He glanced down at his notes. 'If you rest up here for a day or two, take your pain medication as directed and promise to take things easily, we'll discharge you. But if you overdo things, you run the risk of doing more damage.'

'And then what?' Lily said. 'I've got a publishing deadline and a dog to walk.' Lily's legions of fans were already clamouring for a new story.

'I'd encourage you to try to stay active,' the doctor replied, 'but not without the aid of crutches or a walking frame for six weeks. We can book you in for some physiotherapy sessions, which should help to keep you mobile.'

'I'm not using a Zimmer frame,' Lily said mutinously.

'Gran,' Sophie warned, 'perhaps you should give it a go. It might help.'

'I'm not on my last legs yet,' Lily said, 'and I'm buggered if I'm going to look as though I am by using one of those things.'

Unwilling to argue the point in front of the doctor, Sophie didn't reply. So long as Lily agreed to stay put for a few days, she thought, it would be easier to pick her battles.

'The pharmacy trolley will be around at six o'clock with your next dose of pain medication,' the doctor said.

'And I'll see you again tomorrow morning. You're not catheterised, so call the nurse when you need to use a bedpan, and tomorrow we'll see about getting you up on your feet.'

'Heaven forbid.' Lily rolled her eyes.

Sophie felt a stab of sympathy for her bedridden grandmother. Lily was fiercely protective of her independence, and hated to rely on anyone. Sophie knew that being forced into bed was the worst thing in the world for her spirits. But at least she had a private room on the Waterside Suite, and so wouldn't be kept awake by other patients on the ward.

'I'll go and phone Mum,' she said. Then she paused. 'Gran...'

'Yes, darling?'

'You said that Barney got into an altercation with another dog. Was it one he'd met before? I mean, it's just not like him to respond like that.' Weimaraners were known for their liveliness, especially when called upon to be protective of their owners, but not for impulsive acts of aggression. Sophie couldn't remember the last time the dog had acted up in public. On or off the lead, he was the perfect gentleman.

Lily hesitated, and Sophie immediately clocked the expression that flickered across her face, although the instant it did, Lily attempted to hide it.

'What is it, Gran?' Sophie said gently. 'You can tell me. If there was another dog involved, it ought to be reported.'

Lily shook her head. 'If I thought anything would come of it, I'd do something. But it won't. I know it won't.' She couldn't quite meet Sophie's gaze. 'It's better that it's just left alone.'

'How can you say that, when you're lying here in a hospital bed?' Sophie said more loudly than she meant. Seeing Lily's most unaccustomed look of alarm, she apologised. 'It's just that I'm so angry that this caused you so much pain.'

'It's really not that bad,' Lily replied, a trace of the old wryness back in her voice. 'And you've been telling me I should slow down for ages.'

'This isn't quite what I meant,' Sophie said, taking one of Lily's cool hands in hers. 'I was thinking about maybe having more holidays.'

'Well, perhaps this'll be just the break I need; no pun intended.' Lily smiled.

'But that still doesn't change the fact that there's a potentially aggressive dog out there who could do this to someone else,' Sophie said, not to be derailed from her line of argument. 'What if it's even worse next time? What if you and Barney meet this dog again? Are you sure you'll be able to hold him?'

'Look, I know you think that Barney's too strong for me these days, but he, like me, is getting on a bit now. This was completely out of character for him.' Lily looked at her granddaughter again. 'And I'm grateful that you and Alex are stepping in to help with him while I'm in this... mess.'

'You know it's no bother,' Sophie said, wondering how she was supposed to feel about the *you and Alex* reference. It wasn't as if they were a couple, after all, this afternoon on the bench notwithstanding. 'I'm just worried about you, that's all. And you still haven't told me who the other owner was.'

The pause was so long that even between Lily and Sophie it verged on the uncomfortable. 'Well,' Lily said, when neither could bear it any longer, 'I suppose you'll find out through the grapevine soon enough anyway.'

'Who was it, Gran?' Sophie's voice was gentler this time.

'It was Mark, and his dog Jimmy.'

Sophie felt her stomach flip. 'What?'

'Now you can see why I'd rather we moved on,' Lily said. 'You've only just got him out of your life, and I've absolutely no desire to be the reason you come into contact with him again. So, I'm asking you nicely, Sophie, to let this go and move on.'

'How can I let it go, Gran?' Sophie asked incredulously. 'When you're lying in a hospital bed? What on earth happened?'

Lily heaved a huge sigh. 'I'd taken Barney out for his usual midday walk, and we were just on our way back up the high street. He was pretty shattered, since Alex had taken him out early that morning anyway, but I wanted to get out and get some fresh air, so I thought I'd take him for a quick run up the Strawberry Line. Anyway, I was about a quarter of a mile from home when I saw Mark and Jimmy coming up the road. You know how small dogs can react to Barney.' Jimmy was some strange mixture of several aggressive small breeds, and had the temper to match.

'Like small men,' Sophie said with a bleak smile. 'Something to prove.'

Lily grinned briefly. 'Something like that. Anyway, I was going to cross over to the other side of the road but traffic was busy and there were those blessed parked cars all along the side by the zebra crossing, so I couldn't get over in time. Mark was jogging with Jimmy, who was off his lead, and he had his headphones in, so he didn't spot us until he was nearly on top of us. Jimmy's aggressive at the best of times, and as he got closer to Barney he started to snarl. Well, poor old Barney didn't know what to do with himself. My fault really, I should have taken him straight out of the way, but I couldn't move quickly enough to avoid him. Before I knew it, Jimmy had gone for Barney's neck, and Barney was trying to shake him off. He totally forgot it was me and not Alex on the end of the lead, I think, and that was when I ended up on the pavement.'

'And where was Mark during all this?' Sophie asked.

'He'd jogged past without batting an eyelid, but when he heard the commotion, he turned round, too late to see what had actually happened. He did come back and help me up, but he caught the tail end of the altercation, the part where Barney's hackles were up and he was trying to pick Jimmy up by the scruff of the neck, and assumed it was Barney who'd started it. At the time I thought I was all right, but by the time I got home I realised I was hurt more badly than I'd thought, and that was when I phoned my GP, who immediately called an ambulance.'

'So, Mark walks away, with that aggressive sod of a dog, thinking Barney caused it all.' Sophie sighed. 'Figures. He always blames everyone else for everything.'

'I don't want you to do anything,' Lily said. She suddenly looked very old, and very, very tired. 'You've only just moved on from what happened between you and Mark, and I won't be the cause for you two having to speak again. There's no major harm done. I'll be back on my feet in a few days and Barney's fine apart from a puncture wound on his neck. It's not worth pursuing.'

'You might think that now, but what if this happens again?' Sophie asked.

'We'll worry about that some other time,' Lily said. 'But for the moment, my darling, I'm telling you to let it go.'

Sophie knew better than to argue with an elderly woman in a hospital bed, but inside she was seething. As if Mark hadn't done enough to screw up her life, now he'd managed to hurt her grandmother, too. Why was it that some people could just sail through life, hurting others without a second thought, and those who were caught in the crossfire came off worst? Feeling angry with him, rather than hurt, for the first time, she thought again about what a lucky escape she'd had when they'd split up.

16

After she'd phoned her mum with the latest from Lily's consultant, and convinced her that she didn't need to jump on the next plane out of Marseille, and then convinced Lily that she really did need to stay put until the doctors told her she could leave, Sophie headed wearily back from Weston General Hospital. Her cottage felt charmless and empty, and Sophie was definitely in need of some company but she didn't fancy parking herself on a bar stool at The Stationmaster all night and drowning her sorrows. Just as she was reconciling herself to another Netflix box set and Nutella on toast, her mobile rang.

'Hi.' Alex's voice was gentle, concerned. 'Is it a good time?'

Sophie felt her throat constrict with tears at his tone. 'I'm back home, if that's what you mean.'

There was a pause. 'Are you OK?'

'Not really.'

'You shouldn't be on your own.'

'I've got the cat.' Sophie gave a shaky laugh. 'Although she's pretty pissed off that she hasn't been fed yet, so she'll probably sulk on my bed all evening.'

Alex laughed gently. 'That's not quite what I meant.' There was a pause. 'Look, why don't I bring Barney over to keep the cat company and we can talk about how we're going to stop your grandmother from doing any more damage to herself when she gets out of hospital?'

Sophie's heart began to beat faster. 'I'd like that.' She sniffed. After all, it did feel as though they had a bit of unfinished business from the bench on the downs that afternoon, although that now felt like a lifetime ago.

'Do you have a favourite bottle of wine that I can pick up from Kelli's place?' Alex asked, his tone still soft. 'That's if you'd like me to.'

Sophie smiled. 'That would be great. I'm less of a wine connoisseur than Matthew, though, so anything bone dry and fizzy would be great.'

'Consider it done,' Alex said.

As she ended the call, Sophie wondered if, had circumstances been different, she'd now have been racing around like a blue-arsed fly, trying to make herself more presentable for an evening with Alex. As it was, she barely had the wherewithal to run a brush through her hair and clean her teeth. Deciding against getting changed, as Alex was bound to notice if her clothes were different from when they parted this afternoon, she sprayed on a bit of her favourite perfume and checked the pantry to see if there were any nibbles in the house to mop up the wine. Finding a couple of packets of crisps, she decanted them into bowls and set to waiting for Alex.

She didn't have long to wait. Obviously anxious not to leave her on her own to stew, he turned up twenty minutes later. She was reassured that he, too, hadn't smartened up and was still wearing the shorts and T-shirt that he'd worn on their trip to Bristol. He had a bottle of sparkling wine in one hand, and Barney's lead in the other. The dog looked docile and as if he'd had a lot more exercise than he usually got, and, when Sophie opened the front door, it was all Barney could do to raise his nose and give her a sniff.

'I decided he needed to get out this afternoon!' Alex said as Sophie commented on the knackered Weimaraner. 'And I think we went way further than he's used to.'

'I told you he was lazy.' Sophie smiled as, released from his slip lead, Barney wandered through to the living room and collapsed with a martyred sigh on the rug by the patio doors, which Sophie had left open as it was still stiflingly hot.

'He doesn't cope well with the heat,' Alex replied, smiling fondly down at the prone hound. As if he'd forgotten himself, he suddenly started and passed Sophie the bottle of wine, which had obviously just come out of the fridge at the wine shop, as it had condensation on the neck. 'Here, I hope this is dry enough.'

Sophie looked at the bottle of cava he'd passed her. 'It looks great. I'll grab a couple of glasses.' Passing the bottle back to Alex, she smiled.

Hurrying through to the kitchen, she grabbed the crystal flutes from the top shelf of the cabinet and headed back to Alex. The glasses had been a present from her grandmother on her twenty-first birthday, and they'd survived eight years through careful handling. They were made of Edinburgh crystal; Lily had been adamant that you should only drink good sparkling wine from crystal, and Sophie had tried to adhere to that as often as possible. At the thought of Lily, lying alone in that hospital bed, Sophie blinked back the tears. It comforted her a little to think that Lily was probably lying awake plotting her next bestselling novel, and not feeling sorry for herself in the slightest.

Alex undid the foil on the bottle and popped the cork into his palm, obviously doing his best not to make Barney jump. Pouring two glasses, he handed one back to Sophie. She took hers across the room and sat on the sofa, motioning for Alex to join her.

'So how are you doing?' Alex asked once they were settled.

Sophie took a sip from her glass, appreciating the flavour and the exquisite dryness as a distraction from her emotions. 'I'm OK. It's Gran we need to worry about.' Her hand started to shake, and she put her glass down on the side table. 'I can't believe it happened.'

'How exactly did she fall?' Alex asked.

As Sophie recounted the story, she saw Alex's face darken, first in shock and then in anger. When she said that Lily didn't want to take things any further, Alex shook his head in consternation.

'But she could be badly injured. This Mark guy should at least make sure his dog gets a muzzle or something. What if it does the same thing to someone else?'

Sophie sighed. 'I've tried to convince her, but she doesn't want to have anything more to do with him. She knows how upset I was when Mark and I split up. I suppose she thinks she's protecting me if she just lets it lie.'

'And how do you feel about that?' Alex's voice was so gentle, spoke of such concern for her, that Sophie felt her eyes fill with more tears.

'I want to see him held responsible for what he did, even after everything that's happened between us.'

'Why did you break up? If you don't mind me asking.'

Suddenly, after the day she'd had, and all the worry over Lily, Sophie felt an overwhelming need to tell someone, anyone, about the deeper reasons for the split with Mark. Alex had such understanding in his dark brown eyes, and as his hand crept across the sofa and covered her own she felt reassurance like she'd never known.

'I was in a bad place when Mark and I split,' Sophie said quietly. 'If I'm being honest, it wasn't just him screwing around with Jenna that ended it. I wasn't the best person to be around for a couple of months before that.'

'I'm sure that's not true,' Alex murmured. 'I can't imagine not wanting to be around you.'

Sophie smiled, but it didn't quite reach her eyes. 'No. You don't understand.' She swallowed. 'Not even Mum or Gran know this. In fact, I haven't told anyone.'

Alex reached across the sofa and took Sophie's hand. 'It's OK. You don't have to tell me anything you don't want to. I won't be offended.'

'It's not that I don't want to tell you.' Alex's hand was warm around hers, and Sophie was grateful for it. 'It's just that it's hard to go back there. I guess I never really dealt with what happened, and just filed it away. And when Mark was caught out cheating, it seemed easier to be angry with him than admit that I'd actually withdrawn from the relationship long before it ended.'

Alex looked at her with soulful dark eyes, turned even darker in the low light of the setting sun. Neither of them had wanted to move to turn on the lamps in the living room, and now the sun's last rays gradually faded into dusk. 'I'm here for you, Sophie,' he said gently.

Sophie took a deep breath, bracing herself to say it out loud. It had been something she'd shut away for nearly a year, and she'd fooled herself that it was over, but being with Alex made her want to be completely open with him.

'A couple of months before Mark and I split, I found out I was pregnant. It was a total accident. I'd had a bout of food poisoning and my contraceptive pill hadn't been enough to cover me. I was getting complacent; I'd been on the pill for so many years that I just assumed it would all be fine. It wasn't.' She shook her head, surprised that she could sound so matter of fact about it when it had hurt so much at the time.

'Mark and I had been seeing each other for about eighteen months, and, although neither of us had talked about a family, it seemed to be heading that way. I wouldn't have been surprised if we hadn't moved in together sooner or later. Anyway, I've always been as regular as clockwork, so when I realised what was happening, I was shocked, but not overly worried. If Mark didn't want to be around, then I was more than happy to keep the baby by myself. Mum had already been dropping hints about settling down, and, although it wouldn't have been ideal to raise a baby on my own, I knew I'd be fine. Then, just as I was getting used to the idea, I had a miscarriage at ten weeks. I hadn't told Mark about the pregnancy – I'm not really quite sure why. I wonder if, deep down, I knew things weren't going to work out between us, so I was holding back a bit. Don't get me wrong...' she glanced up at Alex, who was listening intently '... I'd have told him soon after that, but then I lost it, and there didn't seem much point. The miscarriage wasn't pleasant, but I was physically all right fairly quickly. I just needed a week or so off work, and I pretended I'd had a stomach bug. No one asked any questions.'

She laughed hollowly. 'Much as I miss Mum, it's actually quite convenient that she lives in Marseille these days. It was easy to pretend I was just ill. Gran wondered where I was, I think, but I texted her and kept up the pretence that I had this awful stomach bug and didn't want to infect her. I don't think she guessed.'

'That surprises me,' Alex observed, thinking privately that Lily was about as shrewd as they came.

'Anyway, after that, I wasn't up to much, if you know what I mean, and Mark started getting frustrated. I can't blame him, really, although it would have been nice if he'd let me talk to him about things in my own time. I couldn't talk about it, you see. It was all such a shock: finding out I was pregnant, getting used to that idea and then suddenly discovering that it had ended before it had really begun. I think if I'd had more time, I'd have managed to discuss it with him, but, as it was, he started looking elsewhere and that's when we split.'

'Still doesn't excuse his cheating,' Alex said. He'd turned away, but Sophie was sure she saw something unfathomable in his eyes before he composed himself and looked back at her. 'I'm so sorry you had to go through that alone.'

Sophie shook her head. 'I know it sounds harsh, but perhaps it was for the best. There's no telling what caused it; the baby could have been damaged, or there might have been something else wrong, something with me. At the time you go on the internet to find answers, but really there are no hard and fast rules. And perhaps Mark and I just weren't meant to be.'

'Perhaps you're right on that score,' Alex said, a husky note in his voice. He pulled Sophie into a warm embrace and she luxuriated in his closeness for a long, delicious moment. 'But for what it's worth, I'm sorry about the baby. Raising a child alone is hard, I know that from what my mom went through in the early years of my own upbringing, but so is losing one before time.'

'Thank you,' Sophie whispered against the soft fabric of Alex's white T-shirt. 'I just felt I needed to be completely honest with you. I value honesty above nearly everything else, and when I couldn't talk to Mark about what had happened, that's when things started to fall apart. I don't want that to happen with anyone else.' She pulled away from him and looked him deep in the eyes. 'Whatever happens, I promise I will never lie to you, Alex.'

Was it the last flickers of the dying sunset, or did Alex suddenly look unsettled? Perhaps she was being too intense for him by saying that, but after what she'd just told him, she wanted to make things completely clear. After all, they were still very much on the cusp; they hadn't even kissed yet, although the traumas of the afternoon seemed to be creating an intensity between them. 'Are you OK?' she asked. 'I haven't shocked you?'

Alex gave a brief smile. 'I'm fine,' he said. 'And no, you haven't shocked me at all.' He raised a hand to her face and stroked her cheek. 'I guess I was just lost for a moment. All this talk of children made me think about Mom.'

'She sounds like an amazing woman, from what you've told me about her,' Sophie said gently, relieved to be off the subject of her miscarriage. 'You must really miss her.'

Alex nodded. 'I do.' The hand that was resting on the arm of the sofa balled into a fist for a moment. 'I just get so angry sometimes that she was taken before she saw me realise this dream of the orchard. For years she wanted me to take the chance, to make the move from law to artisan cider; she even offered to loan me the money, but I refused. I always thought there'd be more time, that when she and my stepdad, Harry, got older they'd be able to retire out to the smallholding, and by then I'd have a family of my own to take care of them. The cancer took her too quickly, and too young. And I guess I'm still coming to terms with that.' He ran a hand over his eyes before he would look at her again.

'I'm sorry for your loss, too,' Sophie said. 'But I'm sure she would have been incredibly proud of what you've achieved so far, and how hard you're working to realise the dream.'

'I like to think she would be,' Alex said quietly.

There was a pause as both of them sat, lost in their own thoughts. Eventually, Sophie spoke again. 'You can tell me this is none of my business if you want, but you mention your stepdad a lot. Are you in touch with your biological dad?' For a moment she'd almost said 'real', but she knew that Alex regarded Harry as his real father, the one who'd brought him up, and so she adjusted her words accordingly.

Alex shifted uncomfortably on the sofa. 'No,' he said eventually. 'Mom didn't tell me much about him when she was alive.'

'Do you know if he's still around?'

'He died a while ago. Mom told me a little about him over the years, but I never really felt like I needed to find him. And now it's too late, anyway.' Alex reached forward and poured them both another glass from the bottle of cava on the coffee table in front of them.

'Aren't you tempted to try to find out if you have any other family?'

Alex paused a little too long. 'Maybe one day,' he said eventually, passing Sophie her glass. 'But I've got a lot to do trying to learn as much as I can about this new business first.'

'Fair enough, but remember what you said about leaving things too late. What if you've got more family out there who might want to get to know you?'

Alex shook his head. 'I don't think I'm ready to think about that just yet.'

'I'm sorry,' Sophie said. 'I'm saying what's in my head again without actually thinking. It's your choice, and up to you when and if you do it.'

'No need to apologise,' Alex said, settling back on the sofa. Sophie hesitated for a moment, and then snuggled closer to him. If she'd looked up, she would have seen a mixture of emotions crossing Alex's face, and would have been hard pushed to fathom any of them. They sat for a long time, cuddled up but lost in their own thoughts.

Some time later, when night had truly started to fall, Alex shifted on the sofa. 'I guess I should get going.'

Sophie sat up. She felt drained by the conversation they'd shared, but also unburdened. The funny thing was, it had felt so natural to curl up with Alex on the sofa that she'd almost forgotten the sizzling chemistry they'd shared on the bench that afternoon. Events, it seemed, had overtaken them once more. They still hadn't kissed, she realised with a jolt.

'Thank you for coming over,' she said as she shifted so Alex could get up. 'I never imagined in a million years I'd end up talking about things so much tonight.'

'Me neither,' Alex said, smiling down at her. 'Look, Sophie…'

'Yes?'

'I know it's been a really hard day. But I kind of feel glad I was here to share it with you.'

Sophie smiled back. 'I'm glad you were too.' She glanced at the clock. 'I'm going to go and see Gran in the morning. I think we need to get the cottage ready for when she comes home, too.' She swallowed. 'Will you help me?'

'Of course.'

Sophie walked with Alex to the front door where they both paused, unsure, after the night's disclosures, what happened next.

'I'll see you tomorrow, OK?' Alex said. He slipped Barney's lead onto the tired Weimaraner and then leaned forward and kissed Sophie's cheek. 'Try to get some sleep.'

Sophie felt the warm brush of his lips on her cheek and the back of her neck started to tingle. Despite everything, she had the sudden urge to kiss him more passionately, but she was afraid to spoil the moment. Alex's reserve was a tricky thing to gauge.

'I will. You too.'

As they parted, Sophie leaned back against the front door and let out a deep breath. Emotions crashed within her for attention, but, too exhausted to process any more of them, she decided to call it a night. There would be time to analyse everything in the morning.

17

Alex had left Sophie just after eleven o'clock, after the sun had set but the light was still the warm smoky grey of a Somerset summer. They'd talked about adapting Lily's cottage so that she wouldn't have to go upstairs for as long as needed, and Sophie had decided to put the plan to her when she went to see her the next day. Visiting hours were from ten until twelve, and she'd agreed to meet Alex back at Lily's place afterwards so they could get the downstairs guest room converted into Lily's temporary bedroom.

Fortunately, between the two of them, they managed to get the room looking more suited to Lily's needs, and it didn't take as long as Sophie had thought. As they straightened the duvet cover and removed the dresser that was a little too close to the door for comfort, Sophie looked at her watch. 'We've done well,' she said.

'We have.' Alex was slightly flushed from shifting some of the furniture around. 'And since Lily's not coming home for another couple of days, we're ahead of the game.'

Sophie smiled. 'Thank you for helping me. I bet this wasn't what you had in mind when you became Gran's lodger!'

FAY KEENAN

'I'm happy to help,' Alex said. 'But I must admit, I'd really like to get outside now.' He paused, looking a little nervous. 'Do you have any plans for this afternoon?'

Sophie shook her head. 'Apart from walking Barney, I didn't have anything in mind.'

'How would you like to show me Cheddar Gorge?' Alex asked. His mouth twisted into a mischievous smile. 'I know we talked about going next weekend, but I'd really like to see it, since you told me so much about it!'

Sophie laughed. 'OK, you're on. And we can take Barney with us as it's all dog friendly.'

Barney, who was sniffing around the newly arranged spare room, raised his head at his name.

'Sounds good.'

'I'll drive if you like.'

'If you're OK with that.'

'Sure. I'll pop home and get the car. Meet you back here in twenty?'

Alex smiled. 'All right. That gives me twenty minutes to get on the web and find out a few more things about the place, since my local tour guide isn't awfully well informed!'

Sophie grinned, but didn't grace him with a response.

'It's not exactly the Rocky Mountains, I know, but it has a certain charm,' Sophie said wryly as she and Alex walked up the main street that bisected Cheddar Gorge. Rising to the skyline on either side of them, the timeless, romantic landscape, inside which weaved countless deep, dark caves and caverns, made the Gorge cool, even on the warmest of days. Despite the influx of tourists, the sounds seemed muffled by the depth of the rock walls, and as they meandered up the Gorge to the entrance to Gough's Cave it felt deceptively peaceful.

'It's lovely,' Alex said, neck craning as he looked up towards the top of the crags on either side of them. 'And I can't think of a better day to see it.' He glanced down at Sophie, and caught her eye before she could look away. 'Do you mind if I, er…?'

'What?' Sophie asked, flustered that he'd caught her looking at him.

Alex coughed nervously. 'May I hold your hand?'

Sophie laughed. 'You really are something else, you know. Do they breed that politeness into you, or is it something in the water?'

Alex grinned. 'You can't blame a guy for wanting to ask.'

'I would love to hold your hand.' Sophie slipped her hand into Alex's, where it fitted perfectly. It felt warm, safe and decidedly right, and as their palms connected she was sure she felt a frisson of electricity.

Moving a little closer to each other, they continued up the street, Sophie keeping up a tongue-in-cheek commentary about the different shops that seemed to do their best business in the summer, and trying not to dwell on how good Alex's hand felt. Passing the Lion Rock Tea Rooms, Sophie wondered if she should suggest a late breakfast between their exploration of the Gorge and Jacob's Ladder, but was unsure whether Barney would cope with all the food on the table without misbehaving. Weimaraners were notoriously naughty when food was involved. As they reached the entrance to Gough's Cave at the top of the main street, where the Costa Coffee franchise surely occupied its most picturesque location, Sophie turned back to Alex. 'We can go up and over the top, if you like, or go into the caves for a tour. Which do you fancy?'

'How about both?' Alex said. 'We've got all afternoon. Which would you like to start with?'

'Let's go into the caves first,' Sophie said. 'It doesn't take long and it gives us a chance to get out of the heat. Then, if you still fancy it, we can climb Jacob's Ladder to the top of the Gorge.'

'Sounds great.'

In very little time, they'd bought their tickets and were walking around the inside of the massive carboniferous limestone structures inside Cheddar Gorge. Despite living in the next village for nearly three decades, Sophie had only visited the caves once, and she was as spellbound as Alex seemed to be by the stalactites and stalagmites clinging to the floor and ceiling of the caves. The dark corners still unnerved her, but as they followed the path into what had been nicknamed King Solomon's Temple, it took her breath away.

'It's like nothing else matters and time just stands still,' Sophie murmured, staring up at the huge ceiling of the cavern. 'Like we're all just some small part of something so much bigger.'

'It's beautiful,' Alex murmured into her ear. He turned her around so that she was in front of him and pointed. 'See that there?' He was pointing to the vast structure of undulating rock that lined the walls to the top of the cave, their stalactites frozen in time, dripping from rock to rock.

'Yes,' Sophie breathed. As if she was enchanted, by the moment, the place, she slowly turned back around so that she was facing him. 'Any minute now they're going to turn the lights off,' she said softly. 'And then you can see what true darkness is, this far beneath the surface.'

Alex gave her a smile. 'We should be ready, then.'

'We should.'

The attendant who looked after this section of the caves called out a warning, and the parents of the two small children who were still looking in awe up at the tiered magnificence of King Solomon's Temple made sure they were holding their hands. Sophie drew a little closer to Alex.

In the space of two heartbeats, the lights went out, and as they did Sophie felt Alex's lips, soft and warm, meeting her own. Her lips parted as she explored his mouth, a hand coming from her side to tangle in his silky dark hair. His mouth was warm and gentle, and Sophie felt such a sense of rightness in that kiss; it was as if she'd been waiting for him all her life. She pushed closer to him, feeling the contours of his body through the T-shirt and shorts he was wearing. A deep, rolling tingle started inside her as the warmth of the kiss began to spread, and she suddenly yearned for things to go further. As the lights came back on again, the change in shadows suddenly obvious through her eyes that had been closed, lost in the moment, and they broke free, she could see Alex's eyes closed still. Long, dark eyelashes feathered his cheeks and she had the urge to just melt further into him. From the way he reluctantly pulled away from her, she was more than sure he felt the same.

'I'm sorry,' he breathed into her ear. 'That wasn't very polite, was it?'

'Oh, I don't know,' Sophie whispered back. Her knees trembled, and she was stunned how much she wanted Alex to kiss her again. She hoped it would be the first of many. His breath in her ear was sending her off balance, and she was amazed how quickly her blood was rushing through her, igniting her from within.

'Does that mean I can do it again?' Alex's lips were tickling her earlobe, his breath warm on the side of her neck.

'It wouldn't be very polite if you stopped now,' Sophie said. 'But perhaps we should find a quieter spot.' She glanced to one side of her to see that, along with the parents and children, a very interested German tourist party, consisting of mainly teenage boys and their parents, was convening in the area, too.

'I think you're right,' Alex murmured. 'Shall we keep walking until we do?'

'Plenty of quiet spots on top of the Gorge, too,' Sophie said as Alex put his arm around her. She was suddenly struck with an extremely erotic vision of the two of them making love against the rocks of the Gorge, and hastily quashed it. Being kissed was one thing, but getting arrested for indecent exposure was quite another. Perhaps she ought to splash herself with some of that chilled cave water on the way past, just in case.

They exited the caves and headed towards Jacob's Ladder, which consisted of two hundred and seventy four man made steps of near vertical incline up the Gorge wall itself. Even Barney was huffing and puffing by the time they got to the top. But the view was more than worth it. Hand in hand, Sophie and Alex wandered across the top flat of the Gorge, from where it was possible to look straight down at the tourists ascending the main road, across the Somerset Levels to Glastonbury Tor and westwards to the sea. The stinging green of the fields of the Levels seemed to stretch endlessly.

'It's so beautiful,' Sophie breathed, blown away by the panoramic views. 'I can't believe I haven't come up here more often.' There was a warm breeze at the top of the Gorge, which whipped a strand of hair over her mouth, but before she could remove it herself, Alex reached out a hand and brushed it from her lips. Instinctively, she turned her head and kissed his palm, feeling a renewed surge of desire rush over her. Perhaps it was the emotional roller coaster of the past couple of days, of Lily's accident and her own unburdening to him, but she suddenly felt as though she wanted to take risks with this man, to see where those risks would lead.

Alex's hand started to tremble as Sophie's lips caressed his palm, and, acting on instinct, he drew her closer until their bodies were touching and their lips were a heartbeat away.

'Kiss me the way you did in the caves,' Sophie murmured, her voice husky with desire.

'With pleasure,' Alex replied, closing the last gap between them.

This time, even though she knew it was coming, Sophie's knees nearly buckled. With the breeze in their hair, and the sun on their backs, and a for once chilled Barney, who'd collapsed at their feet, they deepened the kiss. Sophie's fingers traced the nape of Alex's neck, pulling her towards him until there was barely any space between them, respectable or otherwise. She felt her insides turning to liquid as he kissed her on and on, his desire evident from the strength of his embrace and the hardness of his body.

Eventually, when Barney decided he'd really had enough of playing gooseberry, he parted them in the only way he knew how, which was to shove a big, wet nose in between them and muscle in on the embrace.

Sophie giggled as the Weimaraner started to nibble her wrist playfully, but she took the hint and broke away from Alex. 'Barney, you're such a tart!'

Alex laughed. 'I think he's trying to tell us he's bored.' He reached down and patted Barney on the flank.

'Shall we make sure he's completely knackered, then?' Sophie said. Casting a quick eye around to ensure there were no livestock, or small children who might be intimidated by a dog of Barney's size, she unhitched the dog's lead. Barney took off, jumping over rocks and circling round the flat, keeping an eye on them closely to make sure they didn't abandon him.

After walking for half an hour or so, they decided it was definitely time for a coffee, and, collecting Barney once more, they headed back down the ladder to caffeine and a brief rest. This afternoon was shaping up to be memorable in so many ways, Sophie thought, lips still tingling from Alex's kiss. She wondered what the night would hold.

★

The afternoon, punctuated by a stop at the Cheddar Gorge Cheese Company to buy some of the village's signature product, and, as they passed it, the hut at the side of the Axbridge to Cheddar road to buy what Sophie would argue to the death were the best strawberries in England, extended into evening. Once Sophie had left the car at her place, she and Alex went to The Stationmaster pub, where they spent more time talking and getting to know each other. After the upheavals of the past couple of days, it was as if both of them wanted to cram as much into their time as possible.

'So, when you're not making cider or being a legal eagle, what do you like to do on your days off?' Sophie, relaxed herself by a glass of Carter's Vintage cider, asked.

'Well...' Alex leaned back in one of the comfortable garden chairs that The Stationmaster had in its beer garden, looking up at the darkening sky. 'When I was younger I was really into motorcycles. I'd spend hours locked away in the garage tinkering with engines, taking them apart, putting them back together...'

'Real boy stuff,' Sophie teased.

Alex grinned. 'You could say that. Mom hated me doing it, mostly because I used to track oil all through the house when I was done, but it was the thing that Harry, my stepdad, and I really bonded over. I was pretty mad when he and Mom got together, and convinced he was going to push me out of the family, but working on the bikes gave us some common ground. We bought the first bike when I was twelve, and I used to ride it all around the backyard, desperate to get out onto the road. It kind of spiralled from there.'

'Sounds like he found a way in to a relationship with you,' Sophie replied. She sipped her pint reflectively. 'So, do you still ride?'

Alex shook his head. 'Not for a long time.'

'What made you stop?' Sophie's curiosity was piqued by a second glass of Vintage.

Alex's pause stretched interminably. He gazed up at the sky a little longer, before focussing back on Sophie. 'The only thing that *could* have made me stop. I had an accident. A bad one.' He glanced down at his left knee, where the stitch marked scar Sophie had noticed before was visible as a white line curving over his kneecap and up the inside of his thigh.

'What happened?' Sophie had to fight the urge to run a fingertip over the scar.

Alex's voice dropped. 'I was twenty, and on a break from college. My girlfriend at that time was staying with me back at Mom and Harry's place. We got the sudden urge for potato chips, and the local store was a good fifteen miles away. It was warm, and I was stupid; we got on the bike I'd been working on that summer. I knew the brakes weren't perfect. Harry and I had been trying to work out what the problem was since I'd come home, but we couldn't quite get it right.'

'I'm sensing this doesn't end well,' Sophie said, sliding her hand into Alex's.

'You're right. We took a corner too fast on the way home. The brakes popped and we were both thrown clear of the bike. Thankfully there wasn't anyone else on the road. If we'd had been going a few miles per hour faster, we'd have been hurt far worse. As it was, I took the fall hardest; I'd given Jo, my girlfriend, my protective gear to wear, so she avoided being seriously hurt, which I'm grateful for. I spent the rest of the vacation in hospital and my next semester on crutches.' He laughed ruefully. 'I swore to Mom I'd never get on a bike again after that.'

'Did you keep the promise?'

Alex smiled. 'I did. To be honest, I kind of lost my nerve after that. And then Jo and I broke up at Christmas, which was probably just as well.' He glanced down at his knee. 'This is a permanent reminder not to take silly risks, although I've taken probably the biggest risk of my life so far coming here. After all—' He broke off and took a hasty sip of his bottle of Eloise.

Sophie sensed that Alex had only just stopped himself from saying more. He was such an enigma to her; at times she felt as though she really was getting to know him, and then he'd suddenly close back up, and the Canadian reserve would kick in again. 'What were you going to say?' she asked as his eyes met hers again.

'It wasn't important,' Alex replied, but something behind his warm brown eyes suggested otherwise. He laughed nervously. 'Too much cider brings back painful memories… literally!' He stretched out his scarred leg, as if he was trying to break the moment. Sophie let it go. After all, he didn't have to tell her anything he didn't want to, she supposed. They were still so new to each other. Although, she thought, she *had* opened up to him about losing the baby. She wished he were prepared to do the same.

After a leisurely stroll back from the pub, Alex walked Sophie right to her front door. 'I had a great time today,' he said as they reached the garden path.

'Me too,' Sophie replied. 'Would you, er, like to come in for coffee?'

Alex assumed a very serious expression. 'The real answer is yes,' he said softly. 'And I would like so much more than that. But I don't want to rush you. You're such an amazing woman, Sophie. I want the timing to be right. And I don't want things to be awkward between us tomorrow morning at work, either.'

'Don't you ever take time off from being a gentleman?' Sophie asked. Frankly, if she'd had her way, she'd have pulled him into the house and taken him straight upstairs, but, regretfully, she pulled back instead. After all, they really hadn't known each other that long, and a part of her was still terrified about letting someone get too close to her, after everything she'd been through with Mark. 'I guess you're right. There's no rush.' She stretched up on tiptoe and kissed him long and lingeringly on the lips. 'I'll see you at work tomorrow.'

'You bet,' Alex said huskily as they broke apart. 'And thank you for a lovely day.'

'You too,' Sophie said. As she watched Alex saunter down the garden path, back to Lily's cottage with a thoroughly exhausted Barney by his side, she felt her stomach flutter in anticipation of seeing him again. Work tomorrow was certainly going to be interesting.

18

'Spill.'

Sophie nearly dropped her iPad, which had the latest statistics about the blends in the vats for her attention. Usually, hearing 'spill' on the vat floor would be her worst nightmare. But this time, she suspected it was going to be far worse. 'Sorry?'

Laura looked at her friend and raised a speculative eyebrow. 'You and the Canadian hottie were spotted by virtually the whole village down the pub on a date last night. So, tell me everything.'

'I don't know what you mean,' Sophie muttered, fully aware that her cheeks were starting to burn, and that Alex was somewhere on the vat floor nearby, possibly within earshot.

'Yeah, right. Look, according to Emma Leadbetter, who popped into the pub after her shift at The Cider Kitchen, you and Alex looked very cosy under one of those heated umbrella things that Vern's put in on the back patio. So tell me: what's going on?'

'Nothing's going on,' Sophie muttered. Laura was a notorious gossip and the last thing she needed was any pressure from her colleagues right now. She was still on a knife edge about Lily's long term recovery, and her mother had been flapping about over Skype, trying to organise things that she and Alex had already sorted, even though she was a country away, until late into last night. Besides, two kisses, a dog walk and a few pints at the pub did not constitute a relationship.

'That's not what Emma said it looked like,' Laura persisted. Thankfully, Sophie was saved from further interrogation by the ping of a message in the iPad's inbox. Swiping down, she was relieved to see that she and David had been summoned to a meeting with the sales director. Wondering what that could be about, she made her excuses and left Laura mid-sentence. She only hoped, as she hurried to meet David, that Laura wasn't going to switch her attentions to Alex in an attempt to get answers. Alex's politeness and diplomacy would really be tested if Laura got on his case.

'Any idea what this is about?' Sophie asked as she met David in the quad between the barns and the cannery.

'Not a clue,' he said gruffly. He wasn't a man who liked disruption to his routine, and a meeting with the sales team wasn't a regular occurrence. The cider makers tended to do their thing, and the sales team did the same, only meeting when it was of mutual relevance. David had little time for marketing initiatives and promotions; he just wanted to make the best cider he could. Sophie, while equally passionate about her craft, was more open to input from other areas of the business. She'd even featured in a national television advertising campaign a couple of years back for

Carter's. Although she'd grown exasperated at the time it took to set up a take, and there had only been so often she could smile winningly at the camera before her face had started to ache, she had quite enjoyed the experience. Local fame had meant a few knowing smiles in the pub for weeks afterward. She wondered if it was going to be something similar that Sales wanted to talk to her about.

As they entered the sales department office, Sophie noticed Jonathan Carter was already there. She wondered why he'd be gracing the meeting – after all, it was probably only likely to be a feedback session. Sometimes the sales team liked to relay their latest findings from consumer panels in person. Perhaps that was all this was.

'Thanks for coming,' Tom Edmundson, the sales director, said as they came through the door. 'Coffee?'

'Thanks,' Sophie said, taking the swiftly offered cup gladly. She'd had a pint or two more than was usual last night, especially on a Sunday, and she felt as if she needed the caffeine hit.

As they settled around the conference table, Tom began. 'I won't keep you long, guys.' He gestured to the notes in front of them. 'This'll outline most of what I need to discuss with you, but I wanted to get some input from you both before we proceed.'

Sophie glanced down at the neatly stapled sheets in front of her. *Royal West Country Show*, she read. *Carter's Cider concession*. That was odd, she thought. One of the biggest agricultural and country shows in the South West, it was four days in late July of corporate colours, free samples and brand promotion, usually handled by the sales team, with the odd guest appearance by one of the Carter brothers on the days that the dignitaries came down. Sophie and David, as tasters, didn't really get involved.

However, this year it seemed it was different. Tom began to explain the new strategy to draw the crowds into the concession. 'We're in danger of being outshone by the artisan cider makers this year, since micro cideries appear to be cropping up all over the West Country, and they've got a whole marquee to themselves to demonstrate their presses and do some promotion, so we want to promote a more "getting back to your roots" theme.' He glanced at David and Sophie before continuing; David's face was as deadpan as ever, although Sophie, who had known him a long time, was convinced she saw the slightest twitch of his mouth at the idea. It had been a long time since Carter's could claim to be an artisan brand, with international sales booming and thousands of kegs of Gold a day leaving the farm for far flung climes.

'So, what we'd like to do is send one of you down there for the duration of the show, if that sounds practical.' Tom consulted his notes. 'Sophie, I understand that you've been mentoring Alex Fraser during his internship here. How would you like to take him down with you and show him what an English country fair is really like? You can see how much he's learned from you, and it'll give you the chance to do some public facing work.' He grinned. 'Who knows, you might even get recognised from that ad we did a couple of years ago!'

Sophie was irritated to feel herself blushing again at the mention of Alex's name, not to mention the TV ad. 'OK,' she said, trying to play down her flaming cheeks. 'So we'd be travelling down every day? What about setting up?'

'Oh, didn't I mention?' Tom said, glancing down at his notes again and then looking at Jonathan, who was lounging in the chair next to Tom's desk. 'There's an old friend of Jonathan's who's setting up a glamping business just off the Mendips and who's keen to get a bit of publicity, so she and her husband will be lending us a couple of fully kitted out demo yurts for the duration of the show. During the day, they'll be semi-open to the show goers to look around, so I wouldn't go taking anything too valuable with you, but they're yours for the nights if you don't fancy commuting down every day.'

'That sounds great,' Sophie said. 'Who else is going?'

'Just you two,' Tom said. 'Although Jonathan'll be down at some point, and I'll probably pop down for one of the days with our new sales rep, Steph, to show her how things work. She's new to the West Country and hasn't been to the show before, so she's coming for the experience. You and Alex can do some demonstrations and tastings, and we'll see how it goes.'

Sophie's stomach flipped. Four days virtually alone with Alex, in the open air, selling cider all day, was going to be intense. How would they cope with being in each other's pockets for all that time? And what would she do about Lily? How would she manage in her cottage alone for the duration of the Royal West Country Show?

'Let me just check out a couple of things,' Sophie replied, aware that Tom was after an answer. 'Can I get back to you by the end of the day?'

'Sure,' Tom replied. 'Just let me know if there's anything you need to help make it happen, and we'll get together to discuss some more details next week.' Tom put his papers down and stood from the table. 'The show kicks off on the Wednesday, and runs until Saturday, so I'll make sure you're cleared to go. David, can you spare Sophie for a few days?'

'Looks like I'll have to,' David replied gruffly.

'Lovely. I'll email you with the details once we've got them. It'll be a busy few days, but hopefully good fun as well. The Royal West Country show exhibitors know how to put on a good party when the punters leave, so it should be… memorable.'

Sophie smiled, hoping that 'memorable' didn't mean embarrassingly unforgettable. As she left the sales office, David turned to her. 'Are you sure you're OK to go with just Alex?' he asked her as they headed back to the vat floor. 'You seemed a bit quiet in there.'

Sophie was touched by his concern. 'I'll be fine,' she said. 'And if I don't fancy staying over, I can always come home each night.' She might have to anyway, she thought, if she couldn't organise someone to look in on Lily.

'Good girl,' David replied. From someone else, Sophie would have found this patronising, but David had known her since she was eighteen. She knew he'd always looked out for her best interests, and, although he couldn't possibly know the ins and outs of what had happened to her lately, she knew he'd sensed her vulnerability. She was grateful for his kindness. In the absence of her father, he'd made a pretty good substitute over the years. She'd told him about Lily's fall the moment she'd got into work that morning, and she knew he was keeping an eye on her, trying to make things a little easier today.

'Well, I'd better head off and break the news to Alex that he's going to the ball!' She laughed, to break the moment.

'He won't know what's hit him,' David replied, deadpan again. 'I'll see you back in the office.'

'See you in a bit,' Sophie replied, wondering what Alex was going to make of the news. She hoped their working relationship would stand it. And as for any other relationship... who could say? And then there was the matter of Lily's recuperation, of course. And who would walk Barney if both she and Alex were down at the show? Suddenly the whole idea of going to the Royal West Country Show seemed even more impractical.

Over lunch, Sophie caught up with Alex, who'd been working with the technicians at the cannery all morning. The delay meant that she was even more nervous at the prospect of telling him about the Royal West Country Show, but she screwed her courage to the sticking place, grabbed a sandwich and a drink from the canteen and spotted him sitting on one of the picnic benches outside the dining room that overlooked the Royal Orchard.

'Have you had a good morning?' she asked as she sat down.

'Yeah, thanks,' Alex replied. 'Although I don't think my hearing will ever be the same again after spending the morning in the cannery! Even with the ear defenders on, it's loud in there.'

'I try not to go in unless absolutely necessary.' Sophie laughed. 'I far prefer the relative calm of the vat floor.'

'You and me both.'

They munched in companionable silence for a moment or two. 'So, I had a meeting with Tom from Sales this morning,' Sophie began, once she'd taken a drink from her can of Diet Coke. 'We're going on a jolly.'

'A jolly?' Alex looked quizzical. 'What do you mean?'

Sophie grinned. 'Sorry. A trip. We're going to the Royal West Country Show.'

'Sounds interesting,' Alex said. 'What exactly does it involve?'

'Well, usually it's just the sales team who get to go, but this year the firm wants to play up the blending and heritage side of the business, so we're going to go down and spend some time doing some blending and tasting masterclasses, as well as doing some promotion. You know the kind of thing, smile at the public, hand out some samples while dressed head to toe in corporate colours. Are you up for that?'

Alex grinned. 'Could be fun. So where exactly is it?'

'Just outside Shepton Mallet,' Sophie replied. 'That's about an hour's drive from here, into real Somerset territory.'

Alex looked quizzical. 'What do you mean?'

'You think we're rural here,' Sophie joked. 'Wait until you get past the Somerset Levels and into the darkest shire. David took me on a tour of some of the smaller cider makers in the county when I first started working for Carter's, and it was a real eye-opener, even for someone who was raised in the county; smallholdings in the middle of nowhere, that look like they haven't joined the twenty-first century. But also some really amazing innovations. The Royal West Country Show is the chance to see both sides up close.'

'Sounds great,' Alex replied. 'So, do I need to rent a car or something?'

'No, not unless you really want to,' Sophie said. 'I'm happy to drive, and we've got, er, accommodation for the duration of the show, if we want it, or we can commute there each day.'

'When you say accommodation…?'

'Yurts,' Sophie replied. 'A pair of them. One for you, and one for me. Have you ever glamped before?'

Alex looked quizzical. 'Uh… what exactly is glamping?'

'It's camping, but not as you might know it. Tents, yes, but also proper beds, a fridge and probably several rugs. You'll love it!'

'Sounds like camping but without all the bits that make it camping,' Alex observed. 'But I'll reserve judgement until we get there.'

'Probably best!' Sophie smiled. 'And at least we'll have somewhere comfortable to lay our heads after a hard day's selling.'

'Amen to that,' Alex replied.

Sophie glanced at her watch. 'Anyway, I'd best get back to the floor. Let me know if you're definitely up for it, and I'll confirm to Tom this afternoon.'

'Will do,' Alex replied. 'I'll see you in a little while.'

'No rush,' Sophie said, relieved to be able to make her excuses. The relationship with Alex was at such a delicate stage; they were colleagues, but now also slightly more than just friends, too. What would three nights at the Royal West Country Show bring for them?

19

Meredith was fine; so long as she didn't think too much. She got up, made some time to read a chapter or two from a book on her summer reading list, checked to see if there were any new additions to the family museum and then headed off to a shift at The Cider Kitchen. Provided she didn't let her thoughts wander, she was absolutely, unequivocally, totally, fine. She'd even volunteered to cover a shift at the Little Orchard Tea Shop, although the memory of all the times she'd spent with Flynn there had become a bit too much and she'd had to bow back out again, or her tears would have made Anna's delectable sponge cakes the wrong kind of moist. She was prepared to admit to a moment of not-fineness at that point.

In her downtime, she stuck close to home, trying to be gentle with herself, not assuming that the heartbreak would go away overnight. It was the first time she'd had her heart broken; she was pretty sure it wouldn't be the last. She'd found that taking Rosa, her pony, out for long hacks definitely helped, though. During university term time, she kept the pony in livery at a friend's stable over in Lower Langford, a mile and a half from Little Somerby, but since she was back home for three months, she decided to move Rosa back home for the summer. Her father had tentatively suggested that perhaps the pony should be sold, now that Meredith was spending so much time away from home, but Meredith couldn't bear to take that final step. Rosa had been with her since she was twelve, and she fully intended to keep her until the end of the pony's days. Matthew had acquiesced with a resigned smile; the way Rosa was going, she'd be around until Meredith was at least thirty.

After tacking her up for an early ride one morning, Meredith was just hacking her gently across the cider farm's land when she saw a figure striding across the orchard towards her. Halting Rosa, feeling slightly awkward, she slid down from the saddle and waited for the figure to draw closer. Remembering the tone of their previous encounter in the Royal Orchard, Meredith was torn between wanting to jump back on Rosa and ignore the person, or stand her ground and try to clear the air.

'Hi,' Meredith said guardedly, when Joe Flanagan was in speaking distance. Then, when he didn't respond, 'How's the Royal Orchard going?'

'Fine,' Joe replied shortly.

Meredith felt a flare of irritation. 'Just trying to be friendly,' she said. 'I thought, since our dads are still such good friends, we should perhaps try to be civil, too. Even if you did try to kill me with a tree branch.'

'No, thanks,' Joe said. 'Excuse me, but I've got a job to get to.' He went to walk past her, but Meredith had the strong will and even stronger sense of justice of her father, and she wasn't going to let things lie.

'Don't you think you should tell me what I've done to upset you?' Meredith asked, blocking his path. She had Rosa's reins in one hand, and she wasn't above turning the pony to block Joe further if need be. 'I mean, you've been well off with me since that afternoon in the orchard.'

'You really don't take a hint, do you?' Joe snapped. He went to get past her again, unfazed by both rider and pony, but Meredith blocked his path again. 'I've got work to do.'

'Oh, come on, Joe,' Meredith replied. 'This is getting really stupid now. Just tell me why you're so pissy with me. From what I remember, I was never anything but polite to you when we saw each other.'

'Yeah, it was all very *polite*, wasn't it?' Joe snapped. 'You, your posh boyfriend and your posh mates, nice to our faces and then laughing at the scum from the local comprehensive school behind our backs.'

'No!' Meredith said, her own voice rising. 'It was never like that. I had friends from your school, too.'

'Oh, what, you mean those kids your dad invited to your birthday parties just because they were the kids of the people who worked for him? Don't make me laugh.'

'And what the hell would you know?' Meredith snapped, feeling stung by the harsh tone of Joe's voice. 'You never spoke much to me anyway. What, was I too posh for you? Don't you think that's its own form of snobbery?'

'You have no idea, do you?' Joe stopped walking and tugged a stray dead leaf from one of the line of trees that ran parallel to where they were standing.

'About what? Why don't you just tell me instead of dropping all these stupid hints?' Meredith grabbed Joe's arm and forced him back round to look at her. She still had hold of Rosa's reins in her other hand, but had to resist the urge to drop them and let the pony stand on Joe's foot; he was being so vile to her.

'Why don't you ask your boyfriend?' Joe snapped. 'I'm sure he's got plenty to say.'

Meredith's eyes burned with sadness and hurt. 'He's not my boyfriend any more. We broke up.'

Joe stopped fiddling with the branch. 'I wish I could say I'm sorry,' he said, but his voice was a fraction softer. 'But I'm not. He was a twat.'

'What makes you say that? You didn't know him.'

'Oh, yeah?' Joe turned back to Meredith and looked her straight in the eye. 'Do you remember that time down the rugby club a few summers ago? You were there with him and all your *friends*, but you had to get home by ten o'clock or your dad would worry. Flynn walked you home. All very cosy. Until him and his mates came back. I'd been up there playing football with a couple of my friends and we were just about to head home. They cornered us. They were full of shit, thinking they owned the place. They kept asking us if we wanted to play them, but we knew they were just going to stitch us up. They thought they were so much better than us. In the end, we'd had enough, and when we walked away they jumped us.

'My mate, Louis, had just got a new phone for his birthday – and he had it in his back pocket. His mum had saved up for months to buy it. Your boyfriend grabbed it off him and started chucking it around with his mates. One of them missed the catch and the phone hit the ground. The screen smashed. But that wasn't enough for them. Flynn went over to the phone, and I thought he was going to pick it up and return it to Louis, but instead he just stood on it. They didn't even bother picking it up, they just walked away. Probably wouldn't even have thought about the cost of it – I guess you private school kids just ask Mummy and Daddy to buy new stuff any time something gets broken, but for Louis it was different. He was gutted, and he knew his mum would go crazy if she found out the phone had been broken.'

Joe paused, as if gauging Meredith's reaction. 'I shouted after Flynn as they all left, but all he did was turn round and laugh. If I hadn't stopped him, Louis would have gone after him, but I knew he wouldn't be able to stand up to Flynn and his mates. They were all top rugby players and a year older than us. We wouldn't have stood a chance against them.'

Meredith shook her head. 'You're making it up. Flynn would never do that.'

'Why would I make it up?' Joe asked flatly. 'I don't owe you anything. I just thought you should know that your boyfriend wasn't the top bloke you seemed to think he was back then.'

'He's not my boyfriend any more,' Meredith repeated. 'We broke up at the start of the holidays.'

'Well, if I gave a shit, I'd be glad,' Joe replied. 'Not that it's anything to do with me.'

'No. You're right,' Meredith snapped, hurt by the bitterness in Joe's voice. 'It's got nothing to do with you. You might be working for my dad now, but that doesn't mean you have to talk to me. So perhaps you'd better leave me alone from now on after all.' Confused, head spinning, trying to process the information that Joe had given her, she turned away. How could Flynn have done that? He'd always come across as so caring, so lovely. She'd never seen him behave that way to anyone. But then it was a few years ago; they'd all been younger. Struggling to get her image of her now ex-boyfriend into some kind of shape, and having lost interest in a longer ride, she walked Rosa back to Cowslip Barn. Joe, of course, could be lying, but then why would he? What would he have to gain by it? And something about the way he'd spoken, the outrage and anger in his voice, made her instinctively know he'd been telling the truth. Confused and more heartbroken than ever, she couldn't shake the feeling that she had to make amends.

20

Later that day, over on the other side of the village, Anna had just cleared the last lunchtime table in the Little Orchard Tea Shop when Jonathan poked his head around the door. Back before he'd been reconciled with his brother, Matthew, Jonathan had been a regular fixture at the table in the bay window of the tea room, choosing to work there at his laptop, and Anna still thought of that table as his, even though he'd moved back into his old office on the cider farm these days. Anna's husband, Matthew, was the major shareholder in Carter's Cider, Jonathan having handed his own share of the business that he'd inherited from their father Jack's estate to Matthew in return for the building, deeds and title to the flagship restaurant, The Cider Kitchen, in the spring of last year. Jonathan had then gifted the entirety of The Cider Kitchen, bricks, building and brand, to his now wife Caroline as a gesture of his love for her. The two of them had been running the restaurant ever since, although it was noted by the Carter's Cider accountants that the crockery bills had increased exponentially since the pair had been working full-time together. Either Jonathan was very clumsy, or their rows had involved throwing dinner plates from time to time.

'Hello, stranger!' Anna called as she took the last of the dirty plates to the kitchen. 'Long time, no see.'

'Hi, darling,' Jonathan called, settling himself at the table in the bay window. As Anna came back out from the kitchen, she noticed that her brother-in-law didn't look his usually perky self, and that, far from being busy on his phone, he was just gazing out of the bay window, chin resting on his hand, as if he was mentally somewhere else entirely.

'Everything OK?' she asked.

Jonathan's head jerked up, and, a beat too late, he turned on his usual smile. 'Sorry, Anna, I was miles away.'

'Anywhere interesting?'

Jonathan laughed. 'Not really.' His laugh stopped as soon as it started. 'Look… have you got five minutes for a chat?'

Anna gestured to the now empty tea room. 'I'm not exactly busy after the lunchtime rush, and my high tea regulars aren't due in for another hour or so. Why don't I grab us a couple of coffees and you can tell me what's on your mind?'

'Sounds like a good plan,' Jonathan replied. As Anna walked over to the chrome coffee machine and prepared them a drink each, he began to talk. 'I came to pick your brains.'

'About?'

Jonathan sighed. 'About Caroline.'

Anna was glad that the milk frother was quite loud; it gave her time to formulate a diplomatic response. Since Jonathan and Caroline had married, she'd found herself acting as an intermediary on a few occasions, and it was beginning to become a bit too regular for her liking. Marriage had been a challenge for them both, and at first Anna had put it down to the novelty of the situation, but she was beginning to concede that actually it was because the two of them were just plain set in their ways. She usually had an infinite well of patience, but she didn't like being stuck in the middle.

'What's happened this time?' she said when the milk was ready to pour.

'Nothing, really,' Jonathan sighed. 'That's kind of the problem.'

'In what sense?'

'Caroline's been quite distant lately. Every time I try to get close to her, she backs off. I'm starting to think that maybe...' He trailed off, clearly not wanting to put his fears into words. 'Has she said anything to you?' Jonathan asked as Anna placed a steaming hot latte in front of him on the table.

Anna shook her head. 'Nope. Not a thing.' She looked thoughtful. 'Although you're right, she has been a little bit elusive. She usually pops in to see Ellie after school at least once a week, but it's been about three weeks since she's been over. I did have a quick chat with her when she came in here the other day, but she didn't stay too long.'

'Well, there's something up,' Jonathan said. 'I mean, it's like we're back where we were when we first met. And not in a good way. I feel like she's closed off from me, and I haven't got a clue why. Are you sure she's not said anything to you?'

'Honestly, Jonathan, I think you're having this conversation with the wrong person,' Anna said gently. 'Don't you think you should be talking to Caroline?' She'd offered the same advice to both of them on a few occasions over the year they'd been married, but it obviously hadn't sunk in yet.

'You're right, of course,' Jonathan sighed. 'The problem is, every time I try to do it, she makes up some excuse to talk about something else. She's just so difficult to read sometimes. Even now I'm married to her, sometimes I feel I still don't know her at all.'

'You know the history,' Anna said. 'She struggles to trust anyone. And she's spent so long being her own support, it's likely she's still adapting to having you in her corner.'

'No.' Jonathan shook his head vehemently. 'A year ago I'd have bought that excuse. Six months ago I probably would have, too, but not now. She knows I'm completely crazy about her, and that I would go into battle for her over anything. Why won't she just talk to me?'

'You need to be saying this to her, not me,' Anna said gently. 'If being subtle hasn't worked, then you need to be more direct. She's complicated, Jonathan. You both are. If you think there's something wrong, then there probably is.'

Jonathan shook his head. 'I'd ask you to have a word, but I think that's a bit of a cop out, isn't it?'

Anna smiled. 'Sorry. This is one conversation you need to have yourself.'

'Why didn't anyone warn me that marriage was so hard?' Jonathan grumbled as he took another sip of his latte.

'Would it have made any difference if we had?' Anna said wryly.

'Probably not. It's just that you and Matthew make it look so easy.'

'Oh, believe me, we have our moments,' Anna replied. 'But in the end, everyone's marriage is a mystery to those on the outside. You just have to do the best you can, and love the best you can. And I know how much you love Caroline.'

'I do,' Jonathan said. 'I really do. That's what makes this whole thing so frustrating.'

'Go and talk to her,' Anna said. 'Instead of sitting here in a tea shop, talking to me.'

'OK, boss.' Jonathan finished his coffee and stood up. 'Thanks for the friendly ear.'

'Any time,' Anna replied, taking the coffee cups back to the counter. 'Keep me posted.'

'I will.' And with that, Jonathan wandered back out of the tea shop.

Anna watched him leave and tried to put aside the worry that he'd stirred up. She hoped that whatever was bugging Caroline so much, Caroline would see just how much Jonathan loved her, and that she would confide in him. Jonathan was worth the trust.

2 1

After a busy day, Sophie headed home. She was intending to go and visit Lily that evening, so she didn't want to hang about at home too long. She needed to talk to her mother, too, who was determined to visit Lily. Sophie realised that having Jane back in Little Somerby might be the answer to the logistical problem of the Royal West Country Show. If she could convince her mother to come and stay for the duration of the show, Lily would have someone to keep an eye on her while Sophie was away. She hoped that her mother would go for it. Despite the fact that Jane Henderson had been widowed over a quarter of a century ago, she still adored her former mother-in-law, and was concerned about her since the fall. Dumping her handbag on the kitchen table, Sophie went to freshen up before heading out to the hospital, resolving to contact her mother when she got back. Just as she was pulling a brush through her hair, the doorbell chimed.

'I'll be down in a sec,' she called through her open bedroom window. She couldn't see who was there, as they'd obviously stepped into the shade of the porch, and they didn't reply. Hoping whoever it was would be brief, Sophie hurried down to the door. Her heart sank as she opened it, and for the umpteenth time she wished she'd replaced the old, solid, windowless front door with something a little more transparent.

'What do you want?' Sophie asked as Mark Simpson took a step towards her.

'To talk.'

'You've got a bloody nerve coming here!' Sophie went to close the door, but Mark put out a hand and prevented her.

'Please, Soph, will you at least let me explain?'

'Explain what?' Sophie felt her temper flare, much as she tried not to let it. 'How you and your bloody dog landed my grandmother in the hospital?'

'Sophie.' Mark tried to cajole his way in, but Sophie stood in the doorway. She gave him nothing in height, unlike Alex, who was a good four inches taller than her. 'It was a stupid thing that happened. Come on, open the door before your neighbours start to talk.'

'You've got five minutes. And then I'm going to see my grandmother, who is in Weston General Hospital because of you.'

'I know you're angry with me.' Mark strolled through the cool hallway and took himself into the lounge, almost as if he owned the place. Sophie supposed he knew it well enough to do that, even though it rankled. They'd been together for a long time, after all. 'And if I was in your position, I'd be angry, too. But I've made a lot of mistakes, Soph, and this accident with Jimmy was just the last in a long line of them.'

'Mistakes?' Sophie echoed. 'My grandmother is lying in a hospital bed because of you. And I'd hardly call screwing your admin assistant behind my back a mistake. A cliché, maybe, but a whole lot more than a mistake.'

'I'm really sorry about what happened with your gran. The dogs were both out of control and Jimbo doesn't like big dogs.'

'Oh, and that makes it OK, does it?' Sophie's temper flared up. 'She's got a hairline fracture of her hip, Mark, which could potentially put her out of action for months. And you're *sorry*. It's not bloody good enough.' She started to pace the floor. 'So now you've apologised, you can bloody well get out. And keep that stupid dog away from Barney.'

'I want to talk to you about us, too, Soph.'

'There is no us,' Sophie spat. 'Especially not now.'

'Oh, come on. You and I both know that thing with Jenna wasn't serious. She knew it, I knew it, and if you admit it to yourself, then you know it too.' He shrugged. 'I made a mistake.' Mark plonked himself down on the comfy patchwork fabric sofa that took up most of the lounge. The sofa that Alex had held her on the other night, and made her feel so safe. She didn't want that memory to be tainted by this one, though, so she remained standing. 'I miss you, Soph.'

'So that's it?' Sophie said, despite her determination not to engage with him. 'After all these months, that's all you have to say?'

Mark looked up at her, his blue eyes so clear and unblinking that she instinctively knew he had another agenda. 'Not exactly,' he admitted.

'What is it, then?'

'I came to warn you about that bloke you've been working with. I understand you've been seeing him a bit outside work, too.'

'What's that got to do with you?' The words shot out of Sophie's mouth like a bullet.

'Alex, isn't it? That one who came over for the Carter's internship.'

'So, what if it is?' Sophie snapped. 'It's no business of yours.'

'Sophie, listen to me.' Mark's expression was serious. 'I don't think he's who he says he is.'

'Oh, really?' Sophie snapped. 'I thought you had the monopoly on lying round here.'

'Soph, I'm serious.' Mark stood back up from the sofa and came towards her. 'He's been hanging around Jonathan Carter's house, you know, the cottage that his dad, Jack, used to live in before he died, and the other night in the pub he was asking Vern and Emma Leadbetter a lot of questions about the Carter family. He seems to have a bit of an obsession going on, and it wouldn't surprise me if he was up to some kind of industrial espionage. That he's not a cider farmer after all, or he works for the competition or something.'

'And what is it to you?' Sophie was really riled now. 'You couldn't care less about me, if your little performance with Jenna was anything to go by.'

'I just don't want to see you get into trouble,' Mark said. 'I mean, what if, when your back was turned one day, he dumped something into the vats? Or he's just looking to gain your trust to take the firm down from the inside? Have you thought about that?'

'I think you've been watching too much Netflix,' Sophie said. 'Alex is one of the most honest and honourable people I've ever met. And what I get up to in my private life is absolutely none of your business. You negated the right to pass comment on my life, private or otherwise, when you went behind my back. So, I'll thank you to fuck off and leave me alone.'

'Just think about it, Soph,' Mark persisted. 'I know I'm not your favourite person right now, but I'm saying this because I still care about you. Promise me you'll be careful, all right?'

'Get out, Mark.'

Finally getting the message, Mark walked back to the front door. 'I really am sorry, Sophie,' he said as he crossed the threshold of the door she'd opened for him. 'For everything. But please, think about what I've told you.'

Sophie watched him leave without a word. The nerve of him astounded her. He'd cheated on her and he had the front to turn up on her doorstep and moralise about who she should and shouldn't be seeing. Not to mention his bloody dog putting Lily in hospital. If Alex had heard the conversation, she thought, he'd have laughed his head off. Picking up her phone where she'd left it in the hall when she went to open the door, she saw that she had a text from him. Smiling, she texted an answer to his question. Yes, after she went to see Lily, she was going to be free tonight. Smiling as the message pinged off her screen, she went to change her top before she headed to the hospital.

22

That same evening, Jonathan had quite a while to wait before attempting a conversation with Caroline. In fact, he was starting to get seriously worried when a phone call had come from Emma Leadbetter, sous chef and part-time front of house person, half an hour ago to ask where Caroline was. As he heard the front door open, he strode out to the hallway, relieved and agitated to see his wife coming home.

'Where have you been?' She looked stressed, and tired, and her face was unusually pale. 'Emma's been on the phone all afternoon. It's Gino's night off and she's cooking tonight, as you'd know if you'd checked the rotas, and you're on front of house. She's panicking she was going to have to call Gino back in and take front of house herself, especially with that conference coming in.'

'I'm sorry,' Caroline said. 'I misread the rotas and thought it was my night off. And I've not been feeling very well.'

'Are you OK now?' Jonathan asked, immediately concerned. 'I mean, can you work tonight?'

Caroline nodded. 'I'll be fine. I just needed some... air.' Her gaze slid away from Jonathan's piercing stare and nervously she walked towards the bay window of the living room.

'What's wrong, Caroline?' Jonathan asked, more gently this time. 'You've been a bit off for weeks now.' He approached her, but she moved away from him. He sighed in frustration. It had been that way between them for a little while; every time he tried to get close to her, she seemed to pull further away. He was fed up with it, and he missed his wife.

'I'm fine,' Caroline said, but her sudden smile looked forced. 'Honestly, I've just been a bit under the weather. I'll give Emma a ring in a minute and let her know I'll be in later.' Her hands, which were by her sides, started to shake, and the colour drained from her face. 'Excuse me,' she muttered, and made a dash for the bathroom.

Jonathan let her go, still none the wiser about what was causing his wife's odd behaviour. His heart lurched at the thought that she might be slipping back into old habits; one old habit in particular. Caroline had once been quite a heavy cocaine user, and, although that had been consigned well and truly to the past, the shadow of such an addiction seemed to haunt her from time to time. Jonathan had been sure, up until recently, that Caroline was still clean, but her behaviour was becoming more erratic, and his concern was increasing. Hearing the bathroom door opening again, he padded out to the hallway. 'You're not OK, are you?' he said gently. 'Caroline, please tell me what's wrong.'

Caroline's eyes were bloodshot and her pale cheeks were suddenly and unhealthily flushed. Jonathan prayed she wasn't going to tell him she was taking drugs again. 'Look,' he said. 'Come and sit down for a minute.' Taking her hand, he led her back to the living room and they both sat down on the sofa. 'Tell me what's bothering you,' he said. 'Please.'

Caroline swallowed hard and shook her head. Unbidden, tears started to slide down her cheeks. 'I don't know how to tell you…'

'Tell me what?' Jonathan said, one hand still in hers. 'This is me, Caroline. You can tell me anything.'

'I'm so scared, Jonathan…'

Jonathan pulled Caroline close until her head was resting on his chest. 'You don't need to be scared of anything. I'm your not-quite knight in shining armour, remember?' Once quite the playboy, when he'd met Caroline, Jonathan had fallen head over heels in love for the first time in his life.

Caroline shook her head. 'You don't understand.'

'Try me.'

An age seemed to pass before Caroline drew away again and looked Jonathan straight in the eye.

'I've suspected for a few weeks now, and when I started feeling sick, that pretty much confirmed it.' She paused and then nodded as a look of dawning comprehension appeared on Jonathan's face. 'I'm pregnant.'

Jonathan's mouth dropped open, and, not managing, for once, to articulate anything, he pulled Caroline towards him in a tight embrace. 'That's wonderful, brilliant news.' As he released her again, he looked at her face, and her expression was far from wonderful, or brilliant. 'Or is it? You don't look as though it is good news.'

Caroline bit her lip. 'Oh, no,' she said. 'Most of me, the part that's not being really sick for hours each day, is completely thrilled. I can't think of anything better for us right now. It's just…'

'What?' Jonathan asked. 'Are you worried about The Cider Kitchen? Because we can afford it. We can get a manager in for your maternity leave; it'll be fine.'

'It's not that.' Caroline moved away from him. 'When I suspected I might be pregnant, I started looking at stuff on the internet. About how cocaine might affect things. How it might harm the baby. And I'm really scared, Jonathan. What if I've conceived too soon? What if the baby's damaged by all that coke I did?' She put her head in her hands.

Wordlessly, Jonathan enfolded Caroline in his arms. He hadn't seen her so upset in a long time, and he didn't know what to say. How could he reassure her of something that he himself had absolutely no answer to?

Eventually, they broke apart again, and he stared down at her. 'That was a long time ago,' he said gently, 'and I'm sure that whatever effects the coke had on you, they're in the past.'

'What are you, a doctor now?' Caroline sniffed.

Jonathan was relieved that a little of Caroline's fighting spirit seemed to have returned. 'No, darling, but I do know a thing or two about bad habits. And if you want to ask the doctor about it, I'm sure he or she would tell you there's nothing to worry about. You've been clean for years now, haven't you?'

'Of course.' Caroline tossed her head. 'It's just that, late at night, I've been thinking and thinking about it all, and I can't stop worrying.'

'I'll come with you to the doctor, when you're ready,' Jonathan said softly. 'Just to put your mind at rest.'

Caroline's lower lip trembled. 'Promise?'

'Absolutely.' Jonathan stroked away a tear from Caroline's lashes. 'I will always be here for you, Caroline. You know that.' He checked his watch. 'Except for tonight.'

'What?'

Jonathan smiled. 'Look, I know you don't exactly rate my front of house skills compared to yours, but we can't really have you throwing up all over the clientele, can we? I'll take your shift tonight.' He held up a hand as Caroline started to protest. 'Emma can talk me through it. She could probably do both jobs standing on her head, but I think she'll be better off in the kitchen tonight. You stay here and put your feet up and I'll get away as soon as I can.'

'Are you sure?'

'Totally.' Jonathan helped Caroline to her feet. 'Get in the bath and relax. I'll see you later.' He kissed her forehead. 'I can't believe we're going to have a baby.' Anna was going to be over the moon, he thought as Caroline disappeared upstairs. And he was, too; when he stopped being absolutely terrified.

At the other end of the village, having settled little Jack back down after a nightmare, Anna flopped onto the sofa next to Matthew. He lifted an arm and put it around her as she snuggled contentedly into him, trying unsuccessfully to stifle a yawn as she did so.

'Busy day?' Matthew asked, absent mindedly playing with Anna's ponytail.

'Oh, you know, same old, same old at the tea shop,' Anna replied. 'Although Jonathan popped in this afternoon. He seemed a bit out of sorts about Caroline.'

'Again?' Matthew's brow furrowed. 'They've been bickering a lot lately. And he's not been his usual self at all.'

'Perhaps you should speak to him,' Anna said. A shiver ran down her spine as Matthew's fingers gently caressed the back of her neck.

'He knows where I am if he needs me,' Matthew murmured, kissing the top of Anna's head. 'And I think we can spend our time doing more interesting things than talking about my brother.'

Anna's heartbeat quickened as Matthew's voice dropped and his seductive West Country burr worked its magic. As she raised her face for a kiss, which deepened in intensity as the moments passed, all thoughts of Jonathan and Caroline fled.

'You are *so* good at that,' Anna whispered as they broke apart a little while later. She shifted on the sofa slightly so that she could look into Matthew's eyes. Although they had rather more crow's feet at their sides than they had when they'd first met, and his hair was more silver than black these days, he still had the ability to turn her insides to jelly and her knees to rubber.

'You're not so bad yourself,' Matthew said gruffly, capturing Anna's mouth once again. He pulled her onto his lap so that she was straddling him on the ancient Chesterfield sofa. 'Early night?' he murmured between kisses.

'A room. Get one.' An amused voice came from the entrance to the living room.

Springing apart, Matthew and Anna laughed. 'We didn't hear you come in,' Anna said as Meredith waved sardonically from the doorway.

'So I see,' Meredith replied. 'I'll, er, make myself scarce, shall I?'

Matthew laughed. 'No need. We're turning in anyway.' Getting up off the sofa as Anna shifted over again, he wandered across the living room and ruffled his daughter's hair, as he'd been doing since she was a toddler. 'Goodnight.'

'It comes to something when your parents have more of a love life than you do,' Meredith grumbled, but there was no malice in it, Anna knew. 'Just make sure you keep it down. I wouldn't want you waking up Ellie or Jack.'

Anna shook her head as she joined Matthew at the doorway. 'Why do I suddenly feel like the naughty teenager?' she said as she kissed Meredith goodnight.

23

Lily was discharged from hospital later that week. Because of her age and the severe bruising from the fall, as well as the hairline fracture of her hip, the hospital had advised keeping her in for observation. Lily, of course, had grumbled but acquiesced, primarily because she didn't want to be a burden to her family while still regaining her feet and her balance. True to her word, she'd ignored the walking frame completely, but she had conceded that a medical grade walking stick, custom fitted to her height, would be a good idea once she was up and about.

'Thank goodness for the National Health Service!' she'd said as Sophie had picked her up in the early evening. 'Although, I do have to say, the private room was worth every penny.' Lily was a poor sleeper, and so a few nights in the Waterside Suite had been a luxury she was glad she could afford.

Once Sophie had settled Lily into her newly arranged downstairs room, and Alex had made sure Barney was suitably exhausted with a long evening walk, Sophie had turned her mind to the upcoming trip to the Royal West Country Show, which she and Alex would be attending in a few days' time. She felt excited about spending time at the show itself; it would make a nice change from her usual daily routine. However, she'd be lying if she didn't acknowledge that she was also looking forward to spending time with Alex. The memory of kissing him – in the caves at Cheddar Gorge, on the sofa at her house, and on both of their doorsteps – was so strong, though, that her body was very definitely pushing her in a more intimate direction with him, and, if she was being honest, her heart and mind weren't far behind.

Jane Henderson had arrived on an afternoon flight from Marseilles on the day before the show, and after meeting her mother at the airport and making sure she was settled in at home, Sophie put her mind to packing. For the first time since Lily's fall, now that Jane was back in residence in Little Somerby to look after her grandmother, Sophie felt as though she could get a little bit excited about spending a few days away with Alex; even if they would be working.

The day of the trip to the Royal West Country Show, a Wednesday, dawned bright and sunny, and Sophie reconsidered adding wellies to her packing list. The show, much like the Glastonbury Festival, had been known to be a quagmire in rainy years, but this year the ground was solid and cracking underfoot because of the lack of rainfall, so she figured it would be safe to leave the boots behind. She'd borne the brunt of Laura and her other colleagues' teasing about her 'dirty weekend' away with Alex at the show, and by the end of the working day yesterday she was almost at snapping point from all of the jibes. Not that she could blame them, she thought; virtually everyone in the village seemed to have seen them drinking in the pub after their trip to Cheddar Gorge. Sometimes, though, she wished she lived somewhere a little more anonymous.

After making sure she'd tied up the loose ends in the office, she checked her phone and sent Alex a quick text. He was working over at despatch this week and so she'd not seen as much of him for a few days, at least at work. Since Lily's return from hospital, they'd been spending their evenings with her, and hadn't actually had a lot of alone time. They'd arranged to meet in the staff car park at ten a.m. The drive to Shepton Mallet would take around an hour, and they had an hour or two to settle in before they were due to start manning the Carter's concession at two o'clock.

'All set?' she asked as Alex made his way over to her car.

'I think so,' he replied, hefting his holdall into the open boot of Sophie's car. 'I'm glad I've got you by my side to answer any complicated questions from the public!'

Sophie laughed. 'They generally just want to know the difference between cider apples and eating apples, honestly, and to snag a few freebies. You'll be fine.'

The drive to Shepton Mallet was relatively peaceful, and only hotted up once they approached the showground. Set in some two hundred and forty acres, the ground was used throughout the year for various sporting and agricultural events, but the Royal West Country Show was the jewel in the crown. Four days of farm machinery, heavy horses, local delicacies and more country wear than you could shake an artisan walking stick at, it encapsulated the rural ethos of the county of Somerset like no other show. Sophie remembered coming regularly as a child, and being as enchanted by the Dancing Diggers, huge canary yellow JCBs, as the heavy horses.

As they turned through the gates and followed the signs marked 'Exhibitors' Area', Sophie saw row upon row of motorhomes, horse boxes and tents.

'I'm glad we didn't have to bring our own accommodation!' she joked as they passed a couple who were obviously having an animated discussion about the correct way to erect their tent. Jonathan had assured them that, by the time they got there, the yurts would be fully assembled.

Alex grinned back, and then pointed out of the car window to his left. 'Looks like that's us, over there.'

Sophie pulled off the track and onto the grass as she spotted a handwritten sign tapped into the ground that read 'Somerset Glamping Welcomes Carter's Cider'. Parking the car, it was only when she'd got out that she realised that there was, in fact, only one yurt in evidence. Her stomach fluttered. They had come to the right part of the camping area, hadn't they?

As if on cue, her mobile phone pinged with an email. She scrolled quickly through it, the flutters in her stomach increasing.

'Is everything OK?' Alex asked as he came around to her side of the car.

'I've just had an email from Tom,' Sophie replied, glancing up from her phone. 'He says he's sorry, but there was a problem with the second yurt, apparently. They unpacked it and the canvas had ripped, right down the back, so we're down to one. They've put a bottle of champagne in the fridge to apologise.'

'Well, I'm sure we'll manage,' Alex said, and then a frown wrinkled his brow. 'If you're OK to share with me? If not, we can always go back home in the evenings.'

Sophie smiled nervously. In truth, the thought of sharing a yurt with Alex was both tantalising and terrifying, but she also knew that the atmosphere of an evening at the Royal West Country Show was meant to be well worth staying for. She shook her head. 'I'm sure we'll figure something out. Let's not worry too much until we have to.'

Alex smiled. 'OK.' Popping open the boot of the car, he pulled out his holdall and Sophie's smaller one. 'Shall we go and take a look?'

They approached the yurt, and Sophie simultaneously found herself wishing for two single beds, and the biggest, comfiest king size she could imagine. Her fingers fumbled as she unlaced the fabric door of the yurt and stepped inside. She gave a gasp as the bed situation was made clear immediately. Standing proud in the centre of the space was a large, wrought iron bedstead, complete with patchwork quilt.

'Well, that's interesting!' she said, turning back to Alex, who'd stepped inside the yurt with her.

Alex, however, was looking around, a look of amusement on his face. 'You're not joking,' he said. 'I might be missing something here, but is this really what the Brits call camping?'

Inside the yurt was, along with the huge bed that had caused Sophie such consternation, a dining table, a fridge, and a very swish camping stove. Spread along the floor, covering the ground sheets, was a selection of rugs.

'This is the first time I've seen a fridge and a dining table in a tent,' Alex teased as Sophie threw her holdall down on one of the flat topped packing trunks that sat at the far end of the yurt. He gestured to the centre of the tall dome of the tent. 'And who would want to light a wood burning stove at the end of July?'

'Haven't you learned anything about Somerset weather yet?' Sophie turned back towards him with a smile. 'It can get quite chilly at night, even in the summer.'

Alex, who had frequently camped out in British Columbian temperatures of minus ten and lower, refrained from comment.

Sophie laughed nervously. 'It's not exactly how I remember family camping trips, but at least we'll have somewhere comfortable to lay our heads after spending all day on our feet talking to customers.' She glanced towards the bed again, and her cheeks felt hot.

Alex followed her gaze, finally acknowledging the large bed. He looked away hesitantly, and then grinned when he saw that there was also a chaise longue off to one side of the sleeping area. 'Looks like I'm on that, then.'

'Don't be daft!' Sophie said. 'We can alternate nights if you like.'

'How about we sort it out later?' Alex said. Despite their growing closeness, now that they were actually inside the yurt together, neither of them were too confident about voicing their thoughts, and Sophie was more than happy to let it slide for the moment. She'd not shared a bed with anyone except the cat since she'd split up with Mark, and the fear of how she might react, even with someone she fancied as much as Alex, was starting to nibble at her insides. What if she still wasn't ready? Having the miscarriage alternately felt like a long time ago, and like yesterday, and her emotions were still in turmoil. Was it simply that she was feeling self-conscious about going to the next level with Alex, or would she have felt the same, whoever he was? What if she let him close to her and she couldn't handle it? Berating herself for becoming so distracted, she tried to focus back on the reasons they were at the show in the first place. The rest would have to wait.

'We'd better dump our stuff and get over to where the concession is,' she said. 'We'll be on the stall soon, and we need to be ready.'

Alex nodded. 'OK.'

And with that, all thoughts of the sleeping arrangements temporarily forgotten, they headed back out of the yurt. As they walked, Sophie briefed Alex from the notes that Tom had sent over yesterday afternoon. 'The concession was set up last night, so we just need to go and check it over. We're going to do tasting demos at various points during the day; I think the first one is due to happen at about two-thirty, and then every hour or so after that, but really it's about handing out some samples, connecting with the public and showing a positive face for the brand.'

'If it's OK with you, I'll direct all of the complicated tasting and blending questions your way, then!' Alex smiled. 'I've learned so much from you, but you've got ten years' experience on me, after all.'

Sophie smiled back. 'I'm sure you'll be fine.' She handed him a clipboard that contained notes on the most common blends that Carter's used for their mainstream ciders, and some of the more obscure varieties that had been used to create the more artisan drinks. They had barrels and bottles of all of them to hand out as samples, and conduct tasting competitions with, over the next few days.

'Just remember that you shouldn't taste along with the customers,' Sophie warned, 'or I'll have to carry you back to the yurt!'

'I'll bear that in mind,' Alex said wryly.

The first afternoon of the show was busy; due to the warm weather, it seemed that every visitor was stopping off at the cider tent to sample the Carter's merchandise. Sophie found herself constantly bombarded by curious people, and that she was really enjoying facing the public and answering their questions. From time to time, she glanced at Alex, who was also being kept occupied by show goers. From the look on his face, though, he was enjoying it as much as she was.

'Everything OK?' she murmured as they both said goodbye to a particularly curious couple in their seventies, who had spent quite a while tasting the different samples on the makeshift bar area.

'All good, thanks,' Alex replied, smiling down at her. 'And I think I've learned just as much from some of the customers as they have from me this afternoon.'

'Well, we're only half joking when we say that cider's in the blood around here!' Sophie laughed. 'Everyone's got an apple tree and an anecdote.'

As if on cue, a couple of women wandered into the tent and headed towards the Carter's concession. They were deep in conversation, and kept glancing to where Sophie and Alex were standing. Sophie smiled to herself; Alex was certainly proving to be a draw as far as female cider drinkers were concerned, and these two seemed to be no exception. As they came closer, she caught a snippet of their muttered conversation.

'It isn't…'

'It *is*, I'm telling you…'

'Well, why don't you ask him?'

'Can I help you, ladies?' Sophie asked, gesturing to the bottles in front of her. 'Which one of these would you like to try today?'

'Thanks, love, but we'd like him to serve us.' The brunette gave a mischievous smile. 'And while he's at it, he can tell us how the MD of the company still looks so young.' She turned to Alex. 'What's your secret, love? Your hair's a bit longer than in your company photograph, but it suits you.'

Was Sophie imagining it or did Alex's back stiffen? In the blink of an eye, he'd relaxed his posture again, however, and he gave the two women a bright smile.

'My apologies, ladies, but I'm not the MD, just an intern.'

The other woman gave a ribald laugh. 'That's an accent and a half. And you're the best looking intern I've ever seen. Where are you from?' Clearly having drunk enough already to forego too much tact, she waved a five pound note at Alex in exchange for two bottles of Eloise.

Alex took the money. 'I'm from Canada, ma'am. I hope you enjoy the rest of the show.'

'Fancy enjoying it with us?' the other woman asked. 'We can show you all the good bits.'

'That's a kind offer, but I'm working for all of it,' Alex replied. 'You have a good day, now.'

As they wandered off, arm in arm, Alex turned back to Sophie, who was regarding him quizzically.

'What is it?' he asked.

'Matthew would be flattered that they thought he was still so young,' Sophie replied, grinning.

Alex turned away, and for a second Sophie thought she'd said something to upset him. Then, turning back to her after a beat or two, he smiled again. 'No way,' he said. 'I don't see it myself. Must be the – what's that expression you used the other night? – beer goggles talking.'

Sophie grinned. 'Cider goggles in this case,' she teased. 'Although they seemed to like the look of you.'

Alex drew a little closer to Sophie and reached out to squeeze one of her hands. 'Doesn't matter,' he said softly. 'I wasn't looking back.'

Sophie felt her stomach turn a somersault. They still hadn't fully addressed the issue of the sleeping arrangements, but at that moment, she knew that it was highly unlikely that either of them would be spending the night on the chaise longue.

The rest of the afternoon and the evening seemed to fly by and before they knew it, the summer night was beginning to fall as Sophie and Alex wandered back to the yurt. Having passed the evening in the bar on site with a few of the other cider makers who were visiting the show, they were both relaxed, but not too far gone to lose their way back to the yurt. It had been a good day, and both of them felt they had fulfilled their roles as ambassadors for Carter's Cider admirably, but it was definitely time to relax.

Sophie unlaced the fabric of the yurt and headed inside, mindful of the fact that they had another long day tomorrow. Alex, however, lingered at the entrance. It was a clear night, and the first stars were beginning to peer out from the dark grey velvet of the sky. Orion hovered overhead, the stars of the belt growing in intensity as the sky darkened, and the three quarters full moon was on the rise.

'It's a beautiful night,' Alex said, looking up at the stars. 'Back home, I used to camp out in the backyard a lot in the summer, and in the winter sometimes, too. Mom used to grumble a bit about it, worrying I'd get too cold, but I always liked to grab my sleeping bag and sleep under the stars.'

Sophie rejoined Alex at the door. 'I used to search for Orion in the sky when I was away from home,' she said, staring upwards. 'It always looked as though it was just over my mum's house when I was at home, and I always hoped it was there, watching over her when I was away. Of course, now she's got her new life and home in France, she doesn't need Orion any more.' She smiled. 'That probably sounds really silly, doesn't it?'

Alex looked down at her. 'Not at all.' He swallowed hard, and Sophie felt her hand being taken by one of his. 'Sometimes, after Mom died, I'd look up at the sky and trace the constellations that I remembered seeing from the back yard when I was a kid. She told me all of their names, one night, when she decided to camp out there with me, and now I always look for them when I'm alone at night. It's like, in some way, she's still with me.'

Sophie squeezed his hand. 'I'm sure she'd love to know that,' she said softly. 'Somehow, looking at the stars, you can kind of believe you're never alone, wherever you are.'

Alex turned towards her, and she saw the moonlight reflected in his eyes.

'What is it?' she said softly.

'You look beautiful in the moonlight,' he replied. 'So beautiful, that I'm not even going to ask, this time, if I can kiss you.' And with that, he raised his other hand to her cheek and kissed her squarely on the mouth.

Sophie's knees turned to water and she kissed Alex back hungrily. Standing in the doorway of the yurt, they drew closer together, eventually stumbling through to the inside of the tent.

'I've been wanting to do that all day,' Alex said breathlessly. 'Watching you just out of reach, doing such a brilliant job, I just wanted to drag you back here and kiss you.'

Sophie laughed nervously. 'I've been wanting that, too.'

The solar powered fairy lights that were strung from the beams of the yurt had come on, and filled the tent with a warm, inviting light. Sophie broke free of Alex's embrace and took his hand again. 'Come here,' she said softly, leading him towards the bed. 'I feel like I want to be lying down if you're going to kiss me like that again.' They sat down on the soft mattress, and, taking the lead, Sophie pushed Alex down towards the duck down pillows at the top of the iron bedstead. Hovering above him for a delicious, anticipatory moment, she then leaned down and kissed him, her lips tasting the last of the cider that Alex had drunk. Straddling him, she ran a hand through his dark hair, and felt a shiver of desire as he moaned into her kiss, his hips rising as he pulled her closer. Gasping for air a moment later, she found herself underneath him as he rolled over, raking his fingers through her hair and kissing her as if it were their last moment on earth together.

'Wait,' Alex murmured as their lips broke apart. 'I don't want you to feel like you have to do this.' His eyes were almost black in the warm light, and Sophie smiled into the kiss as she brought her lips to his again.

'I *want* to do this,' she said softly. 'Or hadn't you noticed?' She looked at him, and suddenly all the worries she'd had this afternoon seemed to dissipate. Maybe it was the couple of bottles of cider she'd drunk, or maybe, for the first time in a long while, something just felt right, but all she wanted was to spend the night getting to know this man and his body, intimately.

'Oh, I've noticed.' Alex's voice was husky with desire. 'And I kind of like it.'

'Good,' Sophie murmured, wriggling so that they were torso to torso. 'I'm glad about that.' She continued to kiss him, her mouth wandering lazily from his lips to his neck, playfully nibbling until he was pulling her even closer to him.

'Oh, God, Sophie,' he murmured between kisses. 'You have no idea what you do to me.' His hands roamed from her hair down her body, brushing her breasts and down her waist to rest in the gap between her jeans and her fitted navy blue T-shirt. She shivered again at the warmth of his palm on her bare skin, and reached down to pull his T-shirt out from where it had caught in his jeans, eliciting another low moan from Alex's throat.

'I want you so much, Alex,' she whispered, allowing her fingertips to trace the line of his hips and up his spine, discovering the body that had fuelled her fantasies since the day she'd bumped into him on her grandmother's landing. She didn't even care that she was going to have the most horrendous stubble burn on her cheeks if he kept kissing her that way; she just wanted him never to stop.

Pausing to allow Sophie to pull his T-shirt off, Alex revealed a torso that was just as finely toned as it had been that morning on the landing. Still pale, despite the summer sunshine, his muscular shoulders and chest filled Sophie with desire. Without missing a beat, Sophie slipped her T-shirt over her head and Alex bent his head to kiss her collarbone, hands seeking the rounded fullness of her breasts beneath their campion pink bra. This time it was her turn to groan as his warm fingers caressed her through the thin lace of the fabric, until once again she felt his weight upon her.

'You have the most wonderful hands,' she whispered between kisses. 'I want to feel them all over me.'

Alex pulled back to look at her, and Sophie's heart failed at the intensity in his eyes. 'Are you sure?' he said softly. 'I don't want to rush you.'

'Do I look like you're rushing me?' Sophie replied, knowing her face was flushed and her breathing was heavy. 'I want to feel you… all of you.'

Alex didn't need asking twice. Shifting on the bed to unbuckle his belt, he threw off his jeans, giving Sophie time to do the same. The yurt was still pleasantly warm after the strong sunshine of the day, so she threw back the feather eiderdown and the sheet. She was still clad in her bra and knickers, as Alex joined her, down to his own boxer shorts now; the crackle of electricity between them as their near naked bodies touched sent her senses reeling.

'Oh, God,' Alex groaned. 'I've wanted to do this pretty much since the moment I met you.'

'Would have been a bit awkward,' Sophie murmured, remembering with amusement their first meeting in the vat room at Carter's. 'You'd probably have been fired before you even started!'

Alex smiled. 'It's true, though.' He ran a hand down her side, caressing the dip of her waist and then gliding sideways to the front of her knickers. Slipping past the elastic, his fingers began to caress and stroke, until Sophie was tingling, warm and soaking wet to his touch. Managing, somehow, to wriggle out of her knickers, she parted her thighs and gasped as his warm fingers slid inside her.

'Does that feel good?' he murmured into her ear, sending throbs through her body that centred at her core. Stroking and caressing with a pleasurably relentless rhythm, his touch sent tingles of pleasure shivering through her, and Sophie moved against his hand with her own desperate desire for more.

'Oh, God yes,' she whispered breathlessly, feeling the encroaching lapping of an imminent orgasm. She grew rigid beneath his touch, her breath coming in short gasps as the wave broke and she came.

Alex reared up on one elbow and looked down at her. 'You look like you needed that.'

'So much,' Sophie murmured, feeling ridiculously relaxed. 'But what I really need is to feel you inside me.' She trailed a hand downwards and slipped it inside the cotton jersey of Alex's boxer shorts, encountering a very aroused Alex. As she began to stroke and caress him, he sank back against the pillows once more, surrendering to her touch.

'Oh,' he breathed, although this time his voice was husky with barely suppressed desire. 'You feel so good.' His hips jerked upwards as she increased the pressure of her touch and she could feel how close to the edge he was. Sliding down the bed, she guided him out of his boxer shorts until he was fully naked beneath her. His cock, standing proud, looked incredibly inviting.

Thanking her lucky stars that she still kept a condom in her purse, more from habit than expectation, Sophie leaned down and grabbed it out of her holdall. Alex glanced at her. 'Are you sure?' he asked gently, one last time. Then, grinning, he pulled her back up the bed so they were face to face.

'More than I've ever been,' Sophie replied. 'And are you sure?'

'Oh, yeah.'

Sophie again found herself underneath Alex as he parted her thighs and then slid into her. His length and hardness felt so good. She drew in a deep breath as he started to move, slowly at first, but then a series of deep thrusts that guided her, once again, towards her own climax, pressing, as she was, against him. As she felt the throb and beat of a second orgasm engulf her, she felt his shift in position as he came, and saw the look of naked honesty in his eyes as he tipped over the edge.

Breathing heavily, he collapsed, still inside her.

'You feel so good,' he said, raising his head to look her in the eye.

'You too,' Sophie replied. Sharing one last conjoined kiss, Alex slid carefully out of her. Then, he lay back beside her and she curled into his chest, feeling sated and at peace in his arms.

24

It was around four o'clock the next morning when Sophie woke. The morning sun was on the rise, the solar lights dimmed from the night before. They had slept in a tangle of limbs, one of Sophie's legs looped around Alex's as they'd slept. She should have had the beginnings of a hangover, but she felt strangely calm and very, very good as she stared up at the dome of the yurt. Sleeping with Alex had felt so absolutely right; like being with no one else ever had.

Waking gradually, she took a moment to realise she was alone in the bed. There was a slight chill in the early morning air, and as she came more fully to consciousness, she realised that the fabric doors of the yurt were slightly ajar. Swinging her legs over the bed, she pulled on her T-shirt and wandered over to the entrance. As she poked her head out, she saw Alex sitting in one of the chairs that he'd pulled out of the yurt. He was dressed in his T-shirt and boxer shorts, and his face was turned towards the rising sun.

'Hey,' Sophie whispered softly, approaching him over the dew covered grass.

'Hey,' Alex replied. 'I didn't wake you, did I?'

Sophie shook her head. 'The light did that. And I need to, er, pop to the loo.' There was a Portaloo behind the tents, although they'd have to trek a little further towards the show ground if they wanted to visit the shower block.

'I couldn't sleep once the sun started to rise. Thought I'd spend a little time watching it before the day starts properly.' Alex smiled.

'I might join you when I get back.' When she'd done the necessary, she headed back to where Alex was still sitting. He looked more peaceful than she'd ever seen him; she hoped it was her influence.

Sophie pulled up the other picnic chair and flumped down into it. The silence between them extended for a moment or two, but it was a comfortable one. The sun was gradually rising, casting the sky with a warm pink glow, and bringing even more warmth to Alex's eyes as he turned towards Sophie. 'Come here,' he said softly. He reached out a hand and pulled her to her feet, before dragging her back down onto his lap. Capturing her mouth in a kiss, he brought a hand up to her face, deepening the kiss with a sudden intensity that surprised Sophie. Luxuriating in the moment for a few seconds longer, she eventually broke away.

'Wow,' she said softly. 'We ought to wake up like this more often.'

'Must be the fresh air,' Alex said, a husky note in his voice. Then, his expression became more serious.

'What is it?' Sophie asked, sensing his abrupt change of mood.

'I want you to know... last night. It was special. Amazing.' He paused, and Sophie couldn't tell if it was the rose pink glow of the morning sun or if Alex was blushing. 'Since Mom died, I feel like I've been in a kind of stasis… and last night I felt as though I'd finally broken out of that.' Seeing Sophie's expression, he hurriedly added, 'But I don't want to put any pressure on you, Sophie. I'm going home at the end of September.'

Sophie was stunned at how desolate she felt when Alex said it out loud. Of course, she'd known all along that his internship was only for four months, but somehow, since they'd started seeing each other, she'd managed to block it from her mind. Of course he would be going back to Vancouver; the question was, what did that mean for her?

Raising a hand to Alex's face, she felt the prickle of his dark stubble under her palm, and her fingers tingled at the sense memory of his kiss. 'I know what you mean,' she said. 'Since Mark and I… well, I've not felt like I can get close to anyone. And then you came along and suddenly here we are, sharing a bed in a yurt.' She laughed. 'And to think I was worried about that, this time yesterday.'

'But what about tomorrow, and next week, and when I have to go?' Alex said. 'Sophie, I need you to know that whatever happens over the next few weeks, you mean a lot to me.'

Sophie laughed again nervously. 'You sound very fatalistic. What do you think is going to happen?'

Alex shook his head. 'Nothing,' he said quickly. 'But you know… sometimes things don't exactly turn out the way we expect. I never thought, in a million years, that I'd find you.' He pulled her close.

When they broke apart again, Sophie glanced at her watch, which she'd forgotten to take off before bed. 'We should get going. We've got another busy day selling today, and if it's anything like yesterday, we're going to be rushed off our feet.'

Alex nodded. 'I'm going to head over to the shower. Unless you'd like to go first?'

'No, you go first,' Sophie replied. 'To be honest, I wouldn't mind another half an hour in bed before we get set up for the day.'

'Fair enough. And at least, at five a.m., the showers aren't likely to be busy!'

'Don't you believe it!' Sophie said. 'Some of these farm boys won't have been to bed at all – they're likely just to take a cold shower and keep selling!'

Alex laughed. 'I'll bear that in mind!' Pausing to grab his towel and washbag out of the yurt, he loped off in the direction of the shower block. Sophie watched him leave with a mixture of lust and curiosity. Those long, slightly bowed legs were a sight to behold, but something nagged at her brain. What had Alex meant when he'd said 'whatever happens over the next few weeks'? She couldn't help wondering if there was something he was hiding, and she couldn't help worrying that, whatever it was, it might end up hurting her. She'd made herself vulnerable to him; not just last night but from the moment they'd really started to connect. Was he just going to walk out of her life at the end of the summer, leaving her with nothing but a few good memories and a bruised heart?

25

Bored of spending her free time moping, or reading yet more worthy texts from her book list for September, Meredith decided on Thursday evening that it was time to get out of the house for a more sociable reason than work. Not quite yet ready for a full on night out, she texted her best school friend, Rosie, to see if she fancied a drink or two in The Stationmaster. Rosie seemed just as keen to catch up, so, slinging on a clean T-shirt and running a brush through her long dark hair, Meredith headed out.

'I won't be late,' she called to Anna as she passed her in the hall. 'I'm just going to meet Rosie for a couple of drinks.'

'Have you had something to eat?' Anna looked concerned.

'I'm not really that hungry, but if I do get peckish I'll grab something at the pub,' Meredith replied. She knew Anna was worried about her, and wanted to make sure she didn't make herself ill.

Hurrying down to the pub, she walked through the door and scanned the room for Rosie, who, it appeared, hadn't yet arrived. Most people were sitting out in the beer garden, taking shelter from the still strong sun underneath the parasols and sipping cool pints of cider. As she headed over to the bar, however, she saw, with the exception of Flynn, the last person she wanted to bump into. Chatting to one of the bar staff as he waited for the rest of his drinks order, still in his green work polo shirt and jeans having come straight to the pub from a job, was Joe Flanagan.

Cursing inwardly, Meredith realised it was too late to change direction and go to the other end of the bar without looking like a total muppet. Especially when the bartender caught her eye and gestured that he'd take her drinks order next. She took a deep breath and, deciding to just ignore him, went up to the bar.

'All right?' Joe said as the bartender returned with the two other pints he'd ordered.

Meredith looked straight ahead, determined not to engage with him. She didn't feel like another argument tonight.

Obviously taken aback by her silence, Joe tried again. 'Look, I'm sorry. I shouldn't have lost it with you the other day. It's all in the past.' Joe gestured to his pint glass. 'Can I buy you a drink?'

Meredith dithered for a moment, but she'd never been a spiteful person, and she was disarmed by Joe's apology. He was right; he shouldn't have started the fight, but perhaps he had good reason. She looked round, and into Joe's clear blue eyes, so much calmer than they had been back in the orchard last week. He was smiling nervously, clearly waiting for a response.

'OK, thanks. Apology accepted.' She smiled. 'And I'm sorry, too. I had no idea all that had gone on. Perhaps you never know someone as well as you think you do.' As the bartender approached, she added, 'I'll have a pint of Caffrey's, please.'

Joe raised an eyebrow. 'Odd choice of drink for a summer's evening.'

Meredith laughed. 'I've been drinking a lot of it lately. It's useful in the northern winters to keep out the cold, and I've got a bit of a taste for it.'

When the bartender had poured their drinks, there was a slightly awkward silence. Joe, eventually, broke it. 'Um, I'm meeting some mates here. You're welcome to join us if you want.'

Meredith smiled. 'Thanks, but I'm also, er, meeting a friend. Rosie's just texted me to say she's running a bit late, as usual, so I'm just going to grab a table until she gets here. Thanks for the offer, though.'

'No worries. I'll see you around.'

'Yeah. See you.'

They went their separate ways, Joe to a table at the back of the pub where two lads were already seated, and Meredith to the table nearest the window, where she could keep an eye out for Rosie. It was a warm evening, and the breeze drifting in from the doorway was welcome. Meredith watched as Joe took a seat, and felt her cheeks growing red as one of the guys at Joe's table gestured in her direction. She saw Joe shake his head and mutter something she couldn't make out before he sat down. *Probably telling his mates what a snob I am,* she thought bitterly, before castigating herself for the thought. Joe had just apologised to her, and he was her dad's best friend's son, after all. OK, so they hadn't spent a lot of time together as teenagers, but she remembered playing together when they were kids. She owed him better thoughts than that.

Just as she was contemplating this, Rosie came barrelling through the front door of the pub and straight up to her table.

'Soz!' Rosie panted. 'We got caught in traffic on the way home from Bristol – some crash by the airport – and I needed to get out of my work clothes.' Rosie was working at a branch of Costa Coffee for the university vacation, which alternately left her knackered and wired, depending on how much of the product she'd had herself that day.

'No worries.' Meredith sipped her pint.

'Got one in already, I see,' Rosie observed, gesturing to the Caffrey's.

'Didn't mean to,' Meredith replied. 'Joe Flanagan bought me a drink.'

'Really?' Rosie arched a speculative eyebrow.

'Don't look at me like that,' Meredith replied. 'It was an apology.'

'And what would Joe Flanagan have done to have to apologise?' Rosie smirked.

Meredith flushed. 'It's ancient history.'

'Really?'

'Really. Joe's a nice bloke, that's all.'

'You know what they say, Merry – the best way to get over someone, and all that.' Rosie was staring appreciatively at Joe and his group of mates. 'Maybe it's just boredom, being back home for the summer, but perhaps there are some good reasons to hang out in the village.'

'I think I can do without finding out, thanks,' Meredith muttered, staring down into her pint, which was the same colour as Joe Flanagan's hair. 'Joe's not my type.'

'Yeah, well, perhaps you should start looking at something other than musical geeks, if Flynn was anything to go by,' Rosie replied. 'Joe certainly looks like he'd be a bit of fun.'

'Hadn't you better go and get a drink?' Meredith said, taking a huge gulp of her pint. 'And while you're there, get another one in for me, too.' It was going to be a long night if Rosie was going to insist on trying to suss out who the fittest blokes in the village were, and Meredith was definitely not in the mood for that. She was still hurt over the break-up with Flynn; the last thing she needed was to start thinking about going out with someone else.

Rosie was still staring at Joe and his mates, who had moved back to the bar. She turned to Meredith with a broad smile. 'I'll be right back.'

Meredith tried not to watch, but she found her eyes drawn back to the bar as Rosie, tall, blonde, confident Rosie, immediately attracted the attention of Joe and his friends. Within seconds, she was chatting to them, smiling brightly and nodding. Meredith felt a slight sting as Joe started chatting to her. She was mollified when he glanced in her direction again and smiled. After all, Joe could talk to Rosie if he wanted, couldn't he? Just as Rosie could talk to Joe. Deciding that she was in no way ready to trust her emotions at the moment, she dug out her phone and was, yet again, disappointed to see no message from Flynn. He hadn't contacted her since the break-up. She was surprised to find that it didn't hurt as much as she'd thought it would.

26

After Sophie and Alex had had a busy Thursday selling and demonstrating at the Royal West Country Show, Jonathan Carter arrived at the concession on Friday afternoon, which allowed them a couple of hours off to explore the rest of the show themselves. As they wandered around hand in hand, taking in the assorted sights of country wear concessions, vendors of local produce including the much lauded Yeo Valley ice cream and yogurt and assorted stalls from garden furniture to equestrian supplies, Sophie found herself relaxing into the atmosphere. She'd not visited the show for a few years, and she was enjoying getting re-acquainted with everything that it had to offer.

'This is all pretty neat,' Alex said as they reached the main arena where the police horses were limbering up waiting to do their display. 'Those guys remind me of the mounted police back home.'

'Do the Mounties still ride horses?' Sophie laughed. 'I mean, I remember Mum being addicted to this TV show when I was a kid that had a Mountie as its main character, but I kind of assumed they were more for ceremony than anything else.'

'Of course,' Alex replied. 'Although that's not their only means of transport these days.' Grinning, he whispered in her ear. 'Are you telling me you've got a fetish for a red uniform?'

Sophie laughed. 'That's for me to know and you to find out!'

'Well, well, well, you're looking cosy.' A very unwelcome voice broke into their private world. 'I thought you came down here to work, Soph, not to have a dirty weekend.'

Sophie stiffened and suddenly felt sick to her stomach. 'What are you doing here?' she muttered as Mark sidled up to them.

'Just doing a bit of the hard sell to the punters.' Mark smiled, but there was no warmth in it.

'Mark Simpson,' he said, sticking out a slightly grubby hand to Alex. Alex ignored it, and Sophie felt his back stiffen.

'I know who you are,' Alex said quietly. His expression was dark, and he put an arm protectively around Sophie. 'Excuse us, please.'

'Oh, don't be like that, mate,' Mark replied. 'I'm just coming to say hello.'

'And you've said it.' Alex turned back to Sophie. 'We should probably get back to the concession.'

Sophie nodded, unnerved by Alex's sudden reaction to Mark, given his natural reserve and politeness about everything else. 'Yes, let's get going.'

'Good to see you, Soph,' Mark called after them. 'Text me when you get back, yeah?'

As they walked away, Sophie glanced up at Alex. 'Are you OK?' she asked quietly.

Alex nodded stiffly. 'Of course.' But his set expression suggested otherwise. He was silent until they got back to the Carter's concession, and then they were both caught up in selling and demonstrating for the rest of the afternoon, so Sophie didn't get the chance to question him further. She could understand his reaction to Mark to a point; after all, she knew he was fond of Lily and Mark was to blame for her fall, and, she figured, perhaps Alex felt protective of her, too, after what she'd been through with Mark. She was just surprised that Alex had let his feelings get the better of him when he was so under control about everything else. Hoping she'd be able to get him to open up later, she concentrated on talking to show goers for the rest of the afternoon.

That evening as they headed back to the yurt, Sophie decided the direct approach was best. Alex had been quiet on the way back to their sleeping accommodation, and Sophie felt distinctly unnerved.

'I'm fine,' he replied, in response to her enquiry. 'It's been a long day.'

Sophie forced a smile, hoping that she could help him to brush off whatever it was that had preoccupied him since they'd bumped into Mark. Sliding into his embrace, she tilted her head up for a kiss, but even then, with her body pressed against his, she could tell his mind was elsewhere.

'Tell me what's bothering you, Alex, please.'

Sighing, he drew back to get a better look at her. 'I'm sorry,' he said softly. 'It's just that… I have a real problem with Mark. And not just because he's your ex, or even because of what his dog did to Lily. Although that's reason enough.'

'So what else is it?'

Alex shook his head. 'I guess it's because, when I was in my mid-twenties, I was just like him when it came to women. I didn't care who I hurt, and I was pretty careless with a lot of people's hearts.'

Sophie drew in a breath. She hated to think of Alex and Mark as similar in any way; they seemed like two opposing sides. Surely Alex was exaggerating? 'I find that quite hard to believe,' she said. 'I mean, you were so cautious about us getting involved; what changed?'

'I did,' Alex replied. 'Back then, I was working through a lot of issues. Mom had started to tell me the story of where I came from, a bit about who my father was; well, my biological father. She wouldn't give too many details, insisting that the time would come when I could find them out for myself, and to be honest, on the surface I didn't really care. Harry has always been my dad; I didn't need to know about my *father*.' He shook his head. 'Mom told me that I was the result of a summer fling. She didn't tell me if my father knew about me. That information only came later, just before she died.'

'So how did you feel about that?' Sophie reached out and entwined her fingers with Alex's.

'Frustrated, ten years ago, but not exactly angry. Mom was pretty strong willed, but she'd always made sound decisions. I figured she must have had a good reason for keeping his name from me. But on a deeper level, looking back on it, I can see that only having some of the story was affecting me. I had a string of flings, one night stands, ended things with women I liked because I wanted to prove something to myself. I put myself in danger more than once, sleeping around, running risks, and I'm not proud of that. I guess I must have been dealing with a lot of subliminal stuff, and my way of coping was to turn it all outwards. Mom was worried, I know she was, but I guess I was punishing her, and my biological father, for keeping things from me.'

'Sounds like you had a lot to get your head around,' Sophie said.

'I did,' Alex said. 'The law firm I worked for had a therapist on the payroll. I went to see her and talked things through, got a little bit of perspective. Realised that I was blaming Mom for the fact I felt there was a piece missing in my life, and using those women as substitutes, trying to hurt her.' He shook his head. 'At first I thought it was all pseudo-psychological bullshit, but gradually things started to make sense. Especially when I found out the circumstances of what had happened between Mom and my father.'

Sophie's heart lurched. She immediately started to think the worst; was Alex's mother abused? Was that why she'd kept things from her son? 'So, what did happen?'

Alex smiled sadly. 'He was married, with kids, young kids, when they met. And they lived... a long way apart. According to Mom, there was never going to be a future for him and her. She made a decision that, to her, was perfectly logical; she'd keep the baby, and raise him or her alone. I don't think my father ever knew I existed.'

'And once you found all this out, you never wanted to find him?'

Alex's face clouded over momentarily. He looked as though he was choosing his words carefully; his voice was husky. 'Of course. But it's too late now.' For the first time since she'd met him, Alex looked truly desolate.

'Oh, Alex.' Sophie's eyes filled with tears. She pulled him to her in a tight embrace. 'I'm so sorry.' She could feel him trembling against her.

For a long moment they just held each other; united in their shared sense of the loss of a parent they'd never really known. As they broke apart again, Alex placed a gentle kiss on Sophie's lips.

'Thank you,' he said softly. 'And I'm sorry I was so weird this afternoon. It just brought back a whole lot of stuff I thought I'd put behind me.' He laughed. 'I think being with you is making me want to open up about it all again, to be honest.'

'I'm glad, I think.' Sophie laughed nervously. 'I mean, everyone's got some secrets, right?'

For a second, something unreadable flickered in Alex's eyes, and Sophie itched to press him further, but just as quickly it was gone.

27

On Saturday evening, after another blissful night at the Royal West Country Show, with Sophie marvelling how she and Alex could still function facing the crowds of visitors all day and making love all night, they returned to Little Somerby, and had to readjust to normal life once more. Despite the hard work that the show had involved, to a certain extent it had felt like a holiday. Both of them definitely felt as though they were coming back to earth when they parted.

Sophie had gone back with Alex to Lily's cottage to check on her grandmother, who seemed pleased to see them both. Jane had been taking care of both Lily and dog walking duties for the duration of the show, and Barney was ecstatic to see them back. After a brief cup of tea with her grandmother, Sophie, with more than a little regret, kissed Alex goodbye lingeringly on the doorstep of her grandmother's cottage. Jane was flying back out to Marseille tomorrow afternoon, and mother and daughter both wanted to spend a little time together before she left.

'I'll see you on Monday,' Alex murmured, also reluctant to be parted from her. Neither of them felt comfortable at the prospect of sharing a room under Lily's roof, and Sophie couldn't face answering her mother's Spanish Inquisition should she present Alex at the breakfast table the next morning, so they decided for the moment to sleep separately. Besides, it wasn't as if they wouldn't be seeing plenty of each other at work anyway.

As it was, they both got swept up in the next big event in the Carter's calendar, and this one was quite a bit closer to home. As soon as the Royal West Country Show was over, the team at Carter's were well into preparations for Jack Carter's memorial celebration, which would be happening on what would have been his eighty-fifth birthday in the middle of August.

Carter's Cider liked to host various social events on the site during the year, as a way of keeping in touch with the village that had always been so accommodating and supportive of the business and its rapid expansion, but this particular event also had a deeper resonance. Jack had been a figurehead for the business in life with his charisma, sense of humour and encyclopaedic knowledge of apples. If his son, Matthew, had been the driving force behind the business' expansion in recent years, Jack Carter had perennially been seen as the heart of the brand. His death eighteen months ago had been sudden but not unexpected, but it had still left a hole in the Carter family and also the cider business. The memorial celebration would be a good way of marking his life and his legacy, as well as a reason to have a great night. The last of which, Jack would most definitely have approved of.

All of the cider farm's staff had been invited, and, such was the family ethos of the business, it wasn't going to be a night where they'd be forced to stand on ceremony. Matthew had seen to it that outside caterers and waiting staff had been hired, so no one felt like an employee. The invitation had been clear: wear something colourful, and dance the night away. Meredith had vetoed the use of 'eat, drink and be Merry' on the invitations, for obvious reasons.

Alex, charmed to have received his own invitation to the party, was also feeling distinctly nervous about it. Such a markedly family oriented gathering was an unnerving prospect on one level. He ached, since his nights at the Royal West Country Show, to level with Sophie, but the deeper he got, the harder it was to find the right words. How could he explain to her now, after everything they'd said and done, who he really was?

Sophie, who was looking at her own invitation as Alex opened his, smiled. 'You OK?' They'd managed to maintain a professional distance during the day, partly because Alex had been working with other departments for the past week or so, but he was still at a desk in her and David's office during the down times.

Alex mentally shook himself. 'I'm fine.' He smiled, dragging himself back to the present. 'This looks like fun,' he said, gesturing to the invitation.

'Should be a good night,' Sophie replied. 'Did you, er, want to be my date for it?'

Alex put down his invitation and wandered over to Sophie's desk. He took her hand and pulled her up from her chair, drawing her closer to him. 'There is nothing I'd like more,' he said softly. Just as he was dipping his head to kiss her, a cough from behind them made them both leap apart guiltily.

'Not on work time, if you don't mind,' David said gruffly, passing Sophie a stack of printouts from the latest vat tests. 'You might want to check number fifteen this morning,' he said. 'Its stats aren't quite as they should be.'

'Thanks for the heads up,' Sophie said, feeling the blush creeping up her cheeks. She suppressed a smile; David still preferred to check the numbers as they were spewed out on an ancient dot-matrix printer, rather than carry an iPad around with him at work, so she made a show of looking at the sheaf of paper that he passed her, before logging in to the real time numbers on her own iPad.

'And you'd better head on over to the presses.' David turned to Alex. 'The boys over there don't like to be kept waiting.'

'Sure, right away,' Alex said, feeling like a teenager who'd been caught by his date's father. He was sure he didn't imagine the faintest of twinkles in David's eye as the older man slipped back out of the office, though. Laughing nervously, he looked back at Sophie. 'See you at lunchtime?'

Sophie nodded, still rather pink. 'I'll meet you over in the canteen.'

Alex hurried out of the office and across the courtyard to the cannery. He tried not to think about the invitation on his desk, celebrating the life of a man he'd never known, and never would. For all kinds of reasons, the night would stir up a lot of emotions; he just hoped he'd know how to handle them.

28

Sophie was stunned at how quickly the summer seemed to be rushing by now that she and Alex had become a couple. The days seemed to run into each other, and Alex had taken to spending the short, sweet summer nights in Sophie's bed, always heading off at about six o'clock in the morning to take Barney for his early morning walk. Lily hadn't yet said anything to him about the fact that his bed in her spare room wasn't being slept in a lot of the time, but he was sure he hadn't imagined the pleased, yet rather knowing look in her eye when he'd returned with Barney and grabbed a quick breakfast before heading out to work.

Before Sophie and Alex knew it, it was the evening of Jack's memorial celebration. The party started at seven, but Alex and Sophie were in no hurry to join other people and be sociable. They'd stopped for a quick drink in The Stationmaster before getting to the farm, as both wanted to slip into the party unobserved. Sophie was keen to do this because she didn't fancy getting collared by a knowing Laura, and also because she knew that Mark would be there somewhere. The dairy farm he managed had been collaborating with Carter's on a joint marketing campaign to promote both their cheese and Carter's cider, so he was bound to show his face at the party. She was still very angry about what had happened between Mark's dog and Barney, but had been grudgingly relieved to see that Mark had at least bought his dog a muzzle since the incident. She really didn't fancy making small talk to her ex with Alex in tow, though, especially given their acrimonious meeting at the Royal West Country Show.

Alex had been quiet when he'd called to pick her up, and Sophie felt a prickle of concern worrying at her heart. It wasn't like him not to make some sort of conversation.

'You OK?' Sophie asked Alex as they wandered through Little Somerby towards the cider farm.

'Yeah.' Alex nodded, but still seemed a little faraway. He smiled down at her. 'I guess I'm just a little tired.'

Sophie suppressed a grin. It wasn't really surprising; they'd spent a lot of the past few nights awake. There never seemed to be enough time for sleep before the sun started to rise on another day.

'I just need to make a quick stop before we get to the party,' Sophie said as they passed the large church at the crossroads. She was holding a bunch of pale pink roses, bought from the village florist earlier that afternoon. 'It would have been Dad's birthday tomorrow, and I wanted to put these on his grave. Do you mind?'

'Of course not,' Alex said. 'Do you want to be by yourself? I can wait at the gate if you like.'

Sophie smiled. 'Actually, I'd quite like you to come with me,' she said. 'I know it sounds silly, but I'd like to

introduce you to him. I think you'd have liked each other.'
She opened the wooden gate that led up to the churchyard
and headed up the path. 'Jack Carter's buried here, too,'
Sophie said. 'He's a bit further back in the field. I like to
think he gets a good view of the cider farm by being here.
So much so, he's probably still sticking his oar in from
beyond the grave!' Was she imagining it or did Alex's
hand clench in hers? 'I'm sorry.' She paused, and drew
him round to face her. 'I forget that I've had a lot of years
to get used to being without my dad – you only lost your
mum last year.' She squeezed his hand. 'Forgive me?'

Alex seemed to relax under her gaze. 'Nothing to
forgive,' he said softly. 'I guess it all just takes a bit of
time.' He reached out a hand and brushed Sophie's cheek
with his fingertips.

'Dad's over here,' Sophie said, stepping from the path
onto the grass. About three plots along was a dark marble
headstone, inscribed with:

ANDREW HENDERSON

BELOVED HUSBAND, CHERISHED FATHER AND ADORED SON

and the dates. Sophie unwrapped the roses and picked
up the steel vase that slotted into the headstone.

'Would you like me to get some water for that?' Alex
asked as Sophie removed the dead blooms from the vase.

'Yes, thanks, that would be great,' Sophie replied.
Watching Alex walk off to the tap in the corner of the
churchyard, she murmured, 'He's lovely, isn't he, Dad? I

think so, anyway. I hope you would have, too.' The image of the young man in the photos at home swum before her eyes. It felt strange that she was now two years older than he had been when he died. She couldn't quite get her head around that.

Returning, Alex passed her the vase and seemed to read her thoughts. 'Your Dad was really young, wasn't he?' Alex said, looking at the dates on the headstone. 'I'm so sorry for your loss. At least I had Mom until I was in my thirties.'

Sophie nodded. 'Mum always knew there was a chance Dad's cancer could come back when she married him, but they were so happy together. They might not have had a lot of time, but they made the most of what they did have. Gran was devastated to lose him as well; she hardly ever talks about it, but I know, even twenty-seven odd years on, she still misses him.'

'It must have been so hard to understand, as a kid.'

'I don't have any actual memories of my father,' Sophie replied. 'I was only two when he died. He'd had leukaemia in his teens, but he'd been in remission for years. When it came back, it was aggressive. My mum prepared me as best she could for the inevitable, and I guess I always felt I was lucky in some ways that I didn't have to remember him gradually deteriorating, like she did. She loved him so, so much, and for a long time after he died my grandmother had to carry my mother – even though she was grieving the loss of a son, too. Eventually, she learned to live again. It took her a long time to move on. I think that's why she went to live in France when she met Steve;

she couldn't quite move on from the memories, still living in our house.'

'You must be happy for her,' Alex said. 'I know when Mom met my stepfather, I was about eight, and although I felt jealous at first, that he was taking her away from me, eventually I realised what a good guy he is. We helped each other a lot when Mom passed.'

Sophie slipped her hand back into Alex's, both of them united by their expressions of grief. 'I went through a phase in my teens when I was obsessed with finding out about Dad. I looked at every photo, asked Mum a million questions… I was trying to get my image of him into some kind of shape in my own head, and I got so frustrated that I didn't actually remember anything about him. Then, one day I came across this bottle of aftershave in my mum's perfume drawer. It must have been old – the liquid was virtually gone – but when I undid the top and smelt it, suddenly I started crying. It was as if some long dead memory had woken up inside me, some piece of Dad that I didn't even know I held in my mind.' She shook her head. 'I didn't tell Mum – I was too worried about upsetting her, but I wonder if she knew anyway. Every time I felt like I needed to be close to him from then on I'd sneak into Mum's room and smell the aftershave bottle. It helped me through some pretty dark times, knowing I had that little link with him.'

'Mom always wore the same perfume, too. And when she died, I found myself doing the same.' He shook his head. 'Grief does things to you; sneaks up when you least expect it. I cried my eyes out when I smelt that scent, knowing she'd never put it on again.' He swallowed hard, and turned away, focussing his gaze on the horizon.

Sophie couldn't say anything; what was there *to* say, after all?

'I'm guessing that the headstone with the apple blossom engraved on it must be Jack Carter's, right?' Alex's brow had furrowed as he looked over towards the newer section of the graveyard.

Sophie followed his line of sight to where, a few rows away, was a white headstone, facing in the direction of Carter's. 'Yup.' She nodded. 'Do you want to take a look, since it's him we're remembering at this do tonight?'

Alex seemed to hesitate again. 'It's OK,' Sophie said hurriedly. 'I totally understand if not… coming and standing in a graveyard is a bit of a downer before a party, really, isn't it?'

Alex smiled. 'It's fine, really. Perhaps I should take a look. I've heard so much about him, after all.'

They were about to wander off towards Jack's grave when Sophie bent back down and plucked one of her father's pink roses from the vase. 'Jack loved his roses as much as Gran loves hers,' she said. When they got to Jack's headstone, she tucked the rose into the vase next to a fresh sprig of freesias that someone had placed there. As they stood for a few moments in silence, Sophie's gaze drifted from Jack's headstone to Alex's face. He seemed lost in thought, almost as if he was struggling with something. She was torn between wanting to ask him, and feeling as though she should give him the space. Grief, they'd both agreed, was a strange, unpredictable thing.

After another moment or two, Alex turned back to Sophie. 'We should probably get going,' he said quietly, 'or we'll be late for the party.' They headed back down the path to the church gate, both lost in their own thoughts.

It was only a short walk to the wrought iron gates of the cider farm. Sophie had noticed Alex's pace slowing as they'd approached, as he'd seen the bunting and the fairy lights, and heard the strains of the jazz band playing where a makeshift dance floor had been set up. As the band launched into a cover of Billie Holliday's 'You Could Be So Easy To Love', he stopped altogether and pulled her into his arms.

'I'm so glad I met you,' he said softly. 'You've made being here so much nicer. I thought the only thing I was going to fall in love with when I came here was English apples. I never imagined I'd find my own English rose to love as well.'

Sophie smiled. 'It seems so crazy... we've only known each other a few weeks, but crazy is exactly what I need right now. In the best possible way, of course.' She drew a little closer to Alex, and pressed her lips to his. 'I just don't know why we can't turn around, go back to my place and forget this evening, though. Do we really have to go and be sociable?'

Alex stroked Sophie's cheek with a warm hand. 'Nothing would make me happier than to walk out of those gates and spend the evening alone with you, but we were invited because you and Jack worked so closely together. Don't you want to honour his memory tonight?'

Sophie nodded. 'He'd have loved this,' she said softly. 'He loved a party.' She glanced at Alex. 'I think he'd have loved the idea of Adelaide's, too.'

Alex tensed in her arms. 'What is it?' she asked softly. 'Did I say something wrong?'

'No,' Alex murmured into her hair. 'No. You really didn't.' He pulled her so close that Sophie felt the breath being squeezed out of her. Disquieted, she raised her gaze to meet his eyes.

'Are you OK?'

'Yeah,' Alex replied, a beat too quickly. 'I'm fine. Honestly. Shall we go see who else is around?'

Sophie nodded, but still the worry lingered.

Alex's heart hammered in his chest as he looked around at the assembled partygoers, all there to celebrate the life of a man he'd never known. He felt as out of place as a cheerleader at a rugby match; an outsider; a fraud. When Sophie had asked him if he was all right at the gates, he should have just taken her hand and run as far away from this place as he could. The courtyard was already full of partygoers, all drinking cider and looking as if they were having a great time. There was, obviously, a lot of drink circulating, and laden tables full of delicious buffet food, much of it prepared by The Cider Kitchen. Dotted around the place were mementoes: blown up pictures of Jack, examples of the apple varieties he'd grown, and quotations from interviews. Some guests were dancing already, and Sophie and Alex drifted towards the makeshift dance floor, feeling themselves caught up in the mellow, jazz-infused mood. As they joined the other revellers, Alex noticed Meredith Carter hovering by the bar, a pint of cider in her hand. She smiled as she noticed him, too.

'This definitely feels a little weird,' Alex murmured into Sophie's hair as they began to sway to the music. She was so tall that he could rest his lips on her forehead if she got a little closer.

'Certainly does. Now concentrate,' she chided as Alex's left foot collided with hers for the umpteenth time.

'Sorry.' Alex grinned. 'I don't have the benefit of a classical dance education.'

'It was a long time ago,' Sophie said. She looked up at him, face growing warm as she noticed the desire in his deep brown eyes. 'And it wasn't quite like this.'

'I don't think anything else is quite like this,' Alex said. 'I certainly never imagined I'd be dancing in an orchard.' The uneven ground underfoot was proving rather tricky to move on, but really it didn't matter too much.

'Are you having a good evening?' Sophie asked, still concerned about Alex's earlier mood.

'I am,' Alex replied, mostly truthfully. 'Being here with you is all I could have asked for.'

Satisfied, Sophie slid closer into his embrace. Something still nagged at her mind, but she was prepared to ignore it while they danced.

A little time later, when guests were starting to slip away, Alex and Sophie decided it was time to leave as well.

'Can I walk you home?' Alex asked as, hand in hand, they drifted through the cider farm, smiling at people they knew on the way to the gates. Sophie had been genuinely surprised by how many people had been happy to see that she and Alex had arrived together. The village network could be frustrating at times, but the interconnectedness of everyone and everything also felt like an incredible support. She knew that a lot of people were happy to see her happy.

'I'd like that,' Sophie replied. Sophie knew that Lily wouldn't have batted an eyelid to see her own granddaughter slipping down the stairs and out of the door in the early hours, but she didn't want to put Alex in an uncomfortable position. 'I've got some great coffee in,' she murmured, sliding an arm around Alex's neck and drawing him to her in a deep, sweet, cider infused kiss.

'Get a room!' came the call from Laura's new boyfriend, Sam, as they passed the two of them on the way home.

'We intend to,' Sophie murmured, breaking the kiss and wrapping an arm around Alex's waist.

'Will you excuse me a moment?' he asked Sophie. He gestured towards the toilets at the edge of the courtyard. 'Too much of the good stuff.'

Sophie smiled. 'Of course.' She caught sight of David over by the buffet table. 'I'll just go and catch up with the boss.'

Alex smiled and wandered off. When he was sure Sophie was preoccupied, he abruptly changed direction and headed over to the museum building. There had been some discussion about whether or not to open it for the memorial party, but in the end it had been decided to let people in to see the results of Anna's research in the family archives. Alex slipped in, unobserved, and tried to breathe.

The whole place was both memorial and testament to the Carter family's legacy. Huge photographs of the key players and key places of the Carter family's heritage stood sentinel around the glass and wood building, with carefully curated artefacts in glass cases lining the back wall of the museum. Notebooks, tankards, even the first ledgers of sale for Samuel Carter's fledgling business were on display for all the world to see. Photographs of Jack, the proud father of two such similar but wildly different sons, who now had both followed him into the family business, were everywhere. At the sight of so much that screamed *family*, Alex felt the panic, guilt and fear rising within him. What business had he to be here, in the midst of all this?

Reluctantly, he was drawn back to the last days of his mother's life; when she had finally told him her version of her truth. She'd been frail, close to death, knowing that time was not on her side. Fighting to remain until the very end, she'd told him about his father. '*He never knew about you, Alex. You mustn't bear a grudge against him for that; I never... I never told him.*'

'*Why, Mom? Why didn't you tell him?*'

Addie had closed her eyes for a long while, and Alex had almost been convinced that she'd gone, that the light was starting to die, when she'd looked at him again. '*He had enough at home to think about. We both knew... we both knew that what we had was special, but it couldn't last. I made the choice to raise you alone. But you need to know, now, who he was, so you can make your own decisions.*'

'*Who he* was?'

Addie had sighed. '*I'm sorry Alex. I'm going to leave you soon, so it's right you should know. He died last year. I wanted to tell you, but I couldn't find the right way to do it. But I think it's right that you know now. So you can make your own decisions about what to do with that information, if anything. His name was Jack. Jack Carter.*' She'd reached out and squeezed his hand with one of her own, the veins prominent on the back if it. '*Forgive me.*'

'*Nothing to forgive,*' Alex had said softly. The questions would come later; the onslaught of whys, wherefores and speculative becauses. For then, his mother had been all that had mattered. '*Try to get some rest.*' He'd leaned over and kissed her on the forehead before telling her he loved her; it was the last thing she'd heard as she'd slipped into unconsciousness. Back in the present, Alex could almost hear the last breaths Addie drew, before the life finally left her. Surrounded by the relics of another family, he had never felt so alone.

'You're my father,' he breathed as his eyes alighted on yet another picture of Jack from the early 1980s. The word felt simultaneously alien, yet absolutely right. Irresistibly drawn to the portrait, he reached out a hand and traced Jack's features with a shaking fingertip. 'I wish I'd known you.' Frozen there, trying to keep under control the surge of emotion that he'd known this evening would evoke, he could hear the revellers still enjoying the fruits of Jack and his family's labours, paying tribute to the man himself tonight. They seemed so far away from him here, alone, still carrying his secret but so desperate to share it. But even now, standing in this place, on this site, he hesitated. What good would come of revealing things now? Too much time had passed for it to do any good, and how could he look Sophie in the eye after all these weeks? Perhaps it was just better to finish his internship and go home; close the book and walk away from this library of memories that he had no part in. He didn't want redress, and he didn't feel the Carter family owed him anything. Over the past few weeks, being here at the heart of Jack's empire had allowed him time and space to discover the man that his biological father was; surely that was enough? Perhaps he could lay the ghosts to rest now, and leave no one the wiser about whose son he really was? Taking one last look around the museum, his gaze lingering on Jack's photograph, he made the decision.

So preoccupied with his own thoughts, Alex didn't notice the slight shifting of the shadows in one of the recesses of the museum as Mark Simpson slipped out of the museum door, a look of shocked triumph on his face.

29

Maybe it was the warm summer air, or the fact that this was a commemoration for her grandfather, but Meredith Carter was definitely feeling better. As she sipped her glass of cider and looked out at the assembled partygoers, she smiled as she saw her father and Anna, on a rare night out without the smaller children, looking happy and relaxed. They never strayed far from one another and Meredith felt so happy that they were still so very much in love. This evening was intended to be a celebration of her grandfather's life, and all the people who'd been most important to him were here, along with well wishers and other friends.

Solar powered fairy lights had been strung between the rows of trees in the Royal Orchard and were shining brightly now that darkness had fallen. Meredith had to admit it was looking spectacular now it had been tidied up by the tree surgeons. The apples in the rest of the orchards were about three quarters grown and would be harvested soon, now that the Eloise harvest was out of the way. Under the trees was a Bristol based jazz and blues band, and people were enjoying the barbecue and hog roast, as well as getting stuck into the cider. The ground was so dry that there had been no need to worry about a marquee or a dance floor, and Meredith knew that, as with so many events that the cider farm had held in the past, it wouldn't take long before everyone was dancing.

As she scanned the crowd, hoping to see Rosie or Izzy so that she could mooch over and talk to them, her gaze fell on a much smarter looking Joe Flanagan, who was drinking a pint of cider and chatting to his father, Patrick. Out of his usual green polo shirt and jeans combination, his charcoal grey jacket and white shirt over a darker, more fitted pair of jeans were understated but stylish. Hair that had a tendency to unruliness was carefully brushed back from his face, revealing a clear forehead unblemished by the spots that had dogged him a few years back. Meredith found herself looking at him in a different light from the way she remembered him. His air of self-assurance was decidedly attractive, too, and so different from the blushing sixteen year old he'd once been.

As if aware of her scrutiny, Joe turned slightly away from his father, and smiled when he caught sight of her. Murmuring something to Patrick, he ambled over to where she was standing, slightly away from the crowds starting to sway in front of the jazz band.

'Hey,' he said as he drew closer. 'You all right?'

Meredith, surprised that the smile she gave in return came so easily to her, nodded. Feeling suddenly nervous, she took a gulp of her sparkling cider.

'Nice dress, by the way,' Joe continued. 'Matches the apples.' He blushed. 'Sorry. That was a really crap line, wasn't it?'

Meredith's smile turned into a laugh. 'I've heard better.' She quite liked the fact that Joe still wasn't quite as confident as he thought he was.

'Can I, er, get you another drink?' Joe asked hastily, noticing her nearly empty glass.

'Actually, I'm fine,' Meredith replied, but, seeing Joe's look of disappointment, hastily added, 'but I'd really like you to just stick around for a bit, if that's OK? I mean, if you don't have anyone else to, er, meet, here.'

'Friends not coming?' Joe said archly, taking another sip of his own drink. 'Feeling a bit left out?'

'No,' Meredith snapped back. 'I just don't really feel like talking to people I don't want to talk to tonight.'

'I'm honoured,' Joe said, his gentle smile softening his words. 'I suppose being the heir apparent to all this can get a bit annoying at times.'

'Can we stop with the digs about that?' Meredith said. 'It's getting a bit old. Anyway, technically you're not right; Ellie, or even little Jack, can both have a say in the business now. They might be the ones who run it, one day.'

'Sorry,' Joe said. 'Old habits and all that.'

'Let's just forget all that, please. What's done is done. I just want to try to enjoy myself tonight. I think Granddad would have liked that.'

Joe nodded. 'Fair enough. Your granddad was a good bloke.' He cleared his throat as the band struck up another Billie Holliday tune. 'If you don't want another drink, would you, er, like to dance, then?'

Meredith smiled again at his sudden reticence. 'Yes, I would. Thank you.' Wandering over to the area that was rapidly being taken over as a dance floor, she drew a little bit closer to Joe until, with some nervousness, he slid a hand around her waist. She placed an equally hesitant hand on his shoulder and, as if some greater instinct was taking her over, she slid a little closer to him. Joe was a good few inches over six feet tall, and his arms felt reassuringly comfortable as she breathed in the scent of a lemony aftershave on his jaw.

They swayed gently to the music, both still a little bit tense. 'I've always loved jazz,' Joe murmured. 'I know that's probably not cool to admit, but…'

'Granddad loved it too,' Meredith replied. 'That's why we got this band in tonight. They usually don't come this far out of Bristol, but they had such good reviews that we persuaded them to play this gig in the end.'

'Good choice,' Joe replied.

They swayed in silence for a few more beats, neither quite knowing where to take the conversation next. It felt nice, though, Meredith thought, to be held by someone again. The fact that it was Joe, who had, unsurprisingly given his job, filled out in all the right places, was an added bonus.

As the music stopped, they broke apart again, unsure what happened next. Meredith noticed, to her pleasure, that Joe kept an arm around her waist.

'Now can I get you another drink?' Joe asked, as a rather more upbeat choice of song started.

Meredith nodded. 'Yup. And I think I know where I'd like to drink it, too.'

A little time later, they were sitting on top of one of the oak vats in the barn, working their way down a bottle of sparkling cider. Meredith was stunned at just how easy Joe was to talk to after his initial antagonism towards her.

'So, do you like training to be a tree surgeon?' she asked. She could feel the effects of the sparkling cider, but wasn't too far gone to be aware of sitting thirty feet in the air on top of an antique vat.

'It's all I've ever wanted to do,' Joe replied. 'Mum loved trees. She used to take me to Westonbirt Arboretum when I was little, and I loved seeing the colours in the autumn, and the greens in the spring.' He shook his head. 'Dad and I scattered her ashes there. It was where she seemed most alive. I was eight when she died.'

Meredith's eyes filled with tears. She'd known, of course, about Joe losing his mother at such an early age, but somehow, he'd been so out of her orbit socially that they'd never really discussed it. Just as Patrick's friendship had been a rock for her own father to lean against when Meredith's mother had left, so Matthew had been for Patrick a few years later when his wife had been taken from him unexpectedly.

'It must have been so hard for you,' Meredith said softly. 'She died so suddenly.'

Joe smiled sadly. 'She had an aneurism. Doesn't give you any time to think, really, until afterwards. I went from being sad to very, very angry, and that lasted a long time. School didn't like me very much; *I* didn't like me very much. But then, when I got to GCSEs, I suddenly had a plan. I knew Mum wouldn't want me chucking my education away because she was gone, and that's when I decided what I wanted to do with my life.' He swallowed.

'Dad was brilliant, though. He didn't have a clue what to do with me for a while, but I think it helped that I was a boy; as I got older, we could help each other through it. Then, when I was old enough to start making choices about my future, I broke the news to Dad about the tree surgeon thing.'

'How did he take it?'

'Not very well,' Joe said wryly, taking another sip from his glass. 'He really wanted me to get away from here, get away from the memories, and be the first in the family to get a degree. I got the grades, but I didn't want to go that way. I mean, who wants to end up with fifty grand's worth of debt and no prospect of a job at the end of it? And, this is going to sound really weird, but just before I made the decision to apply for the course at Cannington, I went up to Westonbirt again. It was like the trees were calling to me, like Mum was saying it was OK, that I should follow my heart and do it.' He swallowed another gulp of the cider. 'And that was it. I took up the place, then, when I'd finished the course, I got the job back here.'

'And apart from nearly smacking me with a branch, you seem to be doing really well.' Meredith smiled, trying to disguise how touched she was that he'd confided so much in her.

'To be fair, that was more your fault than mine,' Joe replied.

'You were the one holding the chainsaw.' Meredith gave him a little nudge with her elbow, but the cider was having more of an effect than she'd realised and she overbalanced, nearly ending up in his lap.

'Careful,' Joe said, helping her to sit back up again. There was an almost imperceptible pause.

'I'm a bit pissed,' Meredith said, focussing her gaze on Joe's clear blue eyes to try to ground herself.

'Really?' Joe replied softly. 'I hadn't noticed.' Then, remembering where they were sitting, he shifted. 'We should probably get off the top of this giant barrel before you fall off.'

'I've been coming up here since I was a kid,' Meredith said. 'I'm fine.'

'I'm sure,' Joe said. 'But just to be on the safe side, why don't we carry on talking when we get back to ground level?'

'Are you afraid of heights?' Meredith teased as he stood up and held out a hand to help her to her feet.

'Wouldn't be much of a tree surgeon if I was,' Joe replied.

Meredith had stood up so that she'd ended up very close to Joe again, and he still had hold of her hand. She chanced a look up at him, and found to her surprise that her mouth seemed to have a will of its own. Standing on tiptoe, swaying slightly from the effects of the cider, she placed a very gentle kiss on Joe's lips. He stiffened at the contact, but then seemed to relax into the moment, and she was pleased to feel the pressure of her own lips returned.

'I'm having a lovely time,' she whispered, as their lips parted again.

Joe drew her closer to him once more, and slid his arms around her. Their second kiss was deeper, slower, more leisurely. Meredith forgot, for a moment, that they were standing on a wooden barrel thirty feet in the air, and began to relax into his arms.

'Crikey,' she said as they broke apart again. 'I'm having a lovelier time now.'

'Me too,' Joe said. His pupils had dilated with the sheer pleasure of the kiss, and Meredith could feel his heart hammering against her own. 'But now I really do feel dizzy. How about we continue this on the ground?'

'Probably best,' Meredith murmured. 'I think I could do with a glass of water. Or six.'

Breaking apart a little to clamber back onto the steel gantry that ran around the top of the cider vats, they rejoined their hands as they wandered back down the steel steps, but neither felt too inclined to get back into the thick of the party. Maybe it was the cider, or perhaps the fact that Joe had confided in her, but Meredith was definitely feeling a rush of attraction. So soon after Flynn, she'd never thought it would happen, but she didn't stop to think about it too closely. *Live in the moment,* she thought. And this was a very nice moment.

'Do you want to walk me home?' she said as they came out of the barn. She swayed on her feet.

'I think that would be a very good idea.' Joe slid an arm around her waist to steady her. 'I don't think your dad would be too happy if he saw you like this.'

'Better make sure he doesn't, then.' Meredith let her head drop onto Joe's shoulder.

'Oh, no, you don't!' Joe chided gently, nudging Meredith back upright. 'One foot in front of the other.'

They ambled back to Cowslip Barn, and by the time they'd got back, Meredith was swaying less on her feet. Stopping by the back door of the house, she leaned upwards and kissed Joe's lips again, but before she could draw closer to him, he'd gently disentangled her arms from around his neck.

'Steady,' he said softly. 'I think you need that glass of water.'

Meredith gave a lopsided smile. 'Don't you want to kiss me again?'

Joe's hand in the small of Meredith's back lingered, warm and firm. 'You've no idea how much I want to. But I want to make sure *you* know that you want to, too.'

'I do!' Meredith, prone to bolshiness on the rare occasions when she'd drunk too much, protested. 'Can't you tell?'

Joe shook his head. 'Then let's try it again when we're both sober.'

'Spoilsport,' Meredith muttered, but she let Joe lead her in through the back door, settle her on the sofa in the corner of the kitchen with a glass of water, and put the kettle on for some coffee. By the time the kettle had boiled, though, she'd fallen asleep on the sofa. When she woke, a couple of hours later, she found herself wrapped in a warm blanket, with a cushion under her head. A stone cold cup of coffee, a pint glass of water and a couple of paracetamol were next to her on the side table, and a note from Joe next to it which read:

Text me, if you want to, when your headache's gone.

Grimacing as she felt the thump, thump, thump of a cider induced hangover encroaching on her brow, she swallowed the pills, finished the water and then poured the coffee down the sink. Looking at the kitchen clock and realising it was long after midnight, she assumed that Anna and her father had returned from the party and decided to let her sleep; the sofa was very comfortable, after all. She let Sefton, the family's border collie, out into the back garden for a last pee and then slunk off to bed. Thanking her lucky stars that Joe had seen her to her door and made sure she was OK, she thought about the way the evening had turned out. Perhaps she would call him some time, when it didn't feel as if there were elephants tap dancing in her brain.

30

Sophie was sure she wasn't imagining it, but she and Alex were definitely walking faster. It was as though both of them were gripped with an intensity they couldn't quite understand. There was a tension in the air between them, deeper than their nights at the Royal West Country Show, and seemingly tangible in the warm night. As she slotted her front door key in the lock, she glanced back at Alex, whose eyes were so dark they looked almost black. She felt a shiver run down her spine, and the second the door was open, she pulled him through it. She leaned back against the wall of the hallway as Alex kicked the front door closed behind them, pulled him closer, and for one delicious moment she wanted him to make love to her right there. The way he was kissing her, it was as if they were the last two people on earth.

Parquet flooring was, however, not the ideal surface on which to maintain your balance, especially after several glasses of the current year's Vintage cider. Sophie's foot slipped, and she was saved from crashing onto the floor by Alex's arms around her.

'Now whose footwork is bad?' Alex murmured between kisses.

'Better sweep me off them, then!' Sophie replied, and then gasped as Alex, accepting the challenge, threw her over his shoulder and started to carry her up the stairs.

'Not quite what I had in mind!' Sophie laughed, but her laughter turned to sighs as Alex laid her gently on her bed. The moon had risen, and cast an ethereal glow over the room, and as Alex stood there, the planes of his face low lit by the silvery light, Sophie had a fleeting feeling of total familiarity. She knew this man; knew him like she'd never known anyone, and she wanted to spend the rest of her life getting to know him better. Unsettled, but wildly excited, she dismissed the urge to analyse, and just enjoyed the moment.

Alex knelt on the bed, and Sophie raised her arms and wrapped them around his neck until his body was on top of hers. It was so warm, still, that undressing came easily, and swiftly they were naked in each other's arms. Alex's hands were also warm, and roved over her as quickly as she opened herself totally to him. Never had she felt such rightness in a moment. His mouth, his hands and his desire ignited hers to a white hot degree, and she relished exploring him, feeling the contours that she'd first discovered during their impassioned nights under canvas at the Royal West Country Show.

'Christ, Alex, you have no idea what you do to me,' Sophie whispered as hands, lips and other things drove her to the peak and back again.

'You are the most beautiful thing I have ever seen,' Alex responded between kisses. And as they took each other to the edge, the night seemed to go on forever. Back and forth, they passed the pleasure between them until both were sated and drowsy, the earlier intensity giving way to gentleness and peace.

Some time later, while they were still bathed in moonlight, the mood between them was more contemplative.

'What are you thinking?' Sophie snuggled closer into Alex's embrace, laying her head on his chest and listening to his heart beating.

'How much I don't want to go home,' Alex replied softly. 'I meant what I said earlier, you know. I never expected to fall in love with someone when I came here. But I have.'

'Me too.' Sophie raised her head to look at Alex again. Hair dishevelled, eyes dark with love and sated desire, he had never looked more beautiful to her. 'I really do love you, Alex.'

Alex shifted slightly, suddenly seeming uncomfortable under her scrutiny.

'What is it? You've had something on your mind all evening.'

Alex shook his head. 'I wish I could tell you,' he said softly.

'Tell me what?'

The pause between them felt electric, loaded with a million words that neither could say.

'You can tell me anything, Alex. You know that by now.' Sophie kissed his lips again.

Alex opened his mouth to speak, but as he did so Sophie's phone pinged from her bedside table. Sighing, she rolled over. 'It might be Gran,' she said apologetically. 'I know it's late, but I still worry about her.'

'I know,' Alex replied. Was Sophie imagining it, or did a look of relief flit across his features as she reached over and picked up her phone?

'Everything OK?' he asked as Sophie put her phone back onto the bedside table.

'Fine.' Sophie smiled, but it felt like an effort. It hadn't been Lily who messaged. In fact, it was not a number she recognised, but the message had made it clear exactly who was on the end of it.

Call me in the morning. I need to tell you something. This time you'll want to know. M.

Why couldn't he just leave her alone? She hadn't seen him at the celebration, for which she was grateful, but his yapping presence by text reminded her of that bloody dog of his. Resolving to block him, yet again, she tried to put Mark Simpson out of her mind.

As Sophie snuggled back into Alex's arms, neither of them were quite as at ease as they had been two minutes previously. Mark's timing had, as always, been impeccable. Even now they'd broken up, it seemed, he had a radar for the best moment to cause havoc in her life.

'What was it you wanted to tell me?' Sophie asked sleepily as her heart rate started to slow down again. This was what mattered: being here with Alex.

Alex paused a fraction too long before replying. 'It can wait,' he said softly, gazing up at the patterns of light and shadow cast on Sophie's bedroom ceiling by the moonlight.

31

Far from bringing him peace, Alex found that deciding to keep quiet meant sleep eluded him. Sophie had a long standing engagement on Sunday to go and see an old school friend, who had now moved to Oxford, so she'd kissed Alex goodbye early that morning and set off up the M5, knowing she wasn't going to be back until quite late. As it was, there was an accident on the southbound motorway as Sophie was travelling home, so she didn't get back to Little Somerby until nearly midnight. Alex, who she'd called when she'd pulled over at Leigh Delamere service station for a breather, had suggested they try to get a good night's sleep alone, and catch up at work in the morning. Sophie, although missing his presence in her bed, had agreed. They'd both had far too little sleep lately, and one night apart wouldn't hurt.

Alex had waited up until Sophie had texted him that she was home safely and then found himself unable to sleep anyway. Too much was going through his head: thoughts of Sophie, fallout from seeing Jack's presence *everywhere* at the birthday commemoration, guilt at spending so much time in Little Somerby under false pretences, and a nagging sense that he needed to come clean with the woman he'd fallen in love with. Bleary eyed and unaccustomed to being so lethargic, the last thing Alex needed on Monday morning was to come face to face at the Carter's Cider wrought iron gates with Mark bloody Simpson. Resolving to ignore him, Alex upped his pace. He was going to be late to work if he didn't push it. He'd got up early to run but by the time he'd walked Barney, it was nearly eight o'clock, and he was due at work. As he drew closer, he saw the other man approaching him.

'Snooping around again on Saturday night, were you?' Mark called.

Shaking his head, ignoring Mark, he picked up his pace.

'You can't hide forever, you know. Why don't you come clean, mate?' Mark's voice was like a hammer drill in Alex's brain.

'Can't you take a hint?' he muttered as Mark jogged to catch up with him.

'Bet it's great now you've conned your way into Carter's.' Mark was like a persistent mosquito, and Alex was definitely on the verge of swatting him if he got any closer. 'I mean, this internship story is just what you needed to get in there, with them and with Sophie. You must be loving it.'

'I don't know what you're talking about,' Alex said, a fraction louder. 'And I need to get to work.'

'Not for much longer once everyone knows why you're really here.'

Alex's brain was too addled by lack of sleep to really process what Mark was saying. On a better day he'd have made up some polite excuse, but he was having trouble forming coherent thoughts. 'Just leave me alone,' he muttered.

'What, don't you want to discuss the fact that your connection to the Carters runs a bit deeper than wanting to grow apples? Come on, mate, you can tell me. Spit it out.' Mark's voice was dripping with false sincerity; a tone guaranteed to get on Alex's nerves.

Alex's patience finally ran out. 'Just get the hell out of here, will you?' he snapped as he walked through the gates.

Mark grabbed his arm, a look of understanding dawning on his features. 'That's it, isn't it? Fuck me, until just now I wasn't completely sure I'd heard right the other night, but I'm sure now.'

'Sure about what?' Alex was beyond angry; with Mark for pushing his luck, and with himself for bottling out of coming clean with Sophie and the rest of them. Whatever Mark had to say to him had better be worth his time, or he really would put the other man on his backside.

Mark grinned slowly, savagely, and Alex felt ice dripping down his spine. 'I don't know why I didn't realise it before. Seeing you standing next to that photo of him on Saturday night. It was so obvious. You're not taking the piss, are you? You really *are* Jack Carter's son.'

Alex shook his head, stunned that someone as outwardly clueless as Mark should be the one who finally worked things out and blew his cover. 'You don't know what you're talking about.'

'Don't I?' Mark said, taking a step back from Alex's immediate reach, just in case Alex did decide he wanted to deck him. 'When I heard you in the museum on Saturday night it all fell into place. Jack was a naughty boy back in the day, wasn't he?'

'You're talking bullshit,' Alex replied, his mind racing.

'No.' Mark shook his head. 'No, I'm right. You know I am. I'm surprised no one's found you out before now. You've been here for weeks, sniffing around the Carters and their business, trying to find out about your dead daddy.' He grinned maliciously. 'And I suppose Sophie was just a pawn in your little game, was she? Someone to get information out of.' He paused. 'Or maybe she was just a fuck buddy to keep you warm at night?'

Alex's temper snapped. He lunged forward, pushing Mark back against the railings of the cider farm's open gate. Seeing the other man wince as the spokes winded him, he raised a fist. 'You need to shut your mouth, or I'll shut it for you.'

Mark, despite being several inches shorter than Alex, was unafraid. 'Too close to home, was I? Come on, Alex; you know I'm right. Sophie was just a distraction for you. Well, you can leave her alone now. It's about time she came back to me, anyway.'

'What did you say?' Alex's fist trembled where it hovered in the air, waiting to strike.

Mark let the moment hang in the air before he spoke. 'You stay away from Sophie, *mate*, or I will go to her and tell her why you're really here in Little Somerby, and, if I know Sophie, she'll kick your arse so hard, you'll end up back in Canada without having to get on a fucking plane.'

Alex let his hand drop. 'She won't believe you.'

'Oh, she will.' Alex laughed humourlessly. 'One close look at you and she'll put it all together. You're fucked, mate. And I wouldn't want to be in your shoes if Matthew or Jonathan Carter find out who you are, either.'

'Find out what?' At that moment, on his way to his office, Jonathan Carter appeared. Immediately clocking Alex's fist in the air and Mark up against the gate, he asked, 'What's going on here?'

'Nothing,' Alex muttered, ashamed to have been caught out in such a loss of control. He dropped his arm and released his other hand from where it had balled in the collar of Mark's grubby polo shirt.

'I wouldn't say that,' Mark panted, hauling himself off the gate. Feeling markedly more assured now that Alex had released him, and making the assumption that he'd have Jonathan as back up, whose morals used to be as shady as his sunglasses, he glanced back at Alex, who suddenly looked completely defeated. With a triumphant look in his eye, Mark turned back to Jonathan. 'Mr Carter, I'd like to introduce you to your long lost brother.'

32

Time seemed to slow down, and Alex felt the adrenaline rush of fight or flight kicking in. His legs started to tremble as he stood there, waiting for Jonathan's response.

'What are you on about?' Jonathan said. 'I don't really have time for jokes right now.'

'I swear I'm not taking the piss,' Mark insisted. 'He's your brother. I heard him say it at the party the other night.'

'Is it true?' Jonathan said, his face as bleak as Alex's had been a moment ago as the news started to sink in. 'Are you my brother?'

Alex took a deep, steadying breath and made a gargantuan effort to keep his gaze focussed on Jonathan. Suddenly, all of his noble ideas about keeping quiet, about leaving Little Somerby without a fuss at the end of his internship, seemed to fly out of the window. A yearning to be understood, to belong to the family he'd got to know over the past weeks, overwhelmed his more logical instincts. Now was not the time to look away. 'Yes,' he said softly. 'Yes, I am.'

Jonathan's head snapped round to where Mark was still standing, a look of triumph etched on his weaselly features. 'What are you still doing here? Get off this site, now. You don't work here. You've got no reason to be hanging about.'

Mark's mouth dropped open, but one look from Jonathan's set face to Alex's haunted one convinced him it was better not to hang around. Without another word, he slid out of the gates.

Jonathan continued to stare at Alex, seeming to take in every detail of the man's face, his manner, his bearing, which was strangely diminished now the truth was out. 'I can't believe I didn't see it before,' he said, his voice deceptively soft. 'It's so fucking obvious.' He shook his head. 'You're not taking the piss, are you? You really *are* Dad's son.' Half wonderingly, he shook his head. 'And you've been here for weeks. You've had free fucking rein of this entire place. Christ only knows what you've found out here.'

Alex just stared at Jonathan, whose eyes were as cold as ice chips. Despite the heat of the summer afternoon, Alex shivered. 'I should have levelled with you.'

'Yes,' Jonathan conceded. 'You fucking should have.' Then, ultra casually, his tone belying the harshness of his words, he continued. 'Pack your bags, clear your desk, and get out.'

'Wh-what?' Alex hated that, at this pivotal moment, this moment of revelation, the stammer that had dogged his early school years seemed to return. He suddenly felt like the child who didn't quite fit into the family photo; who'd learned to throw a punch to defend, not just himself, but his mother from the sneers and comments of those who judged them both. He hated it. Jonathan had all the self-assurance of the monarch of the glen, and the way he looked at Alex cut straight through him.

'You heard me. Get out of here, and don't come back. I don't know what you think you know, but I can tell you this: I don't care if you're Dad's son or not. You're nothing to do with us and you are not welcome here.' Jonathan's voice was still calm, but there was no ignoring the thread of steel that ran through it; he meant business.

'You can't do that!' Alex said, all semblance of calm draining away to be replaced by sheer, blind panic. 'I need answers from you; about Jack, about this place… about everything.'

'You're not going to get them,' Jonathan said. 'You've lost the right to any answers by insinuating yourself in here under false pretences, and lying your way into our confidence. I doubt your precious artisan cider farm actually exists at all, does it? Was that all a lie, too?'

'No!' Alex's voice rose, partly in panic but mostly in flaring anger. 'It's all true. Adelaide's is my dream. I came here to learn from you. But you're right, I also came here to find out about my father. I need to know who he really was. And where I fit into all this.'

'You don't fit into it,' Jonathan said brutally. He took a step towards Alex. Alex stood his ground, despite the now rising hatred in Jonathan's eyes. 'And you never will.' His voice dropped lower. 'If you go near any of my family before you leave, I will have you physically removed from this site, and, if I have my way, the whole fucking country.'

'You don't know what you're doing.' Alex's voice shook. 'Please, Jonathan…'

'Oh, I do,' Jonathan snapped. 'My family and I don't take kindly to liars. Especially liars who want to blow our lives apart. So you can get your things, and get the hell out of here.'

Alex thought about arguing, but the look on Jonathan's face told him it would be useless. Feeling his eyes beginning to burn with shame and frustration to have been so close to finding out the truth, his truth, and then been denied, he nodded. He dropped his gaze. 'For what it's worth… I'm sorry. I should have been honest with you from the start.'

Jonathan nodded curtly. 'I won't argue with that. I assume this will be the last I'll see of you.'

Alex nodded, not trusting himself to speak, the emotions churning up inside him too powerful to put into words. He wanted so desperately to keep pleading with Jonathan, but Jonathan had walked away, dismissing him as much with his actions as his words. Head down, Alex went to turn around. It was only as he caught sight of the building where Sophie's office was that it hit him like a brick. How the hell was he going to explain all this to her?

Before he had time to gather his thoughts, he was jolted to see Sophie herself walking across the courtyard between her office and the vat barns with Laura. Her hair was lit up by the summer sunshine, and her eyes sparkled when she caught sight of him. She'd obviously made it to work a lot sooner than he had. Panic stricken, and completely unsure about how on earth he was going to break the news of his sacking and dismissal from the farm to her, he just stood there.

'Hello, stranger!' Sophie said as Laura, with a knowing look, peeled off to the vat floor. 'Where have you been?'

The look of pleasure in her eyes, of delight at seeing him again, tore into Alex's soul. For a long moment he couldn't form the words to tell her.

'What is it?' she asked, obviously surprised by his reticence. 'Don't tell me the old Canadian reserve is kicking in again?' She laughed nervously. 'It's a bit late for that!'

'Can we talk?' He hated the way his voice sounded.

'Of course. Let me just radio David and let him know I'll be out and about, and I'm all yours.'

Without waiting for her to follow, Alex started walking.

'Wait!' Sophie jogged to reach him. She grabbed his arm, and her touch made him flinch. 'Alex, what is it? What's wrong?' The smile she'd had when she'd first caught sight of him faded as she saw the bereft look on his face. 'Tell me what's happened.'

Alex took a deep breath. 'I've been fired, Sophie.'

Sophie took a step back. 'What? By who? Why? What did you do, stick a rat in the Vintage vat or something?' She searched his face. 'This isn't a joke, is it? You're serious.'

Alex nodded. 'Jonathan Carter's told me to get out.'

'But he can't!' Sophie said. 'Why would he do that? What's he got against you?' She began to walk back towards the farm. 'I'll see if Matthew's around. He'll sort this out and overrule Jonathan.'

'No.' Alex shook his head. 'Matthew won't help, Sophie.'
Sophie's brow wrinkled. 'Why not?'

'Because I've been lying.' Faced with Sophie's earnest face, Alex felt his composure starting to fray at the edges. Facing Jonathan was one thing, but facing Sophie felt a hundred times worse. 'I've lied to them, to you, to everyone.'

'What do you mean?' Sophie's voice was so low, Alex had to strain to hear it. 'What have you been lying about?'

'Sophie... I'm not who you think I am.'

Sophie shook her head. 'No. You are. You're Alex Fraser, a lawyer turned cider maker from Canada. You're a kind, decent man with ridiculous manners and too long hair who I'm falling in love with. I *know* you.'

Alex bit his lip. 'I'm so sorry, Sophie.' He put his hands up to touch Sophie's shoulders, terrified she'd bolt when she found out the truth. 'I'm all that, yes, but I'm something else, too.'

'What?' Sophie suddenly went very still in Alex's arms. She drew a deep breath and laughed nervously. 'You're not married, are you?'

Alex shook his head. 'No.' He steeled himself to keep looking into Sophie's eyes. 'Sophie, I'm Jack Carter's son.'

The ground started to shift beneath Alex's feet as he saw the colour drain from Sophie's face when the true impact of his revelation hit her. 'Sophie, I'm so, so sorry. I should have been honest with you. I should have told you. I wanted to, but I couldn't.' He tried to reach out to her as she stepped away from his grasp. 'Can we go somewhere and talk? Please.'

'I can't believe it,' Sophie whispered. 'All this time, everything we've done and said. You were lying to me. Everything I told you.' She shook her head, as if trying to clear her vision, to get a clearer picture of the man in front of her. 'I told you things I haven't told anyone.'

Alex swallowed hard, the tears agonisingly close to the surface. 'I know. And I can't tell you how much that means to me. It doesn't change how I feel about you, I swear.'

Sophie's voice trembled as she still struggled to process Alex's revelation. 'You were just using me for information about Jack.' She shook her head. 'That's all this was, really, wasn't it? You don't care about me, or the cider making. You just wanted to find out everything you could about him. About—' She choked on the phrase. 'About your father.'

'No!' Alex was aware his voice was rising, but it was either that or break down. 'It wasn't like that. Adelaide's really does exist. And so do the feelings I have for you. I never intended to hurt you. What I feel for you... the love I have for you... it's all real, and I want you to know that I intended to level with you as soon as I could. And not like this.' He tried to touch her, but she stepped out of his reach again. Frustrated, he took a step towards her, but she remained stubbornly out of his grasp.

'You knew how much Mark had hurt me by fucking around and not being honest,' Sophie said, her own voice dangerously low, 'and you knew how much I needed you to be honest with me. Christ, Alex, I told you about the miscarriage, how it felt to lose the baby. And you haven't been honest with me. You've been lying to me from the start to get what you wanted.' Suddenly her eyes blazed with fury as she remembered their wonderful nights together under canvas at the Royal West Country Show. The way Alex had pointed out the constellations and explained how different they looked from how they looked in the British Columbian sky. Was that all part of his plan, too? To gain her trust and get her into bed, just so he could get closer to the truth about his father?

'That's not true!' Alex said. 'At the start I just wanted to learn as much as I could from you about blending, but, yes, I knew you were close to Jack before he died, and I wanted to find out what he was like; what the man who was my biological father was really like. My mother talked about him sometimes when I was little, about how he was a charming Englishman who'd swept her off her feet but how their affair couldn't last, and I wanted to know if she was just being romantic. She never told me his name until the day she died. When I came here, with what I'd managed to find out about him on my own, I didn't know what to think. But then I started spending more time with you and I realised it wasn't just Jack and the business I wanted to know about; it was you. The more we were together, the more I realised that I was falling in love with you; that I wanted to know everything about you. The past was one thing, but I want you to be my future, Sophie. I love you.'

'No.' Sophie's anger was rising. 'No, you don't love me, Alex. I was convenient. A silly girl who let herself be swept off her feet like a princess in a fairy tale. Well, you and I both know that life doesn't work like that. You used me to get closer to the Carter family, and now they know who you are, you can leave, can't you?'

'I don't want to leave,' Alex said, trying to take one of Sophie's hands. She quickly snatched it away before he could. 'At least, I don't want to leave without you.'

'Well, you'll have to,' Sophie snapped back. 'I wouldn't go anywhere with you if you were the last man on earth.'

'Sophie, please.'

'Just go,' Sophie repeated. 'I never want to see you again. You used me, you used this place, and for what? Jack would have been horrified.'

'I doubt it.' Exasperated and frustrated at not being able to reach her, Alex snapped back. 'From what I understand of him, he'd have got it completely. I mean, lying must have come naturally to him, too, to have done what he did with my mother.'

The sound of Sophie's hand hitting Alex's cheek resonated in the air. 'Get out of here,' she said, 'before I have someone chuck you out.'

Eyes watering, not entirely from the slap in the face, Alex stared aghast for a long moment. Then, wearily, he nodded. 'I understand. Goodbye, Sophie.'

Turning on his heel, he strode out of the wrought iron gates of Carter's Cider.

33

'We need to talk.'

Matthew was neck deep in paperwork about a potential takeover of a smaller cider maker in Herefordshire when his brother's voice broke into his thoughts. Frankly, the distraction was welcome, as he'd been hard pushed to see the actual financial sense in it, anyway. It had been something Jack had wanted to do before his death, which had been put on hold for well over a year, and Matthew wasn't really sure it was worth Carter's time or capital.

'What is it?' he said, whipping off his reading glasses and gesturing to the cafetière on his desk. 'Help yourself if you want one.'

'Have you got anything stronger?' Jonathan asked. 'You might need it when you hear what I've got to tell you.'

Matthew blinked and gestured to a sealed wooden crate in the corner of his office. 'There's a case of the latest Calvados that the distillery sent over as a taster if you want some. I keep meaning to ask you to take it over to The Cider Kitchen to put on the wine list.'

'That'll do,' Jonathan replied, hurrying to the box and snapping open the lid. 'Glasses?'

'There are some tumblers on the conference table,' Matthew said, sensing Jonathan's agitation. 'What's this all about, Jonno? Is it Caroline? Is she all right?'

Jonathan shook his head impatiently. 'Caroline's fine. Pissed off she can't get into her clothes any more, and still suffering from morning sickness, but fine. Just let me pour this.' Jonathan had filled Anna and Matthew in on Caroline's pregnancy shortly after the twelve week scan had shown her fears about her former drug use were unfounded, and the family were looking forward to welcoming a new addition. The irony that they now also appeared to have a fully grown addition to the family in the shape of Alex Fraser was not lost on Jonathan, who was rapidly starting to regret his cavalier action at the gate.

'Not for me, thanks, I've got a meeting with the charitable trustees this afternoon and I need my head on straight.' The Carter's Calvados had a deserved reputation for ruin if drunk in large quantities, and Matthew much preferred whisky, sacrilegious as it was to admit as a cider maker. Jonathan himself had steered well clear of Carter's Calvados since the night of his father's funeral, when he'd been rescued by Matthew on Wavering Down after getting blind drunk under a hawthorn tree in a thunderstorm. It was ironic, he thought, that *yet again* it was Jack who'd made him reach for the Calvados. Ignoring his brother's refusal, Jonathan poured two large glasses.

'Trust me. You're going to need this one, trustees or no trustees.' He hurried back to Matthew's desk, passed his brother a glass and sat down heavily on the chair on the other side. He took a massive gulp of his Calvados and swallowed deeply.

'Well?' Matthew prompted. 'I've not got a lot of time, Jonno.'

'You might want to cancel that meeting,' Jonathan said. 'I don't think you're going to be in much of a mood for it when you hear what I've got to tell you.'

Matthew sighed. 'Spit it out, little brother.'

'You know how, when we were kids, just before Mum got ill the first time, Dad spent a summer abroad? Did he ever talk about why he was out of the country for so long?'

Matthew shook his head. 'No, not really. As far as I remember, he was doing a kind of tour of international cider producers, gathering some ideas for apple varieties that might sit well with our heritage breeds. If I recall, he brought back some pretty good North American specimens and ended up trying to do some hybrids. I'm not sure if any of them actually took once they hit the Mendip clay soil, but to be honest I wasn't really paying much attention at the time.' He smiled ruefully. 'I was far more interested in rugby and girls aged thirteen!'

'Well, it would seem he wasn't touring the world as much as he led us and Mum to believe,' Jonathan said. 'In fact, he pretty much stayed put once he got to the North American continent.'

'What are you on about?' Matthew snapped. 'I haven't got time for your amateur dramatics, Jonathan.'

'Dad spent three months in British Columbia,' Jonathan said. 'And it wasn't just apples that got his attention. He met a woman out there. Things happened, apparently. Alex Fraser was the result.'

Matthew nearly dropped his tumbler of Calvados. 'Is this some kind of joke?'

'I'm afraid not.' Jonathan poured another slug into his glass. 'I mean, it's not like he's had a DNA test or anything, but it all makes a kind of sense. Dad was away for a long time that summer. Alex even looks a bit like you in the right light.'

'That's hardly conclusive,' snapped Matthew.

'OK, OK,' Jonathan said, seeing Matthew's look of irritation rapidly turning into something deeper. 'Look. He might be a con artist with a sob story, but something tells me, from what we both know about Dad, and what Alex has let slip about himself, that he's telling the truth.'

'How and when did you find this out?' Matthew, unable to resist the Calvados any longer, took a deep pull from his glass.

'About ten minutes ago. That twat Mark Simpson was brawling with Alex by the gates, shouting the odds about Sophie Henderson. Alex and Sophie have become a bit of an item in the time he's been over here. Mark's her ex, and obviously isn't too keen on Sophie spending time with someone else.'

'Thanks for filling me in,' Matthew said dryly. 'But I still don't see how you get from there to Alex being our brother.'

Jonathan shook his head. 'Sorry. Anyway, then it came out. Mark made a leap that none of us have been able to see all summer, and called Alex out on it. Alex looked as though he was either going to pass out or punch him, so I stepped in.'

'And he didn't try to deny it?'

Jonathan laughed grimly. 'To be honest, he looked as shell shocked as I felt. I don't think, on reflection, he intended us to find out that way. Of course, that begs the question when, and if, he was ever intending to level with us at all.'

'So, then what? Where's Alex now?'

Jonathan paused, noticeably unsure what Matthew was going to say when he found out. 'I sacked him and told him to get off the site. And preferably out of the country.'

Matthew nearly spat out his Calvados. 'Don't you think that was a little impulsive, even for you?'

'And what would you have preferred me to do?' Jonathan challenged. 'Sit him down for a civilised cup of tea and a chat? Need I remind you, brother dear, that he's been working here under false pretences all this time? God only knows what information he's had access to since he's been here, about you, me, the business. What makes you think he's not some con man up to industrial espionage? Have you done a full check of the vats lately?'

'I think you're missing the point, Jonno.' Matthew's voice was low, resigned as he finished his drink. 'If what you're saying is true, and he really is Dad's son… we owe it to him to at least talk to him. To find out where all this has come from. Yes, he should have levelled with us from the start, but I can sort of understand why he didn't. I mean, this isn't exactly an easy family to get involved with, even without the fact that Dad kept this rather large bombshell from us.' He shook his head. 'Can you imagine how it must have felt to land in the middle of that?'

'He still should have been honest with us,' Jonathan muttered. 'And what makes you think Dad even knew about Alex? Even if he'd kept it from us while he was alive, surely we'd have found out when he died – there would have been paperwork, evidence… something.'

'That's a fair point,' Matthew mused. 'Do you… do you think, perhaps, that he *didn't* know? That maybe Alex's mother kept it from him?'

'Why would she do that?' Jonathan asked. 'What would she have to lose by telling him?'

'Honesty isn't the easiest thing to practise, as you and I well know,' Matthew said wryly. The brothers had a long and tangled history, which only in recent years had begun to resolve itself. Jonathan's affair with Matthew's first wife, Tara, Meredith's mother, had torn the family apart, and it was only when Anna had come into Matthew's life that the brothers had begun to reconcile.

'Touché, big brother. But now what?'

'Well, seeing as you gave him his marching orders, perhaps we'd better try to get him back in case he actually decides to act on them. If nothing else, he deserves answers, and, if you think about it, so do we.'

'Christ, I wish Dad was here,' Jonathan mumbled gruffly. 'Although I'm buggered if I'd know what to say to him.'

'I can think of a few things,' Matthew said archly. He blinked, focussing his gaze on the bottom of his glass. 'Do you honestly think he didn't know?'

'I can't see Dad not acknowledging Alex's existence if he did know,' Jonathan said. 'He might have been unfaithful, but if a child had come out of it, I think he'd have done his best by him or her. It wasn't Dad's style not to take responsibility. That's what doesn't quite add up.'

'Maybe we need to get Alex back in, find out what he knows,' Matthew replied. 'We might all be holding pieces of the puzzle without realising it.'

'We'd better hurry,' Jonathan said. 'In case he really does take what I said at face value and leave the country.' He put his tumbler down on the table. 'He's staying with Lily Henderson. I'll nip round there.'

'I don't think that's a good idea, given what happened at the gates,' Matthew said. 'Why don't I head over there and talk to him? Although whether he'll agree to open the door to me is a different matter. But we owe it to Dad to try.'

'OK. Shall I meet you back at Cowslip Barn?'

'Sounds good.' Matthew stood up and grabbed his jacket from the back of his chair. 'If Anna's there you'd better fill her in about all this before someone else does. And Meredith. Christ.' He shook his head. 'When I got up this morning I had no idea something like this was going to happen.'

'I think it's knocked us all for six,' Jonathan said.

They headed towards the office door. Before he opened it, Matthew paused. Reaching out a hand to his brother's shoulder, he squeezed it gently. 'I'm glad we're doing this together, Jonno.'

Jonathan swallowed, touched by his brother's intimate gesture. There had been too many years when they'd been separated by time, distance and conflict, and Jonathan relished their rediscovered closeness. 'Me too. I can't imagine what Alex must have been going through this summer. I feel a right twat for bawling him out about it all now, and in public.'

'It's understandable,' Matthew replied roughly. 'It's as much a shock to me as it is to you. But we need to make sure we play this right; find out what the truth is, and, if we need to, do right by him now. Even though he hasn't been entirely honest with us, it's important that we all are from this point on. Agreed?'

'Agreed.' And with that, they prepared to meet Alex for the first time as brothers.

34

Meanwhile, blissfully unaware of the revelations that her father and uncle had unearthed, Meredith hacked her pony Rosa out across country with Joe Flanagan on her friend Izzy's pony at her side. She'd texted him the afternoon after Jack's memorial party, and they'd agreed to meet on Monday, since Joe had a day off and Meredith wasn't working until later that day. Meredith found herself missing Flynn less and less as the summer went on, and when Joe had kissed her on top of the cider vats, the memories of her ex-boyfriend had fled. She'd nervously suggested that he might like to come out on a ride with her, and been gratified when he'd said yes.

Now, pleasantly surprised that Joe could ride very well, she was admiring his excellent seat as the dappled sunlight cut through the woodland on Dolebury Warren, which lay just to the east of Little Somerby and was well within riding distance. The forest trail led up to a hillside dotted with crags of rocks and bundles of sheep, and was generally popular with dog walkers, riders and hikers, although today it was quiet. Joe knew the area well as his father's house was atop one of the small roads that led through the warren. Over the years, Patrick had gradually acquired about three acres of land, which was both field and woodland, and the two were headed there for a bit of privacy and a picnic.

'It's so beautiful up here.' Meredith sighed. 'Rosa loves it too – she's not great with land that's too soft, and far prefers rockier terrain.' She scratched the pony's poll affectionately. 'I think she's got some Welsh blood in her.'

'I spend a lot of time out here, just wandering,' Joe replied, nudging his pony into a trot on the flat path between the wood and the warren itself. 'But I've not done it on horseback for a long time.'

Meredith squeezed Rosa into a trot, and then sat back and let the pony have her head, allowing Rosa to stretch her legs a little on the generous terrain. Joe urged Sunlight, the pony he'd borrowed, to catch up with her, and for a few blissful minutes they cantered alongside each other, enjoying the refreshing feel of the breeze as they upped their pace.

Slowing down as the landscape changed and became woodier, Meredith turned back towards Joe. She felt wide awake and flushed by the exertion, and more alive than she had in a long time. 'I so needed this!' she called as he drew alongside her. 'Thanks for coming out with me.'

Joe gestured towards an old stone outbuilding that marked the outer boundary of his father's land. 'Thanks for inviting me. Do you fancy stopping for that picnic lunch?'

Meredith nodded. 'Actually, I am quite hungry,' she said in surprise. She hadn't been properly hungry for ages, but the fresh air and the riding had whetted her appetite for the sandwiches she'd made, and the leftover slices of Anna's delectable Strawberry Line Gateau from Saturday's service at the tea shop; they had quite a feast to enjoy in the saddlebags slung over Rosa's back.

Joe leaned over in the saddle as they approached the five bar gate that marked the entrance to his father's land. Shoving it open, he waited for Meredith and Rosa to come past then he closed it again behind them. 'It's secure all the way around, so the horses'll be OK to graze for a bit. And you can choose your picnic spot.'

Meredith smiled. The sun was warm, and there wasn't a cloud in the sky. 'How about we tuck ourselves away behind the outbuilding?'

They slid off the ponies and Meredith loosed the saddlebags, then wandered over to the stone building about a hundred yards away. Out of habit, Meredith checked the state of the fences but they were in excellent repair, and so she had no worries about leaving the ponies to graze for a while. When Joe's hand slipped into hers as they walked, Meredith felt a jolt of electricity. She'd been dying to kiss him again since their evening on top of the cider vats, and there was something in the air on this beautiful sunny day.

Setting out the picnic rug, they both fell on the food, neither having felt much like breakfast. Meredith laughed as a succulent piece of Anna's gateau detached itself from the slice Joe was attempting to eat and a strawberry ended up on his lap. Swooping playfully, she took a bite out of it, and then put the other half to Joe's lips. Joe swallowed it down, kissing her fingertips, which lingered at his mouth.

The pause between them seemed to extend to the horizon as both hovered on the cusp of something. Meredith slid her hand around the back of Joe's neck, pulling him towards her for a deep, strawberry infused kiss. Freed up by the total seclusion the peace of the warren offered, Joe pulled Meredith into his lap, intensifying the kiss and murmuring as she straddled him.

'You have no idea how much I've wanted to do this since Saturday night,' Meredith whispered. 'But I wasn't sure how you'd react.'

'You can be sure now,' Joe replied. 'Because I feel exactly the same. I've never been more sure of anything in my life.' Breaking their kiss, he raised a hand and stroked from Meredith's collarbone to her neck, then dipped his head and kissed her mouth again. His lips were firm, and warm, and as the kiss deepened Meredith's eyes closed in ecstasy. 'After all, tree surgeons always say if you fall out of a tree, you should get straight back up it again.'

'I'm not quite sure this is what they had in mind when they said that,' Meredith murmured as they broke apart. She glanced to where they'd left the ponies. Rosa was nose to tail with Sunlight, the two of them nibbling each other's rough patches by way of comfort. Flynn hadn't liked horses, and it had been nice to hack out with someone who could actually ride. Joe had looked so natural in the saddle; Meredith respected the lines of a good rider.

'Come here,' Joe murmured. He pulled her down to him. 'It's all right,' he continued. 'No one's going to burst in on us. Dad's fenced off the land for three acres straight. I know you were hurt by Flynn,' he said softly. 'And I don't expect this to go anywhere if you don't want it to. Let's just enjoy the moment.'

Meredith nodded. Never in a million years did she think she'd be sharing a picnic blanket with the son of her dad's best friend, and somewhere in the back of her mind she wondered exactly what her father would say about it if he ever found out. But Joe had been so kind to her, shown her so much understanding, especially after the way Flynn had treated him in the past, that she was touched beyond belief. The air smelt so sweet, the summer scents of cut grass, with the underlying fragrance of the newly ploughed clay soil giving an earthy undertone. Above them, the sky was stingingly blue and cloudless, and from the woodland nearby the songbirds chirruped lazily in the boughs. It was a moment for love, a moment to seize. Sitting up sharply, Meredith wrapped a thigh around Joe's hips and brought her lips down to his.

'You are absolutely right,' she said between kisses. 'But let's get one thing straight. This is not a rebound thing.' She broke away for a moment and looked down at him. Joe's clear blue eyes were fixed on hers, one hand still in her hair from the kiss. 'I thought you were fit from the moment I saw you up that tree in the Royal Orchard.'

'And I've thought you were fit for much longer than that,' Joe quipped. 'But let's not go there!'

And suddenly, feeling Joe's lips on hers, Meredith knew that it was going to be all right. Surrendering to his kiss once more, allowing him to pull her back down to the blanket, she seized the moment.

'Everything OK?' Joe asked a little time later as he stroked her long dark hair.

'Totally,' Meredith replied, somewhat in amazement. 'In fact, I can't think why we didn't notice each other sooner.'

Joe laughed. 'You were out of my league, remember?'

Meredith sat up and looked down at him. Muscular arms, just smattered with a few freckles, were tucked behind his head, and he was staring up at the sky, a look of contentment on his face. His chest, broad and muscular from the hours spent doing such a physical job, was outlined against the tight blue T-shirt he was wearing. He was the total opposite to Flynn in so many ways; perhaps that was why she'd been so attracted to him. But she mustn't think like that. This had been fun; more fun than she could have imagined, but she was taking things one day at a time.

Time. 'Oh, shit!' Meredith reached for her mobile phone. Glancing at the screen, she groaned. 'Fuck. I'm late for work.'

'I wouldn't worry,' Joe said. 'Don't your aunt and uncle run the place? I'm sure they won't mind if you're a bit late.'

'That's so not the point,' Meredith snapped. 'I've never been late for a shift in my life.' Tearing the hair band off her wrist, she tied her hair back again. 'And Caroline's been really snappy lately. I don't want to be the one who gets a bollocking.'

Joe sat up. 'I'll go and get the ponies,' he said, folding up the picnic blanket. He paused. 'Look, Meredith…'

Meredith glanced up from sending a text to her uncle Jonathan, explaining that she was going to be a few minutes late, which she couldn't seem to spell correctly. 'Yeah?'

'This… this means what you want it to mean. It's up to you what happens next. No pressure. I promise.'

Meredith smiled. 'Thanks, Joe. And it meant a lot. I promise you. But we really do have to get these ponies home, or I won't have a job to go back to.'

'Fair enough.' Joe strode over to the ponies and, catching their reins, brought them both back over to Meredith. 'Let's make sure you get where you need to go.'

35

The walk back to Lily's cottage was the longest of Alex
Fraser's life. What had he done? Why hadn't he just laughed
in Mark's face, denied everything and made the other man
look like the idiot? He'd let that smarmy, cheating ex-
boyfriend of Sophie's get under his skin, and blown his
chances of ever getting to know his father's family properly.
And on top of that, by not being honest with Sophie
sooner he'd blown out of the water any hope of having a
relationship with her, too. Any chance of reconciling with
Jack's family, of getting to know Matthew and Jonathan
as brothers, honestly and without the subterfuge of the
past few weeks, had gone. And he'd betrayed the trust of
a woman who had put her own trust in him despite being
so badly betrayed herself. He deserved to be exiled, to get
on the next plane back to Vancouver and never darken
the doors of Little Somerby again. He knew, now, that
he'd handled everything completely wrongly.

As he walked down High Street, head down, avoiding
the smiles of the people he'd got to know in the time he'd
been in Little Somerby, he thought about how quickly he'd
been accepted here; of how Lily had opened her home

to him, how Sophie had seemed to enjoy imparting her knowledge of cider making to him, how, when he walked into The Stationmaster of an evening after work, Vern had hailed him and poured him a pint of lager without prompting, knowing quickly which brand was his 'usual'. How the long, sunny days and short sweet Somerset nights had been made all the sweeter since he'd fallen in love with Sophie. How, despite the ever present ache of grief for his mother, he'd not once felt homesick. Little Somerby and its residents had beguiled him; he felt as though he belonged.

And now all that was over. It wouldn't take long before the village grapevine, probably headed up by Mark Simpson, went into overdrive about Jack Carter's long lost, illegitimate son. The wrong-side-of-the-blanket Carter, who'd insinuated himself into the family business like a red sock in a white wash. He'd upset the balance, thrown over the applecart and things would never be the same again.

And for what? Jack was dead and buried; never to give Alex the answers he so desperately craved. His half-brothers would close ranks, deny him access to any information. Jonathan had been horrified by the discovery of the truth, and Matthew, with his unimpeachable sense of integrity, would doubtless be at the head of the party to hound him from the village. He knew about as much now as he had when he'd made the discovery of his paternity; so, what had it all been for?

But that wasn't all. Somewhere in the mix had been Sophie Henderson. Tall, beautiful, clever, funny Sophie, who'd stolen his heart on that very first day they'd met, although he hadn't known it at the time. Sophie, that strange mix of confidence and caution, who'd confided in him, trusted him, given him the first feeling of home since his mother had died. Sophie, who'd taught him so much about a subject she loved, and allowed him to share so much more once they'd stopped fighting their attraction. Sophie, who'd shouted at him that she never wanted to see him again, now that she knew the truth.

'I should have told you,' he whispered, earning a surprised look from elderly Miss Pinkham, who was passing by on the pavement with her irritable little dog, Hugo. It was his desire to maintain control, to reveal the truth at a time of his own choosing, that had done for it all in the end. There were some things in life he just couldn't control; that much, now, he knew. And by hesitating, he had allowed his cover to be blown by someone who wasn't even worth the time of day.

'Did you forget something? Everything all right, my love?' he heard Lily call as he passed her living room hurriedly. He knew, if he stopped to talk to her now, he'd break down, and he didn't want to see the look in her eye once she knew the truth of his subterfuge. Almost sprinting up the steep stairs to his room, he closed the door, trying desperately to shut out the world, to stem the flow of emotion that was still bubbling so close to the surface. Sinking down onto his neatly made bed, he put his head in his hands.

Some time later, he raised his head again and took stock. He couldn't hide in his bedroom like a sullen teenager forever, and Lily deserved answers, or at the very least to know that she was going to be losing her lodger a little sooner than she'd thought. But first things first; opening his laptop, he searched the flight listings for Vancouver from Bristol and felt a stab of something unidentifiable that there was a last minute deal on a flight early the next morning. It would mean a transfer in Amsterdam, but the extra time felt like a reasonable penance for his actions. Shame it wasn't today, but, he figured, not even Jonathan Carter could begrudge him one last, sleepless night in Little Somerby. Connecting to Lily's wireless printer in her study, he proceeded to sort out the paperwork.

A gentle knock at his bedroom door snapped him out of his brooding.

'There's someone here to see you, Alexander.' Lily's kindly face appeared around the door.

'Who is it?' Alex asked. He still liked the way she occasionally used his full name, even if it did make him feel as though he were a small boy in trouble. This time, he supposed, he actually was.

'Why don't you come into the living room and see for yourself?'

Alex's heart thumped. Could it be Sophie? Despite everything, had she decided to make the first move? Hope flared in his chest as he hurried down the steep stairs of the cottage, but as Lily opened the living room door he was kneed in the gut by disappointment, and then a wave of anxiety washed over him just as quickly. There, standing stiffly by the fireplace, was Matthew.

'Don't worry,' Matthew said, holding up his hands as Alex took a step backwards. 'I know your last encounter with Jonathan wasn't exactly friendly, but I'm not here to start throwing my weight around. I just want to talk.'

Alex nodded, for once at a loss for words.

'Can I get you a drink, dear?' Lily asked from where she'd stopped in the hallway.

'No, thanks, Mrs Henderson,' Matthew said. 'I'm hoping I'll be able to convince Alex to come back home with me in a sec, where I'm sure there's going to be a fair bit of drinking going on.' He laughed nervously. 'And Jonathan's promised to behave himself.'

'You mean he's not going to try to throw me out again?' Alex finally found his voice.

'If he does, he'll have me to answer to,' Matthew replied gently. 'Look. I'm feeling pretty confused myself right now, and I'm sure you must be, too.' Matthew glanced at Lily, who was still standing in the doorway of the parlour.

'Would you like me to make myself scarce?' Lily asked wryly.

Matthew shook his head. 'No, Mrs Henderson, there's no need for that. You, of all people, won't be surprised to learn that Alex here claims to be my half-brother.'

Lily's right eyebrow twitched in astonishment and there was a long pause before anyone said anything. Eventually, she broke the silence. 'Well, it's about time someone worked it out so that I didn't just seem like a geriatric novelist with an overactive imagination.'

Alex's knees, already trembling, felt as though they were about to give way. 'You knew?' he said.

FAY KEENAN

'I suspected,' Lily replied softly. 'After all, I knew Jack
for a long, long, time.' She glanced at Matthew, seemingly
gauging his reaction, before she continued. 'He was a
good man, but not always a responsible one. He could
charm the birds from the trees on a sunny day. Add to that
your bone structure, which could only come from Jack's
side of the family, and it didn't take much to join the dots.'

Alex shook his head. 'But if it was so obvious, how
come no one else called me out on it?'

'People are preoccupied these days,' Lily said. 'You are
all so busy looking at your phones that you don't really
look at each other. Even my granddaughter's addicted to
Instagram. And...' she paused with a twinkle in her eye,
'... I'm a keen watcher of people. You don't write thirty
bestselling novels without looking around you from time
to time and working out stories.'

Lily, still using her walking stick, walked over to the
dresser in the corner of her living room. 'And now that it's
all out in the open, I have something in here somewhere
that you should both see.'

Matthew glanced at Alex, and as their eyes met an
understanding passed between them. Was this the first step
towards a reconciliation? Alex so wanted to be accepted
by this man; somehow, gaining Matthew's approval was
more important than anything. Matthew was, after all, the
de facto head of the Carter family since Jack had passed
away. And it was more than that; he liked Matthew. He
had a feeling that the two of them had a lot in common,
and he wanted to spend time with the man on an honest
footing now.

Looking back at Lily, Alex wondered what she was up to. The old lady had a shrewd head on her shoulders and was given to big reveals, most of them timely, from what Sophie had told him. Lily reached to the top shelf of her bureau and slotted the key she found there into the lock of the desk. Rummaging around in some papers, she finally found what she was looking for. Silently, she handed it over to Alex.

'When Jack had his last heart attack, he passed me several documents that he wanted kept safe,' Lily said gently. Seeing Matthew's look of alarm, she quickly qualified. 'Don't worry, my love, it was nothing legally binding, or anything that would change your, er, circumstances. They were items of a more sentimental value.' She nodded. 'Go on, Alex, take a look.' She smiled as Alex's hands started to shake. 'Along with the photograph of your mother were several letters. He couldn't tell Jonathan and Matthew, he didn't see the point in enlightening them about something that had happened such a long time ago, but neither could he bear to just dispose of the information.' She sighed. 'I often wish he'd just burned the lot, but he was adamant that he needed someone to take care of these. Perhaps he had a premonition that someone was going to come asking questions one day.'

The pile of letters that Lily handed Alex was yellowed with age, but there was no doubt that it was his mother's distinctive handwriting on the envelopes, and, as he pulled out the first thin airmail sheet inside one of them, his hands started to shake. Taking a deep breath, somehow knowing that there was no going back, Alex steeled himself to read. Not able to speak, he passed the letter to Matthew, whose head nodded almost imperceptibly in understanding as he read.

Darling Jack,

I know that you've been waiting to hear from me, and I'm sorry that it's taken me so long to write this letter. It's taken me this long to get my head together. I'm so sorry to hear about Cecily. You must, of course, do what is right for her and your boys. They will need you in the coming months.

I think, under the circumstances, it would be better if we put this summer to one side now, and keep it as the wonderful memory it was. Please do not try to contact me. I am, and will be, all right.

Ever,
Addie.

Seeing that Alex was still incapable of speech, Lily elaborated. 'It was almost as if Jack knew he wasn't going to be around much longer. He didn't want his sons to find anything that might have led to questions about his affair with your mother, but neither could he entirely let go of what had happened.'

Alex traced the outline of his mother's face in the photograph with a shaky fingertip. She looked so happy, as if whoever had taken it had made her laugh shortly before the shutter closed. She was standing in front of the breathtaking backdrop of Kennedy Falls. Her hair was swept off her face, and she was wearing a loose red shirt and white trousers. She looked young, healthy and very much in love. Then he made the connection; the photo of Jack, the one his mother had given him just before she died, the one he'd carried with him to Little Somerby, had been taken in the same place, at the same time. They were two halves of the same scene; the same moment, much as the letters he'd brought with him from Jack were the other half of the love story his mother had written in hers. Perhaps, in another time, those halves might have been together permanently, instead of separated by greater circumstances.

'Jack told me that this was taken on their last day together. She was determined to think well of him, and she let him come back to Cecily with her blessing. She was in control of it all. From the conversations I had with Jack before he died, I'm also fairly sure he had no idea about you, Alex. And from what I know of Jack, if he had known, he'd certainly have made contact with you.'

'He really did love her, didn't he?' Alex said, half to himself. He'd almost forgotten that Matthew was standing next to him.

'Yes, he did.' Lily placed a cool hand on Alex's arm. 'And I think they both would have wanted you to have these. For all the secrecy surrounding their relationship, they were always honest with each other. They knew it couldn't last, and they'd both made peace with that.'

'How do you know all this?' Alex turned back to Lily. 'If it was all such a secret, how did you know?'

Lily sighed. 'Jack must have known he wasn't long for this world. He could have got a safety deposit box and put all of his things associated with your mother in it, but he wanted to keep the memories closer, and he needed to talk. He went through all kinds of hell after Cecily died. He knew he'd treated her badly in the past, and when she became so ill, he felt it was God's way of punishing him for the way he'd carried on behind her back. I know, over the years, especially after Cecily's death, that he thought about trying to find your mother again.' Lily shook her head. 'Jack was never very fond of computers, or he'd probably have realised he could have looked for her on Facebook. But perhaps it's for the best that he didn't. The guilt of finding out about you, and that he'd never had a part in your life, probably would have killed him. When your mother told you the truth, it allowed you to come here, in your own time and on your own terms.'

Alex shook his head. 'I wish I could have met him.'

Lily smiled. 'I think you'd have liked him, in spite of all the history. And I know he'd have liked you. You're so much like your brothers.'

'You knew all along, didn't you?' Alex said wonderingly. 'You knew who my father was from the day you met me.'

'I had my suspicions,' Lily said. 'But it wasn't up to me to voice them. After all, Jack couldn't have told me what he didn't know. You needed to do that in your own time.'

'Did Sophie... you didn't tell her?'

Lily shook her head. 'No. Again, not my place. And I couldn't be completely sure until you opened your mouth and that wonderful accent came out. Although, having said that, your bone structure is pure Carter, even if your colouring is your mother's. Before long, everyone would have worked it out.'

Alex nodded, remembering with horrifying clarity the way his stomach had dropped through the floor when Mark had called him out by the gates of the cider farm. 'I guess I was fooling myself, thinking I could come here and keep it a secret.'

'Nothing's a secret for long in Little Somerby,' Lily said gently. She turned to Matthew. 'I can imagine this is a bit of a shock for you, too.' She put a hand on Matthew's arm. 'I'm sorry that I kept this from you, but after Jack died it seemed that the secret would die with him. It wasn't until I spent more time with Alex that I realised how he fitted into the things that Jack had left me. That actually, Addie had been trying to protect you and Jonathan from finding out about her own son, and to a certain extent to protect Jack, too.' She sighed. 'You couldn't make it up, really, although I've written some pretty implausible plots myself over the years.'

'I want to be angry,' Matthew said gruffly. 'It would be so easy to be angry with Dad, and with you, Mrs Henderson, for keeping this from me, but after everything that's happened over the past year or so, anger and assigning blame seems pointless. We've all lost people; I think it's time to make the most of what we do have.' He extended a hand to Alex. 'Let's start again, and do it properly. I'm Matthew. The older, and generally assumed to be the wiser, of your two brothers. It's nice to meet you, Alex.'

Alex swallowed hard. The last thing he was expecting from Matthew, after everything that had happened, was such total and unconditional acceptance. He smiled, despite the lump that seemed to be lodged in his throat. 'I'm Alex Fraser, a cider farmer from Vancouver. It's nice to meet you, Matthew.' He reached out and shook Matthew's hand, and in that moment he felt that finally things were starting to make sense.

'Well, that's a start,' Lily said, her shrewd blue eyes twinkling.

Matthew smiled at Lily, before turning back to Alex. 'I think you should probably come back to Cowslip Barn with me and speak to the man who tried to sack you, if you're up to it?'

'Is Jonathan likely to meet me at the door with a rifle?'

'Not in my house, he's not.' Matthew laughed. 'I think you're safe for now.'

As they turned to leave, Alex went back to Lily. Without stopping to think about it, he leaned down and placed a gentle kiss on her cheek. 'Thank you,' he whispered. 'For everything.'

'My pleasure,' Lily replied. 'Although I assume there's still a conversation to be had with my granddaughter.'

Alex nodded. 'I'd like to talk to her but I'm not sure she wants to speak to me again, though.'

'Give her time,' Lily said. 'It's a lot to take in. For all of us.' Watching the two men leave, she was again stunned with just how long Alex had managed to keep the truth quiet. The resemblance between the brothers really was quite startling. *You couldn't make it up,* she thought wryly. Picking up her mobile phone, which lay on the side table in the hallway, she tried to ring Sophie, but was immediately put through to her voicemail. She hoped that once Alex and his new brothers were finished, poor Sophie would get the answers that she, too, deserved.

36

'I think this is going to call for some serious alcohol.'
Matthew poured three generous glasses of whisky with
a less than steady hand. Glancing up as the door to his
study opened, he shook his head as Anna poked hers
around the door. 'It's fine.' Smiling gently, she closed the
door again.

Alex sat down in the leather Chesterfield armchair
that stood on one side of the fireplace, as far away from
Jonathan, who was sitting on the cushioned window seat,
as he could be. Once he'd poured and distributed the
drinks, Matthew sat in the other armchair. Alex was at a
complete loss as to where to begin with the men who now
knew he was their half-brother, so he was warily grateful
when Jonathan began to speak.

'I'm sorry I was so rude to you this morning. I suppose I
was in such a state of shock that I just automatically went
on the defensive. It's a trait that's more often seen in my
big brother, but I guess we're more alike than we realise.'

Alex took a sip of the whisky, which warmed his throat.
'It's understandable, under the circumstances,' he said. 'I
should have levelled with you at the start, not just come

here and waited for it all to come out. I guess I wasn't brave enough.' He laughed hollowly. 'Stupid, isn't it?'

'Not really,' Matthew said, sipping his own drink. 'You walked into one of the most tribal families in Somerset. I don't think I'd have felt too brave, either.'

'My mother would be ashamed of me,' Alex said quietly. Suddenly he had a vision of Addie, serious brown eyes boring into his as they had done ever since he was a small boy. 'She'd have expected better of her son.'

'Perhaps she'd have understood,' Jonathan said quietly. 'Our mother would certainly have kicked my arse for reacting the way I did, and as for Dad...' He laughed, but the sound was hollow. 'He was one of the most hospitable men I've ever known. He'd have bawled me out for throwing you out of the farm, once I knew who you were.'

'Mom didn't talk much about him until the end,' Alex said reflectively, 'but she did say he had the kind of charm that could turn a room to his favour. I'd have liked to have seen that in action.'

'Oh, believe me, it was worth seeing.' Matthew smiled, and this time the warmth reached his eyes. 'He prided himself on being able to sell anyone anything. And most of the time he succeeded.' Swallowing another mouthful of whisky, he put the glass down on the occasional table next to his chair.

'I'm sorry about your mother.' He leaned forward and rested elbows on his knees, hands loosely clenched in front of him. 'We were luckier, I suppose. Mum was diagnosed with lymphoma in the early eighties, but she was in remission for twenty years. When the breast cancer came, it was a different story. She tried to fight it but it was stage four by the time she realised. Dad nearly lost his mind when she died. He spent weeks after the funeral locked away in the bungalow, and whenever Jonathan or I went to see him he'd just ramble on about how he never deserved her, that he wished he'd treated her better.' Matthew swallowed. 'Of course, I had a fair idea that he'd had other women, but I had no clue that your mother had meant so much to him.'

Alex felt his throat constrict at the rawness in Matthew's voice. Since discovering Jack was his father, he'd often wondered if the relationship had meant as much to Jack as it had to Addie. She'd never spoken badly of Jack; in fact, the little she did say about him, towards the very end of her life, had been positive, but he'd always wondered if that positivity had been deserved.

'My mother made the choice for him,' Alex said quietly. 'Just before she died, she said that she'd chosen to walk away, to leave him be. As far as I know he never knew I existed. It was the bravest thing I can imagine. She chose to keep me, and raise me alone. But she didn't bear Jack any ill will for that decision; it was made out of love.' He rubbed his fingertips across the bridge of his nose and over his eyes. 'She didn't want him to feel he owed her anything. And for thirty-five years she kept the secret.'

'She sounds like quite a woman.'

'She was.'

The brothers lapsed into silence, preoccupied with their own memories.

'I did meet him once, though, although I didn't realise who he was at the time.'

Matthew's head snapped up. 'Really? When was that?'

Alex smiled at the memory. 'It was when I was about ten years old. Mom had brought me to England to show me some of the tourist trail. We stayed in the centre of London and did all of the most famous landmarks. I fell in love with Hampton Court Palace just as she'd done when she'd come to London as a student. Just as we were about to go back to the hotel for the evening and go out for dinner, my mother took me into the Rose Garden at the palace. The evening seemed to bring out the scents so strongly, and I remember finding the mixture of perfumes almost overwhelming. There, standing off to one side, looking over the gardens, was a man.' Alex gave a quiet laugh. 'I remember thinking that it was the first time I'd ever seen my mother blush, but she walked straight up to him and said, "Hello, Jack."'

Matthew felt his stomach flip; it was as if Alex was talking about a man other than the father he knew. In a sense, he supposed he was. 'Then what?'

'Jack shook my hand and said he was an old acquaintance of my mother's. I was ten years old and didn't understand quite what was going on, but he was kind, and funny, and he bought me one of those enormous ice creams. While I was stuck into the ice cream, he and my mother spoke briefly, but I never got any indication that he was my father. She'd married Harry by then, so he must have just assumed that I was Harry's son. I was quite small for my age back then, so he might not have put two and two together. My mother never let on that she'd said anything, and Jack certainly didn't seem to make the connection. Then he left.'

'And that was the only time you ever met him?'

Alex nodded. 'It wasn't until just before Mom died, and we'd started going through some of her things, that I found the photo of him at Kennedy Falls and realised.'

'Christ,' Matthew breathed. 'All these years…'

Alex looked out of the large window that overlooked Matthew's rambling garden and clutched his glass of whisky a little tighter. How things had changed since the last time he visited Cowslip Barn. Back then he'd been a guest of his boss; now he had walked through the door as something entirely different.

Jonathan, who'd slipped out of the room during this conversation, suddenly re-emerged, Cheshire-cat-like. Grabbing the whisky decanter, he paused to top up his glass, then Matthew's, and finally Alex's. 'I guess I owe you an apology as well as a top up,' he said gruffly as he pulled up another chair and sat a little closer to his brothers. 'I shouldn't have gone off at you the way I did. I was in shock, I suppose. And Caroline's mood swings have been running me ragged, too.' At Alex's quizzical look, Jonathan clarified. 'She's pregnant.'

'Congratulations,' Alex said quietly. 'And thanks for the apology.' He sipped his drink ruminatively. In a few months' time, both of his half-brothers would be parents. The next generation of Carters would be assured. Once again he felt a churning mixture of guilt, love and frustration about being in the midst of it all.

'I've been thinking,' Jonathan continued. 'With Dad having never been in the picture for you, we want to make it up to you. My big brother, our big brother, is far too diplomatic to just jump right in and say it, but we feel that our father owes you; that he'd want you to benefit from what he built.'

Alex shook his head. 'That was never why I came here.' He turned to face Jonathan and was, yet again, taken aback by the contrast between the two brothers. While he could see the similarities in stature and bone structure, their colouring was as different as night and day. Matthew's dark hair and deep brown eyes must have come from their mother Cecily, whereas Jonathan's chestnut hair and clear blue eyes could only be from Jack. 'I don't need your help financially.'

'We know that,' Jonathan said patiently. 'From what you've told us about Adelaide's, you've potentially got a goldmine on your hands with the apple blends you've been trying. That orchard you bought is something that will last for generations if cared for properly. Adelaide's could be a name to be reckoned with in North America.'

Alex shook his head. 'With all due respect, Jonathan, I'm not sure that I want that. Adelaide's was never intended to be anything other than a kitchen table business; an artisan brand. I don't want what you've got here. It's overwhelming.'

'Oh, come on, Alex!' Jonathan snorted. 'You and I both know that you didn't just come here out of some sense of curiosity. Cider's as much in your blood as it is ours; that's obvious from the fact you bought a fucking orchard! Let us come on board with you. You get your autonomy, but also the backing of a world famous brand.'

'No,' Alex replied. 'It doesn't feel right. I never needed Jack Carter when I was growing up, and I don't need his sons' misguided senses of legacy and loyalty now he's dead. I came here to close a book, not write a new chapter, and I've done that.' He turned from Jonathan to Matthew. 'Please understand,' he said, lowering his voice a little, 'I need to do this for myself, and for my mother. All I want from you is acknowledgement. No more, no less.'

Jonathan shook his head. 'A noble sentiment, I'm sure. But the offer is there, when you need it. I know that Dad would have wanted to make up for his absence somehow, and since he's not here to do it himself, we want to make sure that happens.'

'You've done enough already.' Alex looked from one Carter brother to the other. 'I've learned so much from being here; about Jack, about the business. About...' He stopped himself just in time. Admitting how he felt about Sophie was going to take a lot more alcohol and a lot more courage than he currently had. 'I don't need anything else from you.'

'Well, as I said, the offer's there if you change your mind.' Jonathan turned to Matthew. 'Matthew here's been running this business for over fifteen years now, and if he scents a winning proposition, you can pretty much guarantee you're onto something. He's a good ally to have.'

'I'm sure,' Alex said wryly. He trusted Matthew instinctively; the man's integrity shone out from every pore. Jonathan, on the other hand, he still couldn't fathom. But then he had a lifetime to catch up on, he supposed. Glancing at his watch, he finished his drink. 'If you'll excuse me, I'd better get going.'

'Somewhere to be?' Jonathan asked, a glint in his eye.

'I owe someone an explanation,' Alex replied. 'Quite a big explanation, in fact. And the last time she saw me, she wasn't minded to listen to what I had to say.'

'Good luck,' Jonathan said. He wasn't unfamiliar with the concept of a feisty female; his wife, Caroline, had made him run that gauntlet on a number of occasions. 'If she loves you, she'll listen.'

Alex felt his cheeks burning under Jonathan's scrutiny. 'I hope so.' Placing his glass down on the windowsill, he made his exit.

37

Sophie got home from work that evening and thanked her lucky stars that her mother had put their weekly Skype call on hold. The shock of Alex's revelation was only just starting to sink in. He wasn't the person he'd said he was; he'd been lying to her from day one. And yet, when she'd seen the pain and anguish in his dark brown eyes as he'd finally told her the truth, there was a part of her that couldn't deny his sincerity.

But that didn't alter the fact that he'd lied to her. She'd made it clear to him from the start that she'd been hurt so badly by Mark's dishonesty that she needed better; that she needed *him* to be better. And he wasn't who he'd said he was, so she felt as though everything they'd experienced together had been irrevocably cheapened by that revelation.

Heading to the kitchen, she opened the fridge, and was pleased to see that the bottle of cava she'd put in there in anticipation of sharing it with Alex was nicely chilled. She figured she might as well drink it now. And, feeling mutinous and a bit 'fuck it', she decided to order the hottest curry she could eat from the local takeaway as well. As a taster who had to preserve her palate, she shouldn't have even contemplated it, but after the day she'd had, she was past caring. While she was scanning the menu and deciding what to choose, she heard her phone pinging with an email. Swiping the screen, she blinked; Martingtons Cider was increasing the terms of their job offer. The salary was nearly double what she was currently earning at Carter's. Given her current frame of mind, there didn't seem to be much of a decision to make. Perhaps it really was time to get out of Somerset; to move on.

But what the hell was she going to do about Alex in the meantime? How could she face him after their last conversation? Then, she kicked herself; she wasn't some heartbroken teenager. She was nearly thirty, for heaven's sake! If she couldn't maintain an air of dignity after a break-up then she was nothing better than the silly girl she'd accused Alex of thinking her when they'd had their final, catastrophic row. So what if he'd lied to her? People lied all the time. At least, now Jonathan had fired him, she wouldn't have to share a workplace with him any more. If she happened to see Alex around the village, or bump into him at her grandmother's house, she'd maintain a decent, polite distance. That was the plan and she'd stick to it. Right after she'd spent tonight drinking cava, eating curry and watching as many Keanu Reeves films as she could squeeze in before she passed out.

A little time later, halfway through *John Wick: Chapter 2* and three quarters of the way down her bottle of cava, Sophie was dimly aware of the doorbell ringing. Putting down her glass, she thought about opening it, but, realising she was more than a little the worse for wear, decided to ignore it for now.

The ringing continued. 'Oh, go away,' she muttered, topping up her glass.

The doorbell rang again, and this time someone called through the letter box. 'Sophie. Let me in.'

'You've got to be joking,' Sophie said as Mark's familiar tone echoed through the hallway.

Mark obviously thought otherwise, leaning on the bell. Sophie was forced to get up to make him stop before the neighbours complained.

'What do you want?' she asked, opening the door a fraction.

'I saw your face after that twat Alex spoke to you earlier and I was worried.'

'*You* were worried about me? That's rich, after what you've put me through.'

'Have you been drinking?'

'Not nearly enough to have this conversation,' Sophie snapped. 'Now bugger off and leave me alone.'

Mark, however, had other ideas. 'Let me in, Soph. Please.' Suddenly, despite everything, the gentleness in his voice began to disarm Sophie. Her eyes filled with tears and she opened the door a little wider.

Mark wandered through to the hallway and, taking Sophie's half-empty glass from her hand, put it down on the hall table. 'I think you've had enough of that.'

'I'll be the judge of that,' Sophie said, feeling more than a little patronised. She went to pick up the glass again, but Mark's hand on her arm stopped her.

'Come and sit down.' Sliding his hand into hers, he led her back to the living room and sat on the sofa with her. He regarded her carefully. 'He's messed you up, hasn't he?'

Sophie swallowed hard. 'No worse than you did.'

Mark shook his head. 'If there was any way I could take back what happened with you and me, the way it ended, I would. You didn't deserve it. You deserve someone who'll take care of you.'

Sophie felt the tears sliding down her cheeks, unbidden. Mark's tone was so gentle and reminded her so much of how things had been between them before they fell apart. But there had been so much water under the bridge since then, and there was no going back. Suddenly, though, she felt an overwhelming need to talk, to make sense of it all.

'He lied to me,' she said numbly. 'And you, of all people, worked it out, didn't you?' She shook her head. 'How did I not see it?'

'We see what we want to see,' Mark replied. He squeezed her hand. 'And I might have been a twat to you, but at least I was honest until the end.' His tone was caressing.

Sophie's heart lurched. 'The end was pretty brutal, though.'

'I can't excuse that,' Mark replied. 'But seeing the way you reacted to him this morning, the way he'd hurt you... I just had to come and make sure you weren't spending the evening brooding.'

'Oh, believe me, I've been through worse.' Sophie laughed hollowly. She fought the urge to tell Mark about losing their baby, but, even though she'd had a few glasses of wine, she knew that wouldn't solve anything. What was done was done. It wouldn't get them back together, and that wasn't what she wanted, anyway.

'I know.' Mark hesitated, then slid his arm around Sophie. Much against her better judgement, she snuggled into his embrace. It felt so comforting just to be held, even after everything.

'I should hate you for what you've done,' Sophie muttered. 'If you'd kept your mouth shut, I'd be sitting here with Alex completely unaware.'

'Is that what you'd have wanted?' Mark said. 'Given that honesty is something you're constantly banging on about.'

'Fair enough,' Sophie conceded. 'But I think I just want an early night.' She stood up and, to her surprise, didn't wobble. The wine was obviously wearing off.

Mark stood, too. Pulling her close in a brief hug, he wandered out to the hallway. 'Take care of yourself, Soph.'

'I will,' she replied as he opened the front door. Closing the door behind him a moment later, Sophie didn't see Alex, who, rather the worse for wear after an afternoon that had extended into an evening dissecting the family history with Jonathan and Matthew, was passing her gate and who had paused, full of new uncertainty, in the shadows. On seeing Mark leaving the house, he turned away, his face stricken in the rapidly brightening moonlight.

38

The next morning, Sophie woke with a fuzzy head, but a clearer sense of perspective. She'd slept surprisingly well; perhaps she was glad that for the first time in weeks it was just going to be her and David in the office, now that Alex had been sacked by Jonathan. Just sharing a village with Alex felt overwhelming at the moment. She couldn't imagine how people who had failed office romances coped when they split up; awkward didn't even begin to cover it. She definitely needed time to process what she'd found out over the past twenty-four hours. What a fool she'd been to have broken her 'no romance at work' rule.

Over a breakfast that consisted mainly of strong coffee, Sophie decided to drop Lily a text to see if Alex was at home. If he was, she'd stay away, but if he wasn't, she'd pop round and have a chat with her gran. After all, Lily was going to find out sooner or later what had gone down yesterday, and Sophie wanted her to hear it from her, rather than Alex, if she could manage it. She also texted David and warned him she was going to be a bit late in. She felt slightly guilty about using Lily as an excuse, pretending that her gran had had a bad night, but under the circumstances, it seemed the best solution. As she was pouring the water into her coffee mug, her phone pinged. It was Lily, confirming that Alex wasn't at home. Weak with relief, but with a nagging sense of disappointment, Sophie decided to head over to Lily's for breakfast to go with the coffee.

Opening the front door of Lily's cottage, she was, once again, kicked in the gut with disappointment that Alex wasn't around, despite the fact she wouldn't have known where to start with him if he had been. Lily's voice floated from the kitchen at the back of the cottage, clearly having anticipated Sophie's need for a decent breakfast. As she walked into the kitchen, Lily looked up from her chair and gestured to the coffee pot in front of her. 'I've got some homemade strawberry jam in the fridge if you want it on your croissant.'

'Thanks.' Keen, suddenly, to avoid the moment of revelation, Sophie busied herself with buttering and putting jam on two pastries, before pouring the coffee.

'So…' she began, before trailing off as Lily raised a hand to silence her.

'You should know, before you tell me your version of what's happened with Alex, that I am in some way responsible for this current uncomfortable situation,' Lily said. For the first time ever, or at least since Sophie could remember, the old lady looked uncertain of herself.

'What do you mean, Gran?' Croissant forgotten, Sophie took a fortifying sip of her coffee.

'I knew who his father was for quite a while before all this came out.'

'What?' Sophie swallowed too fast, coughed, and then recovered herself. 'How did you… I mean, why didn't you say something? Did he tell you?'

'That afternoon when you first brought him round, I began to suspect,' Lily said quietly. 'You don't live to my age without picking up a few things here and there. When he spoke, I was racking my brains, trying to remember what Jack had said about his summer abroad back in the eighties. Could Alex's mother be the woman he fell in love with back then?' Lily shook her head. 'Jack never knew about Alex, of that I'm certain, but before he died he wanted to unburden himself to someone who might understand. I kept the secret about his relationship with Alex's mother, and I hoped that Alex would find the right time to reveal it to the Carters, and to you, before you all ended up getting hurt.'

'Why didn't you tell me all this?' Sophie asked. 'You let me get involved with him, fall in love with him, all the while knowing, or at least suspecting, that he wasn't who he said he was. How could you, Gran?'

Lily sighed. 'Believe me, I wanted to tell you, but it wasn't my secret to tell. Alex is a very honourable person; he helped you to take care of me when I had that fall and he's done the right thing by you in all respects except for this. He, I think, loves you very, very much. But he's got to find his own place here, he's got to make sense of what being Jack's son means. And he was terrified that, should the secret come out before he was ready to address it, he'd end up getting rejected by Jack's family, and, ultimately, by you, too.'

Sophie shook her head. 'You still should have told me.'

'I could have been wrong.' Lily sighed. 'I'm going to be eighty next birthday; old age makes you start to question your own powers of deduction a little.'

'Yeah, right.' Sophie snorted. 'Nothing wrong with your brain.' Despite herself, she smiled. 'But I guess I can understand why you wanted to wait for Alex to be the one to come clean. I mean, it would have been embarrassing if you were wrong, wouldn't it?'

Lily gave a relieved smile. 'If I remember correctly, you accused me of imagining too much drama when I so much as suggested that Alex was hiding something. Imagine if I'd told you what I really thought! You'd have packed me off to a secure room at the St Monica's Trust care village in a heartbeat.' Lily had often joked that the path from her front door to the care home to the cemetery was an unnervingly straight one as the crow flew, and she was determined to skip the middle destination for as long as possible.

'So, where is he?' Sophie asked.

'He left very early this morning; I heard the front door closing. It looks as though he's taken all his stuff, too.' Lily sighed. 'When I went into my study this morning, I found the printouts he'd done of the details for an early flight to Vancouver via Schiphol in Amsterdam.' She suddenly looked thoughtful. 'Matthew came round here yesterday to talk to him and they left together. Perhaps the meeting didn't go as well as either of them hoped it would.' Lily sipped her coffee. 'Despite his subterfuge, I think Alex really did fall for you, darling.'

Sophie shook her head. 'He should have come clean with me from the start,' she said, but even as she said it, her voice lacked conviction.

'In an ideal world, yes, he should have,' Lily replied. 'But imagine the pressure it would have put you under. You work for Matthew and Jonathan Carter. You have done for ten years. Could you honestly say that, if Alex had told you who his father was, you'd have been comfortable keeping that secret? Perhaps he was just trying to spare you the heartache.'

'Maybe,' Sophie said, trying to hide how much her gran's words jolted her. She'd been so caught up with the fact that Alex hadn't been entirely honest with her, she'd not considered that if she had known the truth, it would have put her in a very uncomfortable position indeed. Suddenly needing to be close to him, even though she knew he'd gone, she stood up. 'Can I go and have a look in his room?' she said softly. 'I kind of feel like I need to see for myself that he's gone.'

Lily nodded. 'Of course, darling. I'll get more coffee on.'

As Sophie headed up the stairs, she was assailed by memories. She pushed open the door to Alex's room, and gasped. The bed was neatly made, and all of his possessions had gone. Her knees went weak with the reality that he really had left. The silence was deafening as she looked around, taking in the empty chest of drawers, the neatly washed kettle and mugs on the side table by the double bed; everything was in its place. She was just about to close the door again when she noticed a cream coloured envelope propped against the reading lamp on the desk in the corner of the bedroom, with her name written on it in Alex's elegant, cursive handwriting.

With trembling hands, she picked it up and slid a finger under the flap, pulling out the neatly folded letter. Her eyes blurred with tears as she read:

Sophie,

I'm so sorry for keeping secrets from you. I should never have allowed us to become so close without telling you the whole truth about my reasons for being in Little Somerby. Please believe me when I say that I never intended to hurt you. You, and your love, mean so much to me, that the thought of never seeing you again is truly breaking my heart. My mother always said that you should seize every opportunity you can to tell the people you care about that you love them, before it's too late. I'm taking that advice. I love you, Sophie. In time, I'm sure we will both be happy or at least content, apart, but life would be so much more complete if we were able to share it together. If you feel able to respond to this, my phone will be on night and day for as long as it takes. Call me. Please.

Yours forever,
Alex.

'Oh, Alex,' Sophie breathed. Her heart battled with her head; on the one hand, she wanted to get onto the Internet and book the next flight out to Vancouver, but on the other hand, the letter hadn't really said anything that he hadn't tried to explain in person the last time they'd been face to face.

Sophie again looked around the room that Alex had made his own over the time he'd been in Little Somerby. Her grandmother hadn't yet stripped the bed, and as Sophie sat down on it she had to resist the urge to bury her face in the pillow and smell his scent on the bed linen. They'd never made love here; neither one of them could bring themselves to misbehave in Lily's house, but she still had an achingly strong sense memory of his touch, his scent and the rich caramel of his voice whispering her name.

The chat with Lily had given her a bit of much needed perspective. Alex had come to Little Somerby for reasons that she couldn't hate him for. He'd been a little less than honest, not just with her, but with the Carter family, but for justifiable reasons. Throwing a grenade into such hallowed territory was never going to be easy, and he'd tried his best to keep the damage to a minimum. Yes, of course he should have levelled with them all but there was never going to be a right time to do so. Was the reason she had pushed him away because she didn't want to be hurt again? That she feared Alex would do what Mark had done to her? Somehow, she just knew he wouldn't, despite what he'd told her about the flings in his past.

But it was too late. He'd gone. And chances were, he'd move on and forget about her. There was a continent between them now, and an ocean. It was over. A holiday romance that had got out of hand; it could never be anything other than a memory. There was no changing that. Or was there? Heart thumping, Sophie grabbed her mobile from her pocket and dialled Alex's number. The phone went straight through to voicemail. In frustration, she nearly crumpled the letter in her other hand. Shoving it, and her phone, in her back pocket, she hurried downstairs.

'Did the paperwork Alex printed say what time the flight is?' she asked as she came back through to the kitchen.

Lily passed it over from where she'd left it on the side. 'Here, have a look.' She looked hopeful. 'Does that mean you're going to go after him?'

Sophie smiled. 'Maybe I have been a bit harsh,' she conceded. 'And perhaps I shouldn't let him leave the country thinking I'm still angry with him.'

'You'd better get going, then,' Lily said. 'He left a couple of hours ago; even with check-in, you might be cutting things a bit fine.'

Sophie's heart hammered. 'I'll see you later.' She leaned forward and kissed her gran on the cheek. 'Wish me luck.'

'Love will give you all the luck you need.' Lily smiled.

'Come on!' Sophie smacked her palm against the steering wheel and slammed on her brakes as the traffic yet again slowed. She was about a quarter of a mile from the airport, and the traffic on the A38 had been crawling along for the past two miles. The plan she'd had to get to Alex before he got through to International Departures was slowly slipping away from her. As the traffic yet again stopped, she pressed redial on her mobile phone on the dashboard. Once again it clicked through to Alex's voicemail. The signal on her network was pretty appalling, but Sophie kept trying.

After five minutes of staying still, Sophie's patience ran out. About fifty yards away was a bus stop, and then it would be another few hundred yards to the airport. Steeling herself, she pulled over to the grass verge and mounted it, ignoring the furious looks of the other stuck motorists as she passed them on the wrong side. As she thumped down into the bus stop, she was out of the car the second the engine stopped. Not even pausing to lock it in her haste, she sprinted down the road, the tall fences of the airport approaching on her left. She had to get to Alex before he got on his flight.

Ignoring the curious looks of the motorists still sitting in their cars, Sophie kept running, not daring to glance at her watch. She'd have to move faster if she was going to get to him before the gates closed. If he'd already made it through to the departure lounge, she was toast.

Starting to feel the effects of the sprint, Sophie pushed on, past the curving snake of stationary cars. As the sculpture that was at the centre of the airport roundabout came into view, she took a deep breath and picked up her pace even further. Dashing up the lane to the terminal, she made it through the doors of the glass fronted building and then stopped to get her bearings. Red in the face, and breathing heavily, she swept her fringe from her eyes and looked up at the departures board. There it was: the flight to Amsterdam, which was the first leg on his journey back to Vancouver. With a sinking heart, she saw the words change before her eyes: Gate Closed.

She was too late. He'd have been through Immigration and Passport Control, and be in the departure lounge by now. And there was no way she'd be able to get through without a valid ticket or her passport. Rushing up to the KLM desk, she stammered out a question. 'Please… can you tell me if a passenger's checked in?'

The attendant at the desk shook her head. 'I'm sorry,' she said. 'I can't give you that information.'

'But what if it's an emergency?'

'I'm sorry. Data protection.'

Sophie sagged against the desk. That was it, then. The frustration that Alex was likely to be just beyond the escalator bit at her heart like an angry dog, but there was nothing she could do. He was gone. And he might as well be on the plane right now, as close as she could get to him.

'Is there any way of getting a message through to a passenger on a plane?'

The attendant glanced at her colleague. 'We can put out a call to the flight team if it's a genuine emergency.'

Would declaring that she didn't think she'd be able to live the rest of her life without him constitute an emergency in airport terms? Even in her current state of mind, Sophie wasn't sure she could risk it. With a heavy heart, she shook her head. 'It's OK. I'll keep trying to call him.'

Dejected, she headed away from the desk and contemplated the long trudge back to her abandoned car. Swallowing back the sudden tears, she stepped through the airport doors once again, heart sinking even further as her mobile phone battery finally gave up the ghost as well.

39

'Sorry, just say that again.' Meredith sat down hard on the kitchen chair, wincing as the wooden seat jarred her coccyx. 'He's *what*? I mean, *who*?'

Matthew gave a wry grin. 'I guess that means you've got another uncle to keep you out of trouble.'

'That's one way of looking at it, Dad.' Meredith shook her head. 'Although, I have to say, if I was going to get another uncle, there are worse people for the job.'

'I've always loved the way you can put a positive spin on things.' Matthew walked over to his daughter and leaned in to drop a kiss on the top of her head. 'The facts of the matter are a little complicated, but then you always knew Granddad was a... complicated... man.'

'No kidding,' Meredith sighed. A look of worry crossed her face as she gazed up at her father, who still had a protective arm around her shoulders. 'Are *you* OK?' She and Matthew had lived on their own for ten years after Meredith's mother had left, before Matthew had met Anna, and she was still very finely tuned to her father's feelings. She knew that he would be going through all kinds of emotions about this bombshell, and, as his eldest child, she needed him to know she was there for him.

'I'm fine,' Matthew said softly. 'You know Granddad and I didn't have the easiest of relationships for a long time, and, if I'm being honest, this wasn't the biggest shock of my life.' He drew a breath, trying to steady himself. The memories of the different ways his family had nearly been torn apart over the years were still raw. 'I always sort of knew he'd messed Grandma around, but I had no idea how serious his relationship with Alex's mother had been. If things had been different…'

Meredith stood up from the table and snuggled into Matthew's embrace. 'So, you're sure he never knew about Alex?'

'I don't think he'd have kept him a secret if he did,' Matthew said. 'He would have wanted to do right by any child of his, I'm sure.'

'Despite it all, Granddad had a huge heart, didn't he?' Meredith broke away from Matthew again. The irony was that in the end, it was his heart that had failed him. 'The question is, where does that leave us?'

Matthew smiled. 'Don't worry about it all; that's for me, Uncle Jonathan and Alex to sort out. And it could be worse; at least we know he's a decent bloke. I think he's proved as much while he's been here, even if he didn't tell us the truth right away.'

'He does seem quite sound,' Meredith mused. 'So, what are you going to do?'

Matthew paused. 'I'm not sure yet. I do feel like we need to make it up to him for not having Granddad in his life. It's just a question of how we do that. I think Granddad would have wanted to make amends for not being there for him.'

'I think you're right,' Meredith said. 'And I'm sure whatever you and Uncle Jonno decide will be the right thing.' She glanced at her watch.

'Somewhere to be?' Matthew asked.

'Oh, I said I'd meet Joe later,' Meredith said. 'He's invited me over for a movie and a pizza.'

'You've been spending quite a bit of time with Joe Flanagan lately.' Matthew looked intently at his daughter. 'Are you two, er, an item?'

Meredith laughed. 'Dad, you're so twentieth century! We're seeing each other, if that's what you mean.'

'Well, I hope you're not seeing too, um, much of each other,' Matthew replied. 'You've only just come out of your relationship with Flynn, remember?'

Meredith tossed her head impatiently. 'Is that your very roundabout way of telling me to be careful?'

'You've got it,' Matthew replied. 'Although I know you will be, of course. I just don't want to see you getting hurt again.'

'Thanks, Dad,' Meredith replied, giving Matthew a soft smile. 'I'm OK, honestly.' And, as she said it, she realised that she was mostly telling the truth. She was a whole lot more OK now than she had been at the start of the summer. 'But I need to get in the shower and then get going. I've got a lunchtime shift at The Cider Kitchen before I meet Joe later.' Reaching up on tiptoes to kiss Matthew's cheek, she then wandered out of the kitchen.

'Don't be too late back tonight,' Matthew said.

'I won't,' Meredith called over her shoulder. Film and pizza with Joe was just what she needed after the revelations about Alex. She shook her head. Just when she thought she had a handle on her family, something new arrived out of the blue and flummoxed her. All the same, though, it was good to know she hadn't been imagining things when she'd noticed Alex's resemblance to Matthew; she just wondered why she hadn't put two and two together before. 'Granddad, you have a lot to answer for,' she muttered as she went into her bedroom. She wondered if Jack Carter was looking down on them all and feeling relieved that, now he was gone, he didn't have to face a barrage of questions. Joe would never believe it when she told him.

40

Lily didn't need to say anything when Sophie appeared back at her door. Enfolding her in her arms, Sophie smelt the comforting scent of her grandmother's Penhaligon's Bluebell perfume and her eyes filled with tears.

'Come and sit in the living room,' Lily murmured, handing Sophie a tissue as they broke apart. 'I'll put the kettle on.'

Sophie walked through the hallway, wondering how she'd ended up so near and yet so far from Alex. She wished she'd had more time to tell him how she felt; how, even though he'd kept things from her, she did understand why he'd done it. She hadn't realised she'd been living on such a knife edge since losing the baby and splitting with Mark; that she'd been avoiding anything that would actively make her feel. When she'd met Alex, he'd bridged a gap in her heart that she hadn't truly realised existed; and now he'd gone, and that gap felt unbridgeable, especially after the way they'd parted. Grabbing her phone again, which she'd plugged into her car's phone charger on her weary way back from the airport, she tried his number; yet again, it went straight

309

to voicemail. *So much for having the phone switched on all the time,* she thought in irritation, then realised it was most likely because he was thirty odd thousand feet in the air.

Suddenly feeling in need of some air herself, she wandered towards the French windows that led out into Lily's back garden. The bees were drinking lazily from the honeysuckle that rambled amiably over the stone wall between Lily's land and next door's cottage, intertwining like a lover's caress with the clematis, which was just coming to the end of its flowering. In the rows of flowerbeds that lined the walls, the Old English roses that Lily loved so much were pouring forth their scent in their full glory, perfuming the air and consigning the honeysuckle to the background. A riot of colour, their thorns were poised to plunge into unwary fingers. Sophie reached out and took hold of one of the stems, and as the sharp pinprick pierced her flesh she hoped it would give her some relief from her aching heart. She wished so fervently that she'd had the chance to see Alex one more time before he left but it was too late. She didn't even have an address for him in Vancouver. Looking down at the bead of blood on her finger, she watched as it spilt.

'Careful, it'll get infected.' A low voice emanated from the direction of the gate at the back of Lily's garden, the one that led out onto High Street. Sophie tore her hand away from the stem of the rose, the blood from her finger dripping onto her jeans. She was rooted to the spot; all she could stammer out was, 'I thought you'd gone.' Sophie couldn't bring herself to turn around, afraid that if she did, he'd disappear. 'I must be imagining things.'

'I promise you, you're not.' His voice was drawing closer, but his footsteps down the garden path were slowing, sounding more and more hesitant. Sophie could feel the atmosphere between them building, the tension pulling her to turn to look at him. But she couldn't do it. He had to come to her.

'Gran told me you'd taken the next flight back to Vancouver via Schiphol.'

'I was booked onto it. But then Matthew Carter came round and I changed my mind about running away.'

'But why tell Gran you were leaving?' Sophie shook her head in confusion.

'I didn't.' Then, she heard him draw in a sharp breath. 'Oh, God, I was so messed up yesterday afternoon before Matthew came to find me, I booked a flight and used Lily's printer in her study to get a hard copy of the details. I'd ruined things with you, Jonathan had bawled me out and I just wanted to get home. I must have left the extra copy of the booking on the printer. She must have seen it and put two and two together this morning. She probably assumed I'd cleared out early as I shoved my suitcase under the bed, out of sight. I packed everything up before Matthew came over, after writing you that note, of course, which probably made no sense after all the drinking.' He smiled ruefully. 'And when I saw you hugging Mark goodbye on your doorstep—'

'Oh, God,' Sophie groaned. 'He came round last night, I was half-cut, too, and I let him in. He comforted me, that was all. Nothing happened, I swear.'

Alex smiled ruefully. 'It wouldn't have mattered if it had. After all I've put you through, I'd have understood.'

'There's no way I'd ever get back together with Mark,' Sophie said. 'He caught me at a vulnerable moment and was a shoulder to cry on, that's all.'

'It doesn't matter.' Alex shook his head. 'What matters is you and me.' He edged closer to her, as if he was terrified she'd bolt.

'So where did you go this morning, then?' Sophie asked. 'If you weren't planning on getting on that plane.'

'I just crashed out last night, and then I got up this morning without changing and went to the churchyard. It sounds odd but I wanted to talk to Jack. After I'd been there a while, I started walking, and ended up on the other side of Crook Peak.' He laughed. 'It's taken me this long to walk back!'

That all made sense, Sophie thought, especially since Alex's phone kept going to voicemail this morning. Signal was intermittent on the hills.

Alex was only a couple of feet away now. Sophie could see his dark hair in her peripheral vision, but still she couldn't turn and look at him. 'Now that's all explained, can we please talk about us?' he said softly.

'Us?'

'Yes. Us. You and me. And exactly what that means. To me, at least.' Alex stepped off the path and stood alongside Sophie, still hesitant, it seemed. The blood dripped from her finger. She started as a warm hand reached out and wrapped a tissue around it, stemming the flow and holding her hand in his.

'Aren't you going to look at me?' Alex asked softly, still holding her hand.

'I don't think I can.' Sophie laughed nervously. 'I still don't really believe you're here.'

'I promise you, Sophie, here beside you is exactly where I'm supposed to be.'

Sophie's hands were suddenly trembling so much that the tissue slipped from her fingers. As it fluttered to the floor, she could bear it no longer. Turning around, she saw Alex standing in front of her, a look of nervous anticipation in his eyes.

'Oh, Alex.' She flew into his embrace. As his arms enfolded her, she felt as though she was coming home.

'I'm so sorry,' Alex murmured into her hair. 'For everything. Can you forgive me?'

Sophie broke apart from him and looked up into his open, sincere and handsome face. 'I wish you'd told me the truth,' she said softly. 'And although I was angry that you kept things from me, I think I understand why you felt you had to do it. It must have been one hell of a decision to come here, knowing that Jack was your father, and incredibly difficult to keep that secret. And although I wish you'd told me from the start, I guess I can see why you didn't. So yes. I do forgive you. And, Alex…'

'Yeah?'

'I love you. So, so much. It took the threat of you leaving to make me realise that.' She reached up and brushed a lock of hair from his eyes.

'Oh, God, Sophie, I love you too.' He pulled her close again, and his lips met hers briefly before he continued. 'Even when I booked that flight I knew, deep down, I couldn't get on it.'

Sophie swallowed. 'I can't say it didn't hurt that you didn't come clean with me about who you really were,' she said slowly. 'But Gran talked some sense into me about why you might have felt you had to keep it from me. She, of course, had you sussed from the start.'

'I don't doubt that,' Alex said dryly. 'She's the sharpest person I've ever met.'

'I'll take that as a compliment.' Lily, standing at the French windows, smiled. 'Hello again, Alexander.'

'Hey, Mrs Henderson.' With his arm still around Sophie, they both turned to face Lily.

'I take it you two are reconciled?' Lily's eyes twinkled.

'You make us sound like a lovestruck couple in one of your novels,' Sophie said, but she couldn't keep the smile from her face.

'I call it as I see it,' Lily replied. 'Would you like that tea? Or perhaps you'd prefer something a little stronger.'

Sophie smiled back up at Alex. 'I think the tea will be fine.' Hand in hand, they headed back into the house.

41

August fled rapidly, melting seamlessly into September, and before Meredith knew it, it was the end of September and time to return to York for her second year of study. In the weeks since she and Joe had grown closer, the ache in her heart over Flynn had slowly receded, replaced by a warmth of feeling that, while she was still wary of calling it love, was certainly making her very happy. Now, though, at the prospect of leaving Joe, her heart felt sad again. Joe went to pick up Meredith's bag from where it lay beside her on the station platform at Weston-super-Mare, but Meredith got there first. As their hands touched, she smiled, remembering vividly the pleasure his touch and his kisses had given her over the summer. 'It's OK,' she said softly. 'I can manage.'

Joe shook his head. 'I want to make sure you and your belongings get safely on that train.'

They both straightened up again, and there was a brief, expectant pause between them.

'Look, Meredith…' Joe started. 'It's meant a lot to me, this summer with you.' He ran a nervous hand through his hair and swallowed. 'I never expected that so much would happen between us.' His clear blue eyes were serious and sincere, the light reflecting off the strawberry-blond highlights in his hair.

'It's meant a lot to me, too,' Meredith replied, but Joe raised a hand to quiet her.

'Let me finish, please, Merry.'

'O-OK,' Meredith stammered, unsure where he was going to go.

'The thing is…' He paused again, glanced at the clock. There was only a short time before the train was due. 'I know you're still not over *him*. And that's all right,' he said hurriedly as Meredith started to object. 'No, honestly, it is. I want you to know that I'll be here, if you come home at Christmas and you want to look me up. And we can go for a drink, or just have a chat, or whatever. I don't want to pressure you. I know you've got a lot to work through, and you're going back to York where all your friends are, and your new life. You need to be able to enjoy it with no strings, without worrying about what I'm thinking or doing. You need to be free to do that.'

Meredith smiled. 'This sounds like a break-up,' she said softly.

'No,' Joe said. 'It's not that at all. It's me giving you a choice. And telling you that this summer was the best summer I've ever had; being with you was the most amazing thing I've ever felt. But the reality of the situation is that you're there, and I'm here, and I don't want to trap you into something that you don't want. Not while you're still healing.'

Meredith's eyes filled with tears. Joe had been so kind to her over the weeks she'd got to know him; he'd healed her more than he would ever know. Standing on tiptoe, she placed the gentlest of kisses on his lips, increasing the pressure as his lips parted. The warmth of his mouth was both a sadness and a pleasure.

'Thank you,' she said softly as they broke apart again. 'For everything.' She wanted to say more, but the words just wouldn't come.

At that moment, the train's familiar diesel rumble approached, and the platform announcer's tinny voice sounded over the ancient tannoy.

'Take care,' Joe said, as, ignoring Meredith's hand once again, he reached for her bag.

'You too,' Meredith said as the train drew to a halt and the doors began to open.

As Joe boarded the train and lifted her bag into the luggage rack, Meredith waited for him to disembark again before she got on.

'I'll text you,' she said as he lingered, unwilling, herself, to say goodbye.

'Let me know you got back OK,' Joe replied. 'I'll see you soon.'

Meredith nodded. 'Definitely.' Feeling a sudden, inexplicable sense of loss, she reached forward and placed a hand to Joe's cheek, before kissing him gently again. Whether it was a kiss goodbye this time, she wasn't sure, but it was a kiss that would remain with her for a long time.

Carriage doors were closing, and the guard was drawing nearer. Meredith stepped away from Joe, up into the train, and hastily dropped the window, unwilling to break contact with him completely.

'Thank you,' she said as the train's engine started again.
'For what?'

'Being you.' She reached out a hand and grabbed his. 'I *will* see you soon.'

As the train began to pull out of Weston-super-Mare station on the first leg of its long journey back up north, Meredith finally let go of Joe's hand, feeling a mixture of emotions. Time would tell if Joe Flanagan was her future; for now, the cherished memories of a warm summer would sustain her through the turning leaves and snowfalls of a Yorkshire autumn and winter. For a heart thumping moment, she was sure Joe was calling something after her as the train moved, but above the noise of the engine it was difficult to tell. The words forming on his lips and the expression in his eyes made it look as if he'd said *I love you*, but it was probably a trick of the autumn light.

A similar scene was taking place in the echoing entrance hall of Bristol Airport. Standing by the escalators as Alex handed over his plane ticket and passport for checking, Sophie swallowed hard. In a couple of months' time she'd be joining him at the farmhouse in British Columbia for a holiday, but the time between then and now seemed endless. As Alex strode across the airport to rejoin her, she smiled. That slightly bow legged lope of his would be walking through her dreams between now and the time she saw him again.

'All set?' she said softly.

Alex nodded. 'I wish you were coming with me.'

Sophie smiled. 'Me too. But this is the busiest time of year for cider makers, as you'll find out in a year's time when Adelaide's starts really flying. As soon as the last crops are off the trees, I'll be on the next plane to British Columbia, I promise.'

'Won't stop me missing you,' Alex murmured, dipping his lips to meet hers in the next in a long line of goodbye kisses that had started the previous evening, extended into the night and meant neither of them had ended up having a great deal of sleep.

Sophie's knees grew weak. 'I'll miss you too,' she said between kisses. 'Call me when you get there?'

'Of course.' Alex smiled into the kiss. 'And Skype, and FaceTime... Christ, I'm going to miss you.'

They clung to each other, trying to draw strength from the closeness that would soon be divided by an ocean and four and a half thousand miles. As the announcer's final call for Alex's flight echoed over the PA system, they broke apart.

'I'll see you soon.' Sophie smiled.

'You'd better.' Alex smiled back as he went to pick up his carry on bag. They ascended the escalator together, clinging onto every last second. At Passport Control, Alex pulled her into his arms for one last time, murmuring, 'I love you,' into her ear before a final kiss. As Sophie watched him go through security, and then eventually disappearing from view, she was yet again assailed by a mixture of love and longing. She certainly had some thinking to do before she met with him again, and this time it really was going to change her life.

42

'Now, whatever you decide, you need to make sure you're deciding it for the right reasons,' Lily said, a week later, as she and Sophie settled in the garden chairs with cups of tea. 'I mean, a tall, dark and handsome stranger is one thing, but crossing continents is quite a move to make.' The autumn sunshine was still very strong, but the leaves had started to turn on the tall beech trees at the bottom of Lily's garden, gilded by the sunlight into a liquid bronze. A slight breeze lifted the hair on the back of Sophie's neck as the distant rumble of a plane taking off from Bristol sounded in the skies above. With a pang, she recalled where she was last weekend; she'd pulled over into one of the laybys near the airport to watch for the departure of the KLM flight, and as it had soared into the sky, taking Alex away from her, she'd felt kicked in the gut with longing.

'I thought you'd be all for me dropping everything to join the love of my life,' Sophie said dryly. Her grandmother had certainly written enough dramatic but happy endings to her novels for Sophie to assume this would be her opinion in real life.

'Oh, of course, darling, and I don't doubt that Alex is every bit the man you think he is, but I want to make sure you're going for all the right reasons.'

Sophie regarded her grandmother contemplatively for a moment, trying to decide how to respond. In a way, Lily was right; if Alex hadn't been in Vancouver, then she probably wouldn't be crossing continents, but there was actually a little more to it than that, a sounder reason to go.

'Alex isn't the only reason I'm thinking about going to Canada,' Sophie said, after her grandmother had given her a quizzical look.

'Really?' Lily raised an eyebrow. 'Do tell.'

'Matthew Carter called me and David into his office earlier this week,' she began. 'I thought it was to tell me that David's finally going to retire.'

'Not before time!' Lily snorted. 'You should have been given his job years ago.'

'Well, I wasn't offered it,' Sophie said. 'At least, not directly.' She held up a hand as Lily started to object. 'No, it's OK, Gran. They've actually made me a far more interesting offer.'

'Which is?'

Sophie smiled. 'They want to second me as the official liaison between Carter's and Adelaide's. Basically, I'm going to be a cider maker for Alex's company, to safeguard and develop the interests of Carter's Cider.' At her grandmother's look of surprise, Sophie continued. 'Alex agreed during a conference call this week that Carter's *can* actually have a stake in his cider business. He and I spoke about it and it does make financial sense to have them on side to help Adelaide's develop, even if Alex doesn't want it to end up going as global as Carter's. Not only will Carter's be minor partners with Adelaide's, but we'll be producing a unique set of hybrid cider blends that should blow away cider drinkers on both sides of the pond. And they're going to double my salary to do it.'

Lily smiled at her granddaughter's obvious enthusiasm for her subject, but then a look of concern crossed her face. 'You'll have to forgive me if this sounds fatalistic, love, but what happens if you and Alex fall out? Working together as well as living together might not be an entirely sensible decision.'

'It's for a year at first,' Sophie said. 'And if it doesn't work, then I can come home and continue my current job, on my original salary, no questions asked.'

'That's a very generous offer,' Lily replied. 'What happens after a year?'

'I get the choice to come home or make the job at Adelaide's permanent.' Sophie smiled. 'And don't worry; if it all goes tits up in my personal life, I'm a big enough girl to take it on the chin. Besides, I know Martingtons Cider will still have me if I don't fancy coming back to Carters.'

'I know you are, darling.' Lily reached out a hand and squeezed one of Sophie's. 'Adelaide's, and Alex, are lucky to have you.'

'But will *you* be all right if I leave?'

Lily snorted. 'Of course I will. Your mother's talking about me selling this place and moving to France, which I've been considering for quite a while now. Perhaps I'll agree for a year, rent this place out, and if your move to Vancouver becomes permanent, I can stay in the South of France. That's not to say I won't miss you, but I want to see you happy and settled before I shuffle off.'

'Oh, Gran! You've got a fair few years left in you yet. You wouldn't leave Barney all by himself.'

Barney, at the mention of his name, looked up from the rug, sighed heavily and then curled back into a big grey ball. He'd been pining for Alex since he'd left. *You and me both, dog,* Sophie thought.

'And if your father's death taught me one thing, it's that happiness is fleeting,' Lily said quietly. Sophie's heart thumped. Despite the closeness she had to Lily, her grandmother hardly ever spoke about the death of her son, Sophie's father. In twenty-seven years, Sophie could count the amount of conversations she'd had with Lily about him on the fingers of one hand; and that didn't include her thumb.

'You still miss him, don't you, Gran?' Sophie replied, looking down at her hands. Somehow, she couldn't quite meet Lily's eye. She was afraid of the grief she might find there. The loss of a child was a wound that would never truly heal. To some small extent, she identified with that.

'I'm not much for religion, as you know,' Lily said, her voice quiet and steady. 'But shortly after we lost your father, a good friend of mine said something to me that really resonated.' She reached out a hand and gave Sophie's a squeeze. 'When I was at my absolute darkest, when I couldn't see how a god, if there was one, could take my child, your father, the love of your mother's life, so young, and so unfairly, this friend, who was also not much for religion, quoted a little verse from Tennyson to me. "God gives us love. Something to love / He lends us." ' Lily paused. 'I've never forgotten that. Love will always be with us, Sophie, no matter how far away we are from each other. Your father's still in my heart, and your mother's heart, and he's such a huge part of you, too. He'd be so proud of everything you've achieved. He'd want you to be happy, I'm sure.'

Sophie swallowed hard. 'Thanks, Gran,' she said softly. 'I like to think he would be, too.' She didn't need to ask if it was Jack Carter who'd given the advice; she already knew.

'So don't you worry about me, or your mother, or even that blessed dog there.' Lily was brisk once again. 'Do what you know to be right, and what your heart tells you. We only get one chance at this life; make the most of it.'

'I love you, Gran,' Sophie said, jumping from her seat and putting her arms around her grandmother. 'And I always will.'

'I know, dear,' Lily replied. 'Now go and tell those Carter boys that you've made up your mind. And when you get over the Atlantic, you'd better make sure there's a comfortable spare room on the ground floor of that farmhouse for your grandmother to come and stay in.'

'Oh, I will,' Sophie said, breaking apart from Lily once again. 'I definitely will.'

Eighteen Months Later

Spring

The warm sunshine reflected off the new leaves of the apple trees in the orchard as Sophie and Alex did the regular checks on the new apple varieties. Planted the previous autumn, they were a fast growing genus of apple that had taken beautifully to the Canadian soil. One row to their left, straight as an arrow with arms shooting up to the sky, was the prize variety, still rather spindly but reaching ambitiously upwards towards the warming spring air.

Sophie's first winter in British Columbia had been a shock on many levels, not least because of the extreme cold. She'd laughed off Alex's gentle jokes about the wood burner in the yurt at the Royal West Country Show back in the English summertime, but it was only when she felt the oncoming encroachment of the Canadian darkness, saw the huge flakes of snow falling from the wide expanse of grey clouded skies, that she fully began to appreciate the difference. As soon as she'd made the decision to relocate to Canada, she'd swiftly invested in thermal underwear and a goose down winter jacket, as well as a pair of stout winter boots, but she still took time to acclimatise. She'd worn them right through until the following April, when spring finally took hold.

Thankfully, the cider house had taken up a lot of her time. She rapidly found her feet in the fledgling business, and that first autumn she'd put her extensive blending and tasting experience into practice with the native Canadian apple varieties that Alex had revived when he'd bought the place the previous year. Although it would take another season before Adelaide's would be producing enough stock to sell on a larger scale, they'd signed their first contracts with a couple of local bars and restaurants, and initial feedback had been good. With a little consultation from the Carter's Marketing Manager, they'd even come up with decent branding and a fantastic logo for Adelaide's that would stand out on any supermarket shelf or pub pump.

The old farmhouse on site had been another project. Working against the darkening skies and inclement weather, Sophie and Alex had managed to make the place habitable just as the weather closed in, and were now living on site full time. Alex retained his apartment in Vancouver, but was considering selling it now that the farmhouse was nearly finished.

Sophie had kept in regular touch with Lily and Jane by Skype, and was getting ready to welcome them both to Adelaide's now that the weather had warmed up. Despite her misgivings about Lily travelling such a distance, the film rights for Lily's latest novel had been snapped up so she and Jane could both afford to travel Business Class to Vancouver, which softened the prospect of the long flight. Excited to see the taxi drawing up, and tickled to find out that the champagne had been on tap throughout the nine hour flight, putting Lily and Jane in great spirits, Sophie smiled as she welcomed them to the farm, with a nervous Alex pacing a few yards away. As they approached him, a thunderbolt of grey fur hurtled out of the farmhouse door and ran barking up to the three women.

'This is Niyah,' Sophie said as the thunderbolt slowed down, its tail still wagging furiously. 'She's six months old and still at the mad stage.' The Weimaraner puppy, who, being a bitch, was around half the size of the rather more solid and languid Barney, stuck her nose straight into Lily's hand.

'Be prepared for her to be at the mad stage for the next three years!' Lily smiled. 'The dog means you're here forever, you know,' she said in an undertone to Sophie.

'You could say that,' Sophie replied, smiling, before reaching out to embrace first her mother, and then her grandmother. 'It's wonderful to see you! I'm so glad you could come.'

'We wouldn't miss it for the world,' Lily said. The strong afternoon sunlight highlighted the lines on her face, but her eyes were sparkling with excitement. 'It's about time I saw the place you've been talking about for so long. And the pictures you sent don't do it justice.' Lily looked around, first at the two storey white painted farmhouse with the decking area that ran almost around the entire building, its slate roof newly repaired and blue grey in the afternoon sun. Then she looked out at the rows and rows of young cider apple trees, just transitioning from flower to fruit, and then over to the small market garden where Sophie had planted fragrant herbs and the first summer salad vegetables were starting to emerge. 'I see you and Alex have been busy,' she continued. 'You have accomplished a lot this past year or so.' Turning to Alex, she smiled up at him as he leaned in to kiss her cheek. 'I think Jack would have been proud – of the pair of you.'

'I'm so proud of you, too, love,' Jane said, enfolding her daughter in a warm embrace. 'And I'm looking forward to getting to know you a bit better, too, Alex, since we didn't have much of a chance to talk when we were in Little Somerby.'

'I'd like that,' Alex replied.

'Thanks, both of you,' Sophie said. Noticing that Lily was leaning rather heavily on her walking stick, she added, 'Let me show you to your rooms, and then you can have a rest if you like before the other side of the family gets here.'

'Rest, my foot!' Lily snorted. 'Pour me some of your signature sparkling cider and I'll be right as rain.'

Adelaide's first 'hard' cider, a fragrant blend of Dabinett and Goldrush varieties, was proving to be a hit with early customers, and was anticipated, with Carter's investment, to be a success.

'Perhaps you should have a cup of tea first,' Sophie said, leading her grandmother and her mother into the farmhouse.

'Calm down,' she said softly, once she'd seen Lily and Jane safely into their respective bedrooms to unpack. 'What are you so worried about?'

Alex shook his head. 'I know, I know. It's so stupid to get uptight about them coming, but I just feel as though I'm going to be under their scrutiny the whole time. And not just me, but this place, this product...' Instinctively, Sophie knew it wasn't Lily and Jane he was worried about, but their other imminent house guests.

Sophie took Alex's hand and gently kissed his palm. 'They're your brothers as well as your business partners,' she said gently. 'They won't be judging you.'

'I'm so glad you're here,' Alex replied. 'That you made this decision to do this with me.'

Sophie smiled. It had been quite a decision to make, after over a decade with Carter's Cider and a lifetime of living in Little Somerby, to come thousands of miles north west to help set up Adelaide's Cider with the man she loved, and had not been one that she had taken lightly. She and Alex had worked day and night over the past year to get Adelaide's off the ground. Sophie's taste buds had ensured that the early blends of hard cider had been well received by the taste testers, made up mainly of local restaurants and bars, but now there were plans to move further afield to chain stores and outlets across British Columbia. Immediately, though, the challenge was to see if Jonathan and Matthew were prepared to take the brand across the Atlantic as part of their own stable.

As if on cue, Alex's mobile pinged. Swiping the screen, he breathed out. 'They've landed. Matthew's picked up the hire car so they'll be here in an hour.'

'Just enough time for you to calm down and have a cup of tea from the teabags Gran insisted on bringing with her, then.' Sophie smiled and squeezed Alex's hand.

'She does know that we got a box in for her, right?' Alex grinned back. 'I mean, this is BC, not Nunavut. Amazon does deliver out here, too, you know.'

'I know.' Sophie's smile widened. The ability to have Marmite and Yorkshire Tea shipped to this side of the Atlantic had come as something of a relief to her, when she'd made the decision to move. 'But she was determined to bring her own.' Hand in hand, they wandered back to the farmhouse.

A little time later, a large SUV came rumbling up the long driveway through the front facing orchards of Adelaide's towards the farmhouse. Alex jumped up from the kitchen table as soon as he heard the car approaching, and strode out of the front door to greet them. Sophie followed quickly beside him, slipping her hand into his as they went.

'You'll be fine,' she whispered as she felt Alex's shaking hand. Although Matthew and Jonathan had been over to the smallholding a couple of times over the past year, this visit was loaded with significance for a number of reasons. Not least because it wasn't just them doing the visiting. As the doors to the SUV slid back, the car disgorged not just Matthew and Jonathan, but Anna, Ellie, little Jack, Caroline, and, last but not least, Caroline and

Jonathan's new addition, a charming one year old called Emily. Meredith was preparing for finals at university and couldn't join the rest of the family, but sent her love, via Anna and Matthew. She was characteristically charmed that Sophie had to all intents and purposes joined the family when Alex had, and was looking forward to flying out and spending some time with Sophie and Alex once her exams were over.

'You made it,' Alex said, shaking Matthew's, and then Jonathan's, hands and then kissing the assorted other members of the family.

'Remind me to drug the kids for the return flight,' Anna said dryly as, freed from the restrictions of travel, the children dashed off down the driveway and into the orchards.

'We can do that?' Caroline asked, shifting a drowsy Emily from one hip to the other.

'Calpol works wonders.' Anna smiled. 'It might even work on husbands!'

'I think the free booze did enough damage.' Caroline smirked as Jonathan swiftly put on dark glasses against the strong afternoon sunlight.

'So why don't you show me around the place?' Matthew said. 'It's come on a lot since the last time Jonno and I came over.'

'Sure, but let's get you all settled first,' Alex replied. Sophie observed him for a long moment. Now he was receiving his brothers and their families on his own territory, his air of self-assurance had grown; he'd matured into his role as a cider producer over the past year, and he was a long way from the slightly diffident intern he'd been when she'd met him nearly two summers ago. So much had changed since then.

'Sounds good,' Jonathan replied. 'I could do with a cuppa.'

As they headed into the farmhouse, Sophie and Alex stayed back for a moment.

'Are you OK?' Sophie asked, as Alex took in the amiable rabble of family that were crossing his threshold.

Alex smiled and put his arms around Sophie, pulling her close for a long, lingering kiss. 'I've never felt better,' he said softly. 'With you by my side I'm always OK.'

As they broke apart, they could hear the clink of more mugs being grabbed from the cupboards as the Carter family settled into the farmhouse's comfortable kitchen. 'I'd better go and sort out these drinks,' Sophie said, regretfully breaking away from Alex's embrace.

'Uh, before you do...' Alex said softly. 'There's something I want to say to you.'

Sophie's heart flipped as she looked back at Alex, who was standing framed by the backdrop of his flowering apple trees. The sun cast a warm, spring glow over his features, and she thought she'd never seen him looking so relaxed and at peace with himself.

'I'm listening,' she said.

'I was going to wait until later, when we had a bit more time alone, but actually now seems like the perfect moment to do it,' Alex said. He reached out a hand and drew Sophie back closer to him. Fumbling in his jeans pocket with his other hand, he smiled. 'I'm sorry it's not in a box, but I wanted to keep it close by, for the right moment.' He took the palm of Sophie's left hand in his and held it for a moment. Looking into her eyes, he smiled gently. 'I want to ask you to marry me, Sophie. Will you do me the honour of accepting?'

Sophie felt her knees give way as Alex opened his palm and, lying there, was a gold band with a huge, deep emerald at its centre. Surrounding the emerald was a garland of diamonds that glittered in the spring sunshine. She opened her mouth to speak, but no sound came. Looking from the ring to Alex's handsome, expectant face, she tried again. 'Of course I accept,' she said. 'I absolutely, totally and utterly accept, right here, right now!'

With trembling fingers, Alex slid the ring onto Sophie's left hand. 'It was my grandmother's engagement ring,' he said. 'Mom gave it to me as a keepsake shortly before she died.' He laughed shakily. 'She said she wished she could be around to see who I ended up giving it to. But I think she'd definitely approve of you.'

'I hope so,' Sophie replied, before bringing Alex's mouth down to hers to seal his proposal with a kiss.

They broke apart again to the sound of applause coming from the kitchen. There, assembled in the window, were both sets of families.

'It's about time you got your act together,' Matthew called, sipping the tea that Anna had made. 'Now we can officially welcome Sophie into the family.'

'And welcome Alex into ours,' Lily said wryly, from where she was sitting at the kitchen table. 'Not before time.'

Alex laughed. 'I hadn't intended it to be a spectator event,' he said, sliding an arm around Sophie as they wandered into the house, 'but I'm glad you are all here to share it with us.'

'Me too,' Sophie replied. 'After all, that's what being part of a family is all about.'

Acknowledgements

As usual, there are so many people who have made the writing of this book easier, and possible. Firstly, I'd like to thank the amazing team at Aria Fiction for all of their help, encouragement and support. Thank you to my editor, Sarah Ritherdon, Vicky, Nicky and Lucy, and Sue Smith and Rose Fox for their expertise and input. In a similar vein, Sara Keane, my agent, for her continuing support, guidance and encouragement.

This time I have several cider professionals to thank, too. A huge thank you to Martin Thatcher of Thatcher's Cider for being so interesting and engaging to interview and providing me with a real insight into how a multi-national cider firm works from the ground up. Likewise, Julia Barton for answering my many questions, and the tour of the business (and allowing me access to one of my favourite locations to write about, the oak vats!). Finally, another huge thank you to Richard Johnson, Chief Cider Maker for Thatcher's, who is an absolute fount of cider knowledge and expertise, and brilliant to talk to.

There are two real Weimaraner dogs I have to include in the acknowledgements – my own, Bertie (who became Barney in this book) and the gorgeous Niyah, owned by my dear friend Taj. Mad they may be, but they're also the best dogs in the world.

As ever, the family has been amazing at dealing with me when I'm in thrall to a story, and Nick, Flora, Rosie, Peter, Linda, Helen, Michael, Luke and Penny all know just how much I appreciate your support and patience (and in some cases, proof reading!).

Friends, too, have been incredibly patient, and my thanks to Carly, Beth, Tony and Steph, among others, for being brilliantly supportive and constructive early readers. The same goes to Caroline Morris – thank you so much for staying with Little Somerby. I'm blessed to have such a fantastic network around me. I am also fortunate to include the wider circle of inspirational friends from the Romantic Novelists' Association, who have been so wonderfully supportive throughout, especially Rachel Brimble, Teresa F Morgan, Alison Knight, Nicola Cornick and Jenny Kane.

Thanks, also, to the many and varied 'character models' for this novel, especially Keanu Reeves and Adam Driver, who gave me a visual for Alex, and Gwendolyn Christie and Elizabeth Debicki for Sophie. And finally, Paul Gross, aka Constable Ben Fraser of *Due South*, who not only gave me Alex's last name, but also my first teenage crush, and set the benchmark for heroes for a lot of impressionable viewers of 1990s TV, myself included.

Finally, thanks to you, the readers, who have come back for another trip to Little Somerby. I am beyond grateful to each and every one of you, and I hope you've enjoyed spending time in the village once again.

Hello from Aria

We hope you enjoyed this book! Let us know, we'd love to hear from you.

We are Aria, a dynamic digital-first fiction imprint from award-winning independent publishers Head of Zeus. At heart, we're avid readers committed to publishing exactly the kind of books we love to read — from romance and sagas to crime, thrillers and historical adventures. Visit us online and discover a community of like-minded fiction fans!

We're also on the look out for tomorrow's super-star authors. So, if you're a budding writer looking for a publisher, we'd love to hear from you. You can submit your book online at ariafiction.com/we-want-read-your-book

You can find us at:
Email: aria@headofzeus.com
Website: www.ariafiction.com
Submissions: www.ariafiction.com/we-want-read-your-book
Facebook: @ariafiction
Twitter: @Aria_Fiction
Instagram: @ariafiction

Printed in Great Britain
by Amazon

64941342R00200